A Right Fine Life

by

Gency Brown

This is a work of fiction. Names, characters, places, and incidents are either the product of the author's imagination or are used fictitiously, and any resemblance to actual persons living or dead, business establishments, events, or locales, is entirely coincidental.

A Right Fine Life

COPYRIGHT © 2023 by Gency Brown

Cover Art by *Jennifer Greeff*

The Wild Rose Press, Inc.
PO Box 708
Adams Basin, NY 14410-0708
Visit us at www.thewildrosepress.com

Publishing History
First Edition, 2024
Trade Paperback ISBN 978-1-5092-5179-7
Digital ISBN 978-1-5092-5180-3

Published in the United States of America

"Listen, Charlene Sampson is your go-to here tonight. Real class act. This one sold out and should be a breeze."

"Sounds good. We'll set up for sound check in a half hour." He stared into Neil's questioning eyes. "I'll be fine, ya know. Feels wrong, but I know it's what I have to do. Don't worry."

For two hours, including three encores, he channeled all his hurt and frustration into the music. Every rejection on music row and all the dark bars and street corners that held and crushed the dreams of young people like Angie. The pain of the backbiting, lying, and broken promises he knew she had experienced flowed out of him and sailed across the crowd with his songs. He could hear her laughter in the shrill tones of the lead guitar. He saw her smile on the faces of a hundred girls at the edge of the stage. The band members kept looking at each other in disbelief after songs they thought never sounded so good. When at last he stumbled off stage, sweat soaked his shirt and hair, matted down under his hat. He left every emotion out there, and the audience paid him back with ear-shattering applause. The one thing he could not do was spend another hour signing autographs and smiling for photos.

Praise

"Written in the tradition of a memorable country ballad, A RIGHT FINE LIFE takes the reader into the dreams and daily life of a talented yet struggling musician. Author Gency Brown knows her way around a touring musician's life and captures Randy's world authentically."

~ Bobbi Jean Bell - Host Rendezvous With A Writer on LA Talk Radio

"Finally, someone has written a book about the life of a country musician that isn't one dimensional. For every moment of glory and glitter, there are a thousand moments of exhaustion, despair, uncertainty and sacrifice. Gency Brown captures the passion and commitment that keeps an artist chasing a dream while striving to maintain his artistic integrity."

~ Jim Jones, Western Writers of America and International Western Music Association award winner.

Chapter 1

Randy Walters crammed his hand into the mouth of the old pickle jar to grab wadded, crinkled strips of green paper, likely damp from the inside of a two-stepping woman's bra or a puddle of beer on the bar. Thirty-seven dollars in tips, a meager reward for the three hours he poured his heart out singing for people half listening in a noisy bar. He had to wonder, *is this worth the heartache it has caused in my life?*

He moved his head side to side in frustration as he folded the money into his pocket. Sitting next to the stage, he used a ragged tee shirt to wipe fingerprints from his Martin guitar. Each caress of the shiny wood reminded him of his mother saving from the household money to buy the instrument for his sixteenth birthday. He didn't want to let her down.

He jerked around as the jukebox swirled to life behind him. *Are you kidding? They barely waited for me to get off the stage to plug that thing in again.* After fastening the two latches which still functioned on the road-worn case, he smoothed the peeling souvenir stickers from bars and towns left behind. The miles of performing across California started when he was scarcely seventeen. The case would have to do a while longer until talent, grit, and determination made him a country music star.

"You comin' back through next month? I have to

schedule it now," said the bartender and owner of the fifth bar Randy played that week. The Red Rose Grill, with its neon lights and smell of nachos and spilled beer, was a regular stop for him in Riverside. He had a feeling it wasn't moving his career forward anymore.

"Not sure, Lucas. I'm trying to change it up some. How about I call you?"

Lucas wiped a bar towel across his sweaty brow. "I can't hold it. Jerry's bugging me for more nights, and his band brings in a crowd."

"Oh, okay, put me down for the usual." He wouldn't keep his old friend hanging. Nor could he afford to burn bridges.

"Great, I thought you'd come through for me." Lucas called over his shoulder as he headed to the bar. "Hey, how's that pretty little wife of yours? I haven't seen her around lately."

After all this time, the question burned like a hot dagger in his heart. Though Randy didn't look up, his voice grew louder as the anger of his response boiled over. "Ex-wife. Don't you remember we divorced over a year ago?" He stood and growled. "Does everybody have to keep reminding me I've already failed once in life?"

"Aw, listen, man, I just forgot. No need to go ballistic on me. Geez."

Randy put the guitar in his pickup and sat, hands and head on the steering wheel. *Man, what's wrong with you? It's not his fault you got Carrie pregnant before either of you was eighteen. You're the one put the music first and lost her. Get over it.*

Because of his constant travel to shows, which didn't always pay the bills, their young marriage had been a series of missed dinners and broken promises. She finally made it clear one of them needed to make plans for a stable home for their son. He knew she was right, but the breakup had been hard to take.

He stashed away the fifty Lucas paid him. The tips from the jar would cover gas for the trip to the next event and a burger at Sally's Truck Stop on his way out of town. Tomorrow night, he was opening for some famous act at a regional fair, which would pay enough to make the truck payment and give a little to Carrie. She deserved more, if only for putting up with his crazy lifestyle for as long as she did. He'd call soon to tuck in his boy, Jimmy, over the phone.

****

Fairs had never been his favorite gig. They meant dust, heat, drunks, bad food, and dust in the bad food. He drove most of the night to arrive at the Del Mar fairgrounds in the early morning. He parked outside the horse barns, settling in as best he could for sleep in the pickup. The aroma of fresh hay and livestock reminded him of home. Randy relived the argument with his father the day he announced he didn't want to take over the ranch. His dream was music instead. The men had discussed, yelled, and fought about it for three days. Randy said things which still haunted him. Memories of standing his ground now brought pain over the decision, which broke his father's heart. Randy's unspoken apology remained stuck in his throat at his father's funeral a year later.

He drifted off with thoughts of Carrie and Jimmy, aching for the closeness of the family he left behind. *Dammit, Jimmy doesn't even realize how it would be to have a dad around all the time. I want to teach him baseball and building things. This career better be worth it.*

The morning sun peeked under the western hat, covering his resting eyes, when the truck door jerked open. Only a quick grab of the steering wheel kept him from hitting the ground.

"Wake up, you lazy bum." The words startled Randy awake, ready to fight, until he recognized the voice of his friend Bobby Wilson. He raised a hand to shield his eyes from the sun while he verified Bobby's face through a thick, black beard.

"What the hell are you doing, Bobby?" Randy gave him another look. "And what's with the mound of fuzz on your face?" He stood to shake the wrinkles from his clothes.

Bobby's hand stroked the beard. "Aw, I just got tired o' shavin'. Saves me a few minutes and, anyhow, the ladies love it." Bobby gave his signature head-shaking laugh.

"Yeah, you need all the help you can get. What are you doing here, anyway?"

"I'm in the house band for the fair. Pay's okay and they give me a room for the whole two weeks. We'll be backing you tonight. Like old times, eh?" Bobby scratched the new beard, laughed again, and shouted to his friend as he turned to go, "Follow me to the food tent for breakfast. We have rehearsal in an hour."

Randy grabbed his guitar. There was no way to secure it in his truck since someone knocked out the rear window a few weeks ago.

The night's full arena held a curious mix of fanatics shouting for the main act, a sixties rock band on a comeback tour. Though his pulse raced with excitement, his heart sank when he stepped into the spotlight to only polite applause. *No worries, they're gonna love me. After all, my usual fans like the smooth country lyrics I write about love, home, and the working man.* Bobby and the other players were good. Luckily, the young man on the sound board made them even better. After a while, he saw the audience slow dancing to his ballad, "Don't Take Your Heart When You Go." *Finally, I've got 'em.* He kept up a friendly banter with the audience. When he belted out the lively number, "Shoot Me Now, Or Let Me Go," the crowd yelled out his name and the applause grew. He bent to shake hands with sunburned girls in tank tops and jeans, cut off to kingdom come, who crowded the stage until security moved them away. The applause and the thump of the music matched the pounding in his chest. The sweat running down his back fueled his energy. He dove into his performance and lived the dream in front of thousands. After the program, he sold a few homemade CDs and stood for dozens of photos with new fans. As he packed up to leave, he relived his half hour on stage. Hard work was paying off at last.

****

Randy bought gas and a six-pack of Bud Light at a filling station before heading to the neon lights of the Starlight Motel, which resembled a dozen others he frequented over the years. Hat on the desk and duffle bag on the bed, his long fingers ran through the waves of his brown hair. He covered the beer cans with ice in the bathroom sink, popped one open, and flopped his six-foot two-inch frame onto the bed to call his mother.

The number of rings caused him to worry until she answered, "Yes, hello."

"Mom, I guess I woke you, didn't I? I'm sorry. I had

5

a late show."

"I'm glad you called. Was it a good one? Where are you, anyway?" she asked through a yawn.

"At the San Diego County Fair. It was great. They loved my songs. You know the one you like." He crooned the lyrics.

"As I brushed the arena floor from my jeans,
You watched from the stands, like you always do
Remember, whenever you might need me,
I'll be there watching over you."

"Yes, I love that one. It makes me think of your father."

"You feeling okay? Has Sherry been coming by?" He depended on his older sister to keep an eye on their mother, with him gone so much.

"Yes, I said you shouldn't worry. She and Dan came by with the kids this evening, and we went to the grange hall for a spaghetti supper. I ate too much," she said with a giggle. "When will you be home, son?"

He surveyed the Picasso-like design of cracks in the ceiling as he answered, "About two weeks. They asked me to stay on here a few days. Then I have a couple more stops. I'll stay home awhile this time. I need to work harder to make my career go faster. Remember, I turned twenty-three in June."

"Honey, don't be hard on yourself. Your dad and I always believed in you."

"I know, but Dad didn't show it as often as you. Maybe I'm still trying to prove to him choosing music was right for me."

"I think deep down he knew it was, dear. It simply wasn't his dream."

After each phone call, the beer helped relieve

Randy's guilt over leaving family responsibilities behind to pursue his career. When sleep came, hit singles and adoring fans filled his head. Then the recurring nightmares about car trouble, half-empty dance halls, and broken contracts took over. After waking in a cold sweat around three a.m., he flipped through the few TV channels until a black-and-white John Wayne movie appeared. The pain hit him again with the memory of watching those with his dad. Two more beers and he rested.

****

Randy was right to worry over whether his aging tires would make it home. A new set and a rear window would take most of his pay from the fair. He'd use his dad's old Ford pickup while he made repairs on his. He planned to stay around home a lot anyway, contacting venue operators and promoters for better jobs. At least he was home. His mom worked at the kitchen counter while he made calls.

"Yes, sir, hello. I'm Randy Walters, and I wondered if you'd listened to the CD I sent you. I really want to play your venue, and I'm sure the crowd…"

"Well, yes, sir, I know your place. I'll fill it if that's what you're…"

"Yes, sir. Maybe if you want an opening act sometime? I've worked with…"

"Yes, sir, I am planning a better CD. Thanks anyway. Yeah, next time."

Most of the calls were the same. A few said they could use him on a weeknight for tips only. He didn't turn them down.

"What a racket." He hung up the phone hard on his mother's kitchen wall. "You can't get anywhere if you can't get hired, and you can't get hired if…oh hell. I've gotta get ready for tonight anyway."

"Where're you going tonight, son? I'll fix you a plate." He knew his mother enjoyed having him around to fuss over.

"A quick trip over to Oak Grove. Some church doin's, but it'll put a healthy lump in my savings. And the ladies are fixing a big supper, so don't bother cooking. If I'm going to stop by Carrie's on the way, I'd better shower and get out of here." He leaned over to kiss her cheek.

****

Knocking at the door to the house he and Carrie had shared always made him queasy. He was glad she stayed there after the divorce. At least he knew she and Jimmy were in a nice place. He spoke through the screen. "Hi, you remembered I was coming?"

Carrie met him in her uniform, stained with ketchup and chocolate pie from a hard day at Hank's Hamburger Haven. She took off the apron, straightened her tousled hair, and pushed open the screen. "Of course. Sit while I get Jimmy out of the tub. Want something to eat?" she offered on her walk down the hallway.

"No, I'll pick up something at my gig tonight. Smells good, though." He squirmed on the couch where she used to watch late-night movies, waiting for him. He'd slept there more than a few nights when he arrived home too late for her anger to tolerate him in their bed.

Familiar splashes and squeals came to his ears after Carrie told Jimmy his father had arrived. "Hi, Daddy!" With the slap of damp feet on wood flooring, the curly haired little guy ran across the room and leaped into Randy's arms.

A rush of loving emotion and remorse flowed over him. *It kills me to miss these things.* "Whoa, you're getting so big. How's the kindergarten school? You the smartest one?" He relished the smell of Sponge Bob Bubble Bath as his child squirmed in his arms.

"Mrs. Jacobs says I need to be more quiet. It's Billy's fault though." Randy laughed as Jimmy's impish grin gave him away.

"Oh well, I used to hear that a lot, too. You have fun and learn all you can." Randy hugged him tighter.

"You gonna come see me play T-ball Saturday morning, Daddy? Grandma bought me a new glove." This four-year-old wouldn't understand what it meant for his dad to work late on Friday night in a town sixty miles away.

"I'll sure try." He gave his son a pat on the bottom after standing him on the floor. "I need to talk to Mom for a bit."

Carrie finished buttoning the boy's superhero pajamas and sat him down at the table with his plate of warmed-over fried chicken.

Randy stood before her. "Here's a little cash. I wish it was more. I'm real close to catching up, though, right? Work is coming more regular now, Carrie. I think this may be my year." He recognized her smile at the excuses he still offered.

She looked at their son while taking the small stack of bills. "I sure hope so, Randy, for his sake now, more than you." She turned to face him. "I mean, I want you to be happy, of course, but he's growing so fast and needing things."

Old, familiar feelings flowed through him as she looked up into his eyes. The blue ones everyone said she got lost in as a teenager.

"He needs to see you more, too, Randy."

"I'm trying, Carrie, for all of us. I have to get going." He waved to his child. "So long, Superhero Dude. I'll try to be at the game. You be Mom's little man, okay?" With his black hat in hand, he turned to leave.

A chill ran through him as her soft words called after him. "Randy…we'll call it even on the money for now. Take care of yourself out there."

His palm lay on the doorframe, his upper teeth bit into his lip, and he hung back, reminded of the happy times they had shared. To him, her smile was still like turning on every light in the house. The only sound in the vacuum that surrounded him was the creaking of the screen door as he pushed it open in slow motion. His body shook as it slapped shut behind him. Reaching to fit his hat down tight, he released an unsteady breath as he stepped off the porch. *I sure let a good one get away.*

Chapter 2

"Where are you so hot to be headin' off to, Randy?" His brother-in-law Dan was a nice guy and always showed an interest in Randy's career, so he didn't mind answering his questions again.

"In the music business, there are always a few pivotal places you have to make it, to prove you're for real. In country music, one of the biggest is Bakersfield." He continued while turning meat patties over on the grill. "Hand me those buns, Dan. I know I can make it there, which will get me on the road to Nashville and real success.

"I'm doing okay, but I need a professional CD for the powerful people to pay attention to me. Saving is hard. I get ahead, and then something like the tires happens. There's not a lot to be made around here, but at least Mom keeps me fed and a roof over my head while I save. Staying here a few months will cut out most of the overnight travel expense."

"Well, Sherry and I figure you'll make it. You sound just like the guys on the radio." Dan put extra salt on the meat. "How much does it cost to make one of them CDs?"

Randy chuckled. As a construction worker, Dan couldn't possibly know. "Well, it is 2008, Dan, and nothing's cheap. To do it right is eight to ten thousand, maybe more. It depends on a lot of things."

His well-intentioned brother-in-law fumbled and caught the mustard before it hit the ground. "Wow, that's a lot." Dan was a fan and family, but Randy understood he couldn't help with the finances.

****

Two months went by, then five. He worked all the odd jobs he could find to fill the days. At night, he sang at every bar, steak house, wedding, and county fair for a hundred miles around until he could feel his goal within reach. At last, he traveled to the best Los Angeles area studio he could afford, clutching a stack of songs he'd written over the last three or four years.

As he exited the freeway onto a quiet side street in North Hollywood, excitement rushed through him. He double-checked the directions scribbled onto a scrap of paper as he parked his truck outside a bungalow-styled house. It didn't look like a professional studio. He double-checked the house numbers before getting out. Sweaty fingers gripped the handle of his guitar case as he walked through the garden gate to find a state-of-the-art studio in a converted garage. The long-haired engineer in a Hawaiian shirt didn't sound encouraging as he looked up from his crossword puzzle.

"You didn't bring your own band? Well, that adds to the price. It'll take me a day to gather up players, too."

Randy gazed at photos of music business dignitaries and stars with arms around this man who didn't seem impressed with him. On one wall hung two gold records. He tried to show experience as he said, "I only need a steel player, drums, and I can double on lead guitar and bass, if need be. A nice fiddle could fit in, too. I'm used to pickup bands when I can get one. I'm sure whoever you bring in will be fine." He wanted to get the sessions started.

The next day, Randy returned to the studio to find four musicians settling into position and warming up their instruments. Introductions completed, they listened to Randy describing his music and the emotion he wanted to have come through on the recordings.

Janie, the fiddle player, offered, "If you'd like, I can sing harmonies with you."

The engineer burst into the studio. "Let's get this thing going. Randy, you set up in the glass cubicle in the back. Get comfortable with the mic, headphones, and everything."

The week passed quicker than he could imagine, with full, passionate days in the studio. He would have liked a couple more days but couldn't afford them or the motel prices. He loved working with the talented musicians. They only polished ten songs, but he knew quality over quantity was most important anyway.

Randy headed home with a rough copy of the recordings and a promise from the engineer he would have it mastered and ready for manufacturing in a week, no more than two. He agreed to take care of everything for his price. Gruff as the eccentric man had been the day Randy met him, he had warmed up to the young cowboy and his music. Deep in thought on his long drive home, Randy mused, *there's enough money left to make the trip to Bakersfield and get my career established there. Now I'm on my way.*

****

A few weeks later, Randy came home from a painting job, taken with an old high school friend, to find a small stack of boxes on the living room floor.

"They're here, they're here." He tore at a box and

pulled out a copy of the CD he believed would make everything happen. "Mom, come look."

His mother stood in the doorway to the kitchen, drying her hands on her apron. "Your father would be so proud."

He held the CD tight. "At least he'll know I gave it my all. I'll get these out of your way, then I have to shower and change. Tonight, I'm opening for Ben Mathews. Remember, he used to perform with me sometimes? How about that? He's doing all right. I'll take a few of these and ask if he'll let me sell them alongside his. Don't wait up, Mom." He let out a cowboy whoop and got to the work of moving boxes.

He continued to perform around the area for a couple more weeks while he confirmed gigs along his path to Bakersfield. His Mom, Sherry, and Dan helped address and stuff envelopes with the new CD and his 8x10 glossy photograph. He mailed one to each of the radio stations on his route and made calls to arrange meetings with DJs for interviews about where he'd be performing in their listening areas. His dream and his future started now. This move to Bakersfield would get the right people to hear him. Then it was on to Nashville.

The gang at Carl's Corral and Family Dance Hall wanted to give him a nice sendoff, a night of music and dancing with BBQ, drinks, and potluck dishes enough for an army. It was the place that provided his first stage as a scared kid at an open mic. His impression on Carl that night meant his old friend always had a job for him.

Jukebox music and girls wanting one more dance with the good-looking cowboy before he left town filled the night. Carrie dropped in for a while early on, and Dan and Sherry brought his mother by for dinner.

Around midnight, Carl took to the mic and motioned Randy to join him on the stage. "It seems like only last night this skinny kid with his Wranglers dragging and his hat dirty from working his dad's herd came in here wantin' to sing. Shaky? Oh, my Lord, if you were here, you remember he started over a couple times from forgettin' the words. But when he settled in, there would be no stoppin' him. Now, our boy is heading off for the big time. We can say we knew him when. Sing us a few, Randy."

It was fitting to start with Carl's favorite song, an old Merle Haggard tune. Carl swore Merle debuted it right there in his place. Randy couldn't be sure, but the autographed picture on the wall added to Carl's story. He sang a couple of crowd favorites, then a few from the new CD. His friends savored every word and rewarded him with applause, hugs, and goodbye tears.

****

Randy left early on a cloudless March morning. It took almost two weeks to make the 160-mile trip across the state because of stops at radio stations and playing shows along the way. The new CD sold well. The sun hung low as he pulled into Bakersfield, where the traffic was heavier than he was used to. He followed the signs to Buck Owens Blvd. and the Crystal Palace. The Palace, as everyone called it, was the performance venue and museum country music legend, Buck Owens, opened in 1996. Buck and his band played concerts there and hosted many other famous country stars until his death in 2006. As Randy drove under the massive archway entrance, he stopped and surveyed the complex before him. He saw the large Victorian mansion in the forefront. Flashing lights rimmed the colorful roofline to remind visitors this was the always flamboyant musician's house. It did indeed look like a palace to Randy. Every nerve in his body tingled as he realized he had finally arrived. He believed playing at The Palace would put him before significant people in the business. He parked the pickup and walked through the main entrance.

The grey-haired attendant in a flashy embroidered western shirt gave him a friendly smile. The old man looked familiar, but Randy was so nervous he couldn't place him.

"Hello, young man. Are you here to see the museum? We'll close in another hour. Come on in. Buck would want you to enjoy your visit."

Randy could hardly catch his breath to speak but finally managed, "I actually wanted to meet, or at least make an appointment, to talk to the person who books the acts here."

The greeter shuffled from behind the kiosk and placed a hand on Randy's shoulder. "I figured. The guitar gave it away. Well, son, you're a little late today. They already closed the offices. Enjoy looking around, though. There's a lot to see. You a Buck Owens admirer?"

Randy tried not to sound like a silly fan as he explained. "My dad owned all of his records and cassettes. I played those things 'til I wore out the old stereo. He wanted to visit this place but never got away from the ranch. He said what Buck played was right fine music. I learned guitar by trying to copy Buck's lead player, Don Rich. I guess it was pretty tough losing him in that awful accident back then."

He waited as the old man settled onto his stool again, then looked up to say, "Yeah, it was hard on all of us, but especially Buck. I can still hear those opening licks of his instrumental, 'Buckaroo.' " After a few thoughtful seconds, the friendly smile returned. "Well, young man, I'm Tom. You let me know if you have questions about anything. Otherwise, I'll signal with the lights when closing time comes."

Randy lost himself in all the memorabilia, pictures, awards, and fancy suits in the museum. And then he saw it—Buck's famous red, white, and blue guitar. Seeing Buck's personal items made it like he was meeting the man himself. The hour went by much too fast. He'd have to finish his tour another time. After all, he'd be living and working close by now and could come anytime.

At closing, Tom came over to lock the door behind him. "Sorry to rush you off. They have to get ready for the show tonight. You should come, there's lots of seats left. The feature is a new country kid, and a comic opens the show. Otherwise, come back tomorrow. I'll get you in to meet Stan."

Deciding to save the ticket price, Randy booked a motel room and searched out dinner. The rest of the evening he spent in his room with the local want ads. There were plenty of apartments listed for him to check out as soon as they hired him at The Palace. He fell asleep thinking of all he had seen. His plan was off to a good start, but even his excitement didn't keep away the usual nightmares of failure.

****

The next morning, Randy rose early and headed to a nearby diner for breakfast. He made one more review of his promotional material over a second cup of coffee. With two hours to kill before the Crystal Palace offices opened, Randy thought *maybe I should go back to the room and warm up my voice and guitar licks a bit.* He wanted to put his best boot forward to impress whoever he would be meeting. A glance down revealed boots in need of polish. He took a coffee to go and headed to the register. As he paid his check, he thought it odd the pretty red-haired waitress said, "Good luck today."

Randy parked the pickup away from the front doors of The Palace and waited until quarter after opening time so he wouldn't appear too anxious. When he entered, Tom, the man from the night before, met him with a grin. "Are you ready? Give Stan a few minutes to get his coffee. I'll go tell him you're here." Randy found a bench to relieve his shaky knees, his guitar on the floor by his feet. His hand gave the hat in his lap a light brushing. The friendly man returned to sit down beside him.

"Thanks, Tom. I'm a little nervous, I guess. Anything I should know first?"

"Oh, so, so many things," Tom said seriously before his face broke into a smile. "Maybe sometime we can have a drink and go over them all." They both had a laugh, which helped Randy relax. "Be yourself, son. He sees so many like you, and, believe me, the first thing to send you out the door is trying to be something you're not."

Randy grinned. "My dad used to say something like that." He repeatedly turned his hat in anxious hands.

"Sounds like a guy I'd like." Tom continued. "Why do I think there's a story behind the fine Resistol hat you're holding?"

"It was my dad's. Mom gave it to me before the funeral." Randy put it back on his head and sat up straight. "I only get it out for special, ya know?"

A booming voice came from across the lobby.

"Well, let's find out if that hat has some magic in it, young man. Hi, I'm Stan Miller." The man in the three-piece suit thrust his hand out to greet his visitor.

Randy jumped up and gripped the hand in his most determined handshake. "Hi, I'm Randy Walters. I sure appreciate you seeing me."

"Come on in and sit down. I have a meeting at eleven, so let's talk quick." Stan motioned Randy to a leather chair facing his desk. "You want coffee or something? What do you have in the folder?"

Randy sat his guitar down, declined what would have been a fourth cup of morning coffee, and handed the package to the man he thought could shape his future. "The bio sheet there talks about me and a few of the places I've played. The CD is new, and everyone likes it so far. Those are mostly my own songs."

Stan leaned back in his chair and took a fleeting look at the page. He turned the CD over to study the liner notes. "You worked with Jim Myers' studio. He's a different guy, but he definitely knows his way around the board."

"Yes, sir. He was sharp. I'm real proud of how it turned out for me." Randy used a hand to calm his bouncing leg as he got up more nerve to talk. "I, uh, I think my next step is to play a well-known place like this and make a better name for myself. I can start right away, of course."

Stan's office chair creaked and slammed down as he sat up to lean toward Randy. "Hold on, cowboy. First, there are a few things you need to understand. I can't hire you today. We're booked for seven, eight months. Even most of the house band has been with us steady for two years. If the CD is any good, we might put you on a call-in list, for when players are sick or something. I'm talking to you today because Tom saw something in you and I trust his judgment. Things are tough in this business. My primary job here is profit, any way I can keep the doors open. This isn't the old days, when Buck could bring in stars and sizeable crowds. You'll see a country act here one night, then a folk or rock group the next. I haven't resorted to trained dogs yet, but some of the comedy acts make me wonder. Country isn't always the biggest draw, even here. I can hardly get the name acts anymore, though they get first dibs, of course. I probably have two or three young hopefuls in here a week. I can't do much, if anything, for most of them. Like I said, this is a tough business. You understand?"

Randy sat quietly through his education. His head spun as the nervous leg froze to a stop. He struggled to breathe and get his heart back out of his throat. To his burning ears, the man couldn't have said anything closer to "No, go home."

Stan stood up and came around the desk. "Look, kid, I'm going to give the CD a listen. If it sounds like you've got something, I'll share it with the guys here and keep you in mind. Book gigs around town and get your name out there. You've sure got the looks going for you. You never know." He led Randy to the door.

Randy offered him a shaky hand at the doorway. "Thanks for your time, Mr. Miller. Would it be okay if I checked back with you? I'd like to know what you think of the CD."

"Oh, sure." Stan's voice rose as he slapped Randy's shoulder. "I always enjoy helping a kid when I can. Tom, fix up our friend with tickets to Saturday night's show, and welcome to Bakersfield, Randy." The man in the three-piece suit shut his office door.

Stunned, Randy heard little Tom said. He looked at the tickets and didn't recognize the band's name.

As they walked to the exit, Tom advised, "Hang in there, son. I meant what I said about us getting together sometime. We'll have a nice long talk."

Randy sat in the truck, dazed at what had happened. He thought about heading back home fast. Was it over? Had he failed? He stayed in deep thought while driving around Bakersfield all afternoon. Busy streets had him lost more than once. He noticed a bar or honky-tonk advertising live music on every corner in parts of town. *Okay, I'll start finding my way around those places for work. Like Stan said, I need to get my name known here. I won't give up my dream so fast.*

He bought a city map at a gas station, picked up dinner at a fast-food drive through, then made his way back to the motel. He reviewed the map, spread over the bed, and memorized the main streets and freeways. The phone book from the nightstand helped identify venues he could visit right away.

Chapter 3

Randy slept later the next day but still made it to the diner for breakfast. As he laid his hat at his side in the booth, the red-haired waitress brought him the menu and smiled. "Well, hello. You're still here."

"I am. You'll find I usually hang on 'til the buzzer." He gave her his best smile. "This place will take some getting used to, that's all."

"Where're you from?" She set down a cup and poured his coffee.

"Lakeview, a little place southeast of Riverside. How about you, or are you from here?"

"Hmph, is anyone really? No, I came from Nevada for the music scene a few years back. Well, not for me, the jerk I was with back then. You going to order? I'd better get busy."

He ordered the Farmer's Special of three eggs, bacon, hash browns, and toast. As he downed two cups of coffee, he looked over the classifieds, then the sports page. When the waitress laid his check on the table, he saw her name badge.

"Sarah. I like that. I'm Randy Walters. I guess I'll see you tomorrow."

She looked over her shoulder while slipping Randy a paper with a phone number. "A bunch of us will go over to The Purple Den tonight. Some of the guys are musicians, so they do the open mic there." She smiled.

"Call if you want to go, Randy Walters."

He tucked the paper into his shirt pocket, grabbed his hat, and left her a nice tip. A grin crossed his face as he started his pickup. *Good to know some things work the same in Bakersfield.*

One club, bistro, or dance hall after another filled his day. Most he crossed off his list after failing to book gigs. He located a country bar offering auditions on Monday nights. He might try it next week. After he paid for his lunch in a small café downtown, he convinced the owner, Phil, he should let him set up in a corner to play a few songs for tips sometime. "I've just gotten to town, so I'm open for any night but Mondays right now." He hoped this business man would feel lucky to get him, before he started playing other places.

Phil had his speech ready. "I've tried music in here before. This is a family place. Don't be too loud and no off-color stuff. You're on your own, no star treatment. You bring the tip jar, stool, everything. And you show up, got it? We'll try Thursday night at six first and see how you do."

"That sounds fine. I'll be here early to set up," Randy said as he shook Phil's hand. At least the day hadn't been a total loss. Still, by four o'clock, he was tired and frustrated when he reached into his pocket for Sarah's number. They agreed he would meet the group at the place with the strange name, and she gave him directions. He had to admit he was ready for some fun, and it wouldn't hurt to meet other musicians.

As Randy arrived at the address, his eyes grew as large as half dollars. *This can't be the right place.* The brightly colored neon sign flashed The Purple Den with the large P flickering off and on. He parked under a light and covered his guitar with his coat before locking the pickup. The place looked more like something he imagined from San Francisco in the 1960s than a country bar. Ragged, outdated concert posters and beer advertisements covered the windows. He saw a bearded, gorilla-sized guy in a leather vest and Grateful Dead tee shirt he thought must be the bouncer outside talking with Sarah. Randy figured he would at least have a drink and relax a little since he was already there.

Sarah waved to him as he walked toward the front door. When he approached, she asked, "You bring a guitar? I told the guys you'd do a few songs."

He walked back to the pickup and grabbed his instrument in a daze. *What am I going to sing in a place like this? Maybe I can get by with an old Eagles or Marshall Tucker tune without them throwing things at me. How does she even know I perform?* As they entered, he heard George Strait's music blaring from the jukebox. He unwound a little as his eyes adjusted in the dark to reveal a few couples two-stepping and several cowboy hats around the room. He shot around at her in disbelief.

Sarah threw her red hair back with a laugh. "I wish you could see your face. You look like you've just been saved from the devil. Come on, let's order something cool."

"Damn, girl. You knew what I'd be thinking as I drove up to this off-the-wall place, right? This must not be your first time bringing somebody new here. I'm not sure you play fair." He joined in her fun.

They took their drinks to sit with her friends at a table in front of the stage. She introduced him, and he surveyed the faces, trying to remember all their names. "So, some of you play the open mic here regularly?"

Frank shared first. "Yeah, most every Wednesday night. This is a real friendly crowd."

Beth looked Randy over as she said, "You'll hear all types. Johnny and I do a little country/folk duo. Some nights, mostly rock is what you hear. You never know."

"How about you? Sarah says you perform." Bill asked the question of the night. They all waited for Randy's answer.

"I grew up on country. You know, I can do enough styles to fill whatever the job might be. I'm not sure how Sarah knew, though. We haven't even talked much." Randy gazed at her, and the group gave him a knowing smile.

Sarah explained, "I can spot you guys a mile away. I get a steady stream coming into the diner with it so close to The Palace. Of course, most I only see once. Besides, your promo stuff spread across the table the other morning might have been a clue, don't you think? Hey, you'd better get on the list so you get a good slot. Frank, take him over to the sign-in table and help him decide which acts he doesn't want to follow."

He enjoyed his new friends and all their fun. They all came to Bakersfield following a dream. Most, like Randy, were the hometown star. A few enjoyed minimal successes, but most were still struggling. All worked other jobs to support themselves. When Randy's turn came around, the emcee held the clipboard at arm's length to read the name in the dim light. He introduced Randy as a newcomer and renamed him Ralph Waters. Randy's teachers told him he had the handwriting of a fifth-grade doctor, but this was too much. When he got to the mic, he made sure he corrected the name. Each set consisted of three songs or fifteen minutes so he didn't waste any time. He sang a Kenny Chesney tune and two of his own. The crowd reacted well. Sarah and her friends were giving him a standing ovation, yelling and whistling at him. They responded almost as well to all the acts, even if some made listening and smiling at the same time a little hard. This would be a fun, encouraging group to know. He told them about his small café job, and they wanted to support him. He thought bringing in customers would impress the owner, so he gave them the when and where.

At the end of the night, Sarah spoke as they walked to his pickup. "I'm glad you came, and the gang sure likes you. Friends are important around here, and these are some of the best." She gave him a kiss on the cheek and turned to join the others. "See you tomorrow night."

"Thanks, I needed this tonight." Randy didn't know what to think about the kiss on the cheek, but he was glad she introduced him to the group. He gave her a wave as he got into his pickup to go.

****

Randy slept through breakfast and made mid-morning coffee in his room. He telephoned his mother. "Mom, I'm sorry if I worried you. Yeah, I got here a couple of days ago. I'm still in a motel right now, but I've made musician friends, and they can show me around and introduce me to folks. How are things there?"

His mother filled him in on her ladies' Bible study group and family news. "Jimmy's learning to ride your first little bike. Dan put the training wheels on for him, and I think Carrie took pictures."

Another milestone he missed with his son. Right now, he couldn't change things. He would make a quick trip home when he got comfortable in his new home.

"Mom, this will have to be short. I've got lots to do today. Tonight, I'm starting a regular gig at a nice café here." He promised to call again soon.

He arrived at the café at five thirty to set up without sound equipment in the small space. A stack of CDs fit beside the tip jar at his feet. Only a few customers dotted the place, but he thought it might be early for a dinner crowd and shrugged it off. Soon after he began playing, his new friends arrived and sat at a table close by. When Sarah waved, he nodded to her and thought sure his face reddened. They eyed the menu and ordered burgers or appetizers to share. They applauded wildly for him and appeared earnest in their enjoyment of the set.

On his break, he sat at their table and thanked them for coming. "Sure, Randy. Hey, this place is a little nicer than we thought."

Randy was sure Frank meant pricier. He shifted his hat. "Yeah, sorry about that. I don't expect you to come every time. Hey, where are Chase and Bill tonight?"

Beth nearly spewed her soda, trying to speak. "They both got hired to back some girl singer at The Palace tonight. Cool, huh?"

Randy's ears perked up at the news. "No kidding? That's great! I guess I need to stay in touch out there. The guy told me they might put me on a call-in list. I figured he was feeding me a line."

Frank talked as if he knew from experience. "No, that's for real, man. If you can get Stan and the bandleader, Jake, on your side, you might get work."

More people were in the café now, and he finished his set to better applause. It was meager tips, but he welcomed the twelve dollars in his jar. Not too bad for his first night there.

Phil came over as Randy packed up and said, "Hey, you're good. The customers made some nice comments. I told them to come see you next Thursday, too. That's right, isn't it? You won't bail on me for something better?"

"Phil, I'll give you as much notice as I can when Nashville calls me." They laughed together. "Don't worry, I think I may be here for a while."

"Look kid, we've got meatloaf left back in the kitchen. Why don't I bring you a plate? The meal can be part of the deal each time. I'll have Mary make a flyer to put in the window, too."

When leaving, he thanked Phil and the staff for the meal. If he didn't get steady work soon, those once-a-week meals would come in handy.

Before calling it a night, the friends offered a last beer at the house where Frank, Beth, and Johnny lived. He followed directions to a three-bedroom duplex north of town. Randy asked as he entered the sparsely furnished house, "Hey, the sign back there said Oildale. Holy cow. Isn't this the area where Merle lived?"

"You're right," Frank offered. "We were hoping it would be another chance for some of the Bakersfield sound and success to rub off on us. Can't say the plan works out too well, but the price is right out here, even better if we had another roommate. What do you think? You'd have your own room, and we share everything else. The guy before you left a bed and a little dresser, so you won't need much."

The offer took Randy by surprise. "I hadn't thought about something like that. You sure? You hardly know me."

Johnny said, "Look, you'd better get used to taking

a little help. Besides, you seem like an all-right guy. We'll agree to try it until you screw up. How about it?"

Randy didn't see how he could refuse. "I know I need to get out of the motel. I'll try it. Thanks, guys."

Before he left, he pulled Sarah aside and invited her to the show at the Crystal Palace on Saturday night.

"Sounds like fun, Randy. Who's playing?"

He showed her the tickets, and she knew the band. "They're pretty good. They've been knocking around the southwest the last few years. About time they come through here again."

He shook his head and grinned as he drove back to his room. He'd gotten work, found a place to live, and a date, all in his first week. A lot of work loomed ahead, but at least he hadn't completely failed.

Chapter 4

He checked out of the motel on Saturday morning and stopped by Walmart for things he needed around the house. His mother sent him off with towels, bed linens, a coffee pot, and the likes, which would save him a lot. A new cell phone had to be on his shopping list. He had to make sure he didn't miss jobs because his old one dropped a call. The move into his new home was finished before noon, then from a quick glance in the refrigerator and pantry, he determined there probably wasn't too much cooking done in the place. His first contact with the new phone would be Sarah to give her his number and set a time to pick her up for their date.

Sarah introduced him to people at the concert. He looked around for Tom or Stan but didn't see either. Monday, he would follow up on his meeting with Stan to make sure his new address and phone number were on file there. After a night of music and dancing, he and Sarah sat in his pickup outside her apartment, talking about hometowns, families, hopes, and dreams for the future. He finally said good night with a promise to see her again.

****

On Monday morning, Tom answered at the Crystal Palace. "Stan's not in this morning. He had to make a trip into LA. I'll tell him you followed up like you said you would. I heard your CD, and, Randy, there are great songs on there. Jake thought so, too. I can't say what will happen, but keep busy and stay in touch. I'll make sure he has your new information. Is everything going okay?"

Randy gave him an update and said he would check back soon when he had more news. He sensed a connection with Tom.

Randy stayed busy with small gigs in the city and nearby towns over the next two months. He worked hard and put miles on his truck. His new friends helped him keep a decent attitude. They had all experienced the same frustration in their careers. After returning to The Palace to tour the full museum, he got to speak to Stan, who had positive things to say about the CD, but no work to offer.

Once he prepared all day for a job with a band that had recently lost their bass player. He found out the hard way that the bandleader never paid on time, if at all. Randy stayed after him for two weeks to even get part of the money he promised. He knew better. *Have to stay on my toes in this new environment.*

Money was tight. He dipped into savings to supplement what he earned from performances. The tips at Phil's café were a little better, and now he played there two nights a week. The free meals were most welcome. Randy wondered how long he could continue like this. Sleep was still scarce. It was not the life he had envisioned in Bakersfield, but he followed Stan's advice to find work and make his name known around town.

One Friday night of a hard week, he walked the downtown area to clear his head. He heard a Moe Bandy song coming from a corner bar and stopped for a cool drink before heading home. After a couple of sips of a local brew at the bar, he commented to the pretty bartender, "The band sounds good."

She leaned toward him to make herself heard as she wiped a glass. "Yeah, Tom and the guys have been playing here a long time. Our crowd loves them."

Randy turned toward the music and squinted through the stage lights to see the man he'd met at the Crystal Palace, singing at the mic. He had a strong voice and handled the guitar with ease. During the band's break, he went up to speak to him. "Tom, I did not know you performed."

The man introduced the other players, then sat with Randy to talk. Tom still hadn't addressed Randy's surprise.

"I mean it. Why didn't you say something? I only thought you were another fan or something."

Tom sat his hat on the table and ran his fingers through sweaty, grey hair. He sipped his beer before saying, "My real performing days are long gone. I mostly do this for fun now, and anyway, the guys in the band keep me young. Hey, I told you we'd spend some time together, and we need to catch up."

"I'd like to. When can we meet?"

"Why don't I tell the wife you're coming to Sunday dinner? I'll bet a home-cooked meal sounds pretty good right now." He reached for a pen and napkin. "Here, let me give you my address and phone number. Three o'clock Sunday, okay?"

"I'll be there. I don't want to put your wife to extra work, though. You sure she won't mind?"

"Jennie loves feeding young musicians. She's been doing it since I met her way back in Tennessee," Tom said with a smile of memory. "So, we'll see you then and have our nice long talk."

When Randy got home, Johnny and Frank were still

up, playing cards. He told them about his night and plans for a meal with Tom and his wife. "I knew I liked the guy when I met him my first day at The Palace. I mean, we sort of clicked, you know?"

After his friends stared at him in silence for what seemed an eternity, Randy asked, "What? What's wrong?"

Frank spoke, "Do you not know who that is, for heaven's sakes? He's Tom Murphy."

Randy's eyes grew large. "You don't mean *the* Tom Murphy? I thought he seemed familiar, but I never could place him." Tom had been a solo artist for a short while in the late eighties, then played guitar and sang backup harmonies with some of the well-known stars. "I heard he finished up a Tim McGraw tour in the mid-nineties, then fell off the scene. What is he doing here?"

Johnny answered, "He came to work with Buck. They had been friends in Nashville, and Buck made him a part of his operation here. He's a real nice guy, and even though he's cut back on his involvement at The Palace, he's a good one to know."

Randy felt lucky and a little overwhelmed that Tom had taken an interest in him. He could learn so much from his experience and wanted to take care of the friendship. His father's voice rang in his ears. "You can't rely on anyone else to do the work." Having someone like this in his corner couldn't hurt, though. He thought Tom must know a lot of people in the business. What luck to run into him here. He fell asleep compiling a list of questions he was sure Tom could answer.

****

On Sunday, Randy dressed in his best creased jeans and button-down shirt for the visit. He stopped by the grocery store to buy a small bouquet of cut flowers for the table.

When Tom introduced him to his wife Jennie, she made him feel at home. "You boys take your tea out to the porch and chat while I set the table."

"Oh, Mrs. Murphy, I'd be happy to help. That's my job at home."

"I wouldn't think of it, at least not your first time here. And, young man, you learn my name is Jennie." He liked her sweet and infectious laugh.

Their modest home sat in an older neighborhood with other well-kept houses. The front yards with flower beds, college flags, and tire swings swaying in the wind made him think happy families had lived there over the years. Randy soaked up the view of the quiet, tree-lined street. Quiet he hadn't enjoyed since he left home.

Tom said with a grin, "Your eyes fairly sparkle as you look around here."

Randy let out a sigh before responding. "It's beautiful, and so calming."

"We like it here and never needed anything fancy. We bought the place when we moved here in '95. Our two boys went to school right around the corner. Bakersfield has been a nice place to settle down."

"Can I ask why you left Nashville when you seemed to do so well?" Randy didn't want to be disrespectful but wanted to know.

Tom drew a long breath before responding. "Yeah, we might as well get that conversation over with." He sipped his tea and began. "I had my dreams of a solo career, and some came true. It was exciting in my younger years, and very lucrative. There's no denying that. Then, when Jennie and I married, the babies started coming, and it got harder to be gone so much. Some live in the life their entire careers. I wanted something different. So, I stepped back and worked for a few highly successful folks. Even tried studio session work for a while, which kept me home and paid well. The music changed, too. I liked it but wasn't sure how long I would fit into the younger crowd. Later, when Buck Owens offered me a way out, I accepted his offer and haven't looked back. My time in Nashville had come and gone."

Randy summed up what he understood. "It kept you around the music business, and you could have the family life you wanted."

Tom turned to Randy and spoke as he would to a son. "Like I said, there's nothing wrong with the life, but it's not for everyone. One day, you come to a crossroads and you have to make your own choices. Was it easier for me to choose after I had some success and money? Of course it was. If the business is your dream, give it a shot. I'm only saying this has been right for me and my family."

Jennie called through the screen door to announce dinner. The two men rose, and Tom took Jennie's arm to walk to her place at the table. She invited Randy to sit across from her. They got to know each other through lively conversation about music and family. The meal reminded him of his mother's cooking. After the blueberry pie, he pushed back from the table to speak. "Mrs. Mu… I mean Jennie, this meal was so great. I'm afraid I have really made a pig of myself."

"I'm glad you enjoyed it. You'll have to tell me what you like for next time. I know how you boys try to live on sandwiches and TV dinners." She looked at him with eyebrows up and a sly smile that said, *don't try to fool me.*

Randy thought he probably couldn't get anything past this wise woman. "Tom told me you like feeding starving musicians."

She and Tom shared a glance and memory as she said, "We've always had a stream of young people through our house. Either musician friends or when our boys brought home half the football team. The kitchen has always been a way for me to be a part of their lives and success. Anyway, I love to cook."

Tom took her hand. "I always told her she could have had a career like Paula Deen, but she says she's happy. Without her, I wouldn't have had the success I've had."

"So, were you always so organized and focused about the business, like you talk now?"

Tom had to chuckle before answering. "Oh, heavens no, that's mostly Jennie. The cute, level-headed, business major I snatched out of Vanderbilt in her sophomore year. Like you, I was struggling. She could see how much I wanted to at least try to make it."

She added, "I told him, fine, but we will not waste precious time we could spend together."

"She asked me a million questions about the business and what I'd done so far. We made charts and calendars, and over time, had a plan that served us well. Even when I gave up the solo work to be a backup guy, she made sure every decision was a smart one. I tell you, she got me through it all."

Jennie refused to let Randy help clear the table and sent the men back to the porch to enjoy the evening. She joined them later with coffee as they were getting guitars out to share music. Randy watched and listened as Tom played and sang songs any country fan would recognize.

"I know that opening lick. You mean you played on The Judds' second album? Man, this is so much fun for me. Wanna hear the song I'm working on now?" Randy surprised himself at his comfort with this man, who was making his way into the music business when Randy first learned to strum a guitar. They continued to trade songs and stories until the sunset shone through the elm trees. "I have to thank you both for a time I will never forget."

The couple made it clear he was welcome anytime. Tom enjoyed the day so much they agreed to meet there every Sunday afternoon. The exception would be the next one. Talk about their kids led Randy to know he would spend that weekend with his son.

****

Randy made sure he had nothing booked on Friday so he could travel. It gave him that night and all of Saturday with Jimmy. He drove past familiar storefronts and service stations of his childhood hometown, which looked different and in need of paint. A turn at the end of main street found him on the road to his mother's place southeast of town. He got more excited as he crossed the noisy cattle guard, which used to announce his after-curfew arrival to his waiting father. Maybe he would have time to fix her mail box, which leaned to the left since the neighbor boys nearly knocked it down a year ago. He hadn't let his family know about his trip home and hoped they would enjoy the surprise.

"Mom, come on, stop crying. I thought you'd be glad to see me." He teased her. His arms enveloped her until she calmed down, and, of course, she immediately started taking care of him.

"You're so thin, son. I'll fix you up real quick. Why

don't you call Carrie? Let her know you'll surprise Jimmy by picking him up from school. How long can you stay?"

"I'll head back on Sunday. I've got a lot going on right now. Still not going as fast as I'd like, but I'm doing all right." He sat with her on the porch swing. "I've missed everyone and this place. Sometimes so much I wonder if I'm doing the right thing. Even though he disagreed with my career choice, Dad wouldn't want me to give up, would he?" He realized he held her hand a little too tightly and released it.

"Son, we all understand. You're working hard and doing well. Take it a day at a time and keep moving forward. We're fine here."

Randy's stomach rumbled. "Can I help you in the kitchen, Mom? I am ready for lunch, after all."

The weekend went by too fast. He spent Saturday with Jimmy playing in the park, then seeing a movie before they joined the family for hot dogs and hamburgers on the grill. Later, as he tucked the little boy in, Jimmy asked why his daddy had to leave again.

"My job, son. I have to help Mom pay bills and keep up with all the hot dogs you put away." He ruffled the blonde curls as he added, "Anyway, it's something I enjoy. You'll learn when you're older, you want to have a job you like."

Jimmy crinkled his nose and cocked his head to the side. "You think Uncle Dan likes his work? He sure comes home tired."

"I don't know, Jimmy. I hope he does. Sometimes people decide to stay with something because they're good at it and it seems the right thing for their family. Life can't always be fun. You understand?"

"Nope, I just wish you could like your job around here, that's all. I sure had fun today, Daddy."

"Me, too, son. I'll try to make it happen more often." Randy fought back emotions that would only make parting harder.

****

The following Sunday, Randy again sat on the porch with his new mentor. "Tom, will you help me get things going faster? What am I doing wrong? Am I missing something?"

Tom set down his tea and locked eyes with his young student. "You're serious, aren't you?"

Randy's commitment came through his voice. "I am. A music career is all I've ever dreamed of. What else would I do? I didn't go to college. It was no surprise this would be hard, but the few months I've spent here have been a little overwhelming."

Tom stood and walked along the wooden planks of the porch. "Okay, here's the deal. I'll work with you as long as I think your dream is what's right for you. I won't help you down a path I don't think you're suited for. That means listening to me, the tough talk, as well as the pats on the back. I won't pull punches."

Randy grabbed the arms of his chair. "I'd be nuts if I didn't agree. I will work hard every day. You'll see."

Tom was in teacher mode now. "Fine. First thing tomorrow, I want you to go out and get a job." He stopped his pacing and turned to his student. "An actual job you can count on every payday."

Randy uncrossed his legs, and his boot thumped the porch boards as he sat up straight. "What? How does that help? The guys I live with all work, but I thought it was holding them back."

"Don't worry about or compare yourself to anyone else. They have their dreams and have to follow their own path. Right now, you feel pressure, don't you? Bills come in like clockwork. Rent, car payment, your son needs school supplies, braces, new sneakers. You eliminate that pressure with a regular payday, and the rest of the time you concentrate on your music and getting the right gigs. You don't jump into a booking for a few bucks only because you need the money. Believe me, you'll feel better about yourself because you've gotten rid of that evil monster called guilt. You've given yourself permission to be here. Understand?"

Randy sat back and let out a full breath. "I hadn't thought of it that way. It sure makes sense. My friends have been telling me there's work in the oil fields around here. I pass the feedlots every time I come into town. I might be more comfortable working the livestock there or one of the sale barns. Yeah, I'll find something right away."

"One more bit of advice. Make sure the work schedule allows time for music gigs and you protect those hands, you hear me?" He gave the young man's shoulder a shake. "Smells like Jennie has her pot roast just right. Let's go in and wash up for dinner."

Even though he knew the plan meant a lot of work, Randy went to sleep that night feeling lucky.

Randy had worked summers at a livestock auction back home and remembered how hard it had been. The dirt and summer sun under the huge metal building were unforgiving. He could move, clean up after, and feed the animals but wasn't ready for the size of this facility. His experience impressed the boss enough to let him use a horse and saddle from the stock to work the cattle. After a few weeks, his tired body recorded every hour he put in but hardened into muscle.

For once, he didn't have a Friday night gig, and his friends had a movie night planned. Getting away for fun with friends sounded great. The superhero movie kept them all engaged although it seemed a little hokey.

Later, over burgers, Bill got them laughing with his usual antics. "Yeah, the guys that fly are my heroes. I flew off the roof of our barn when I was about eleven, and, boy, was I glad for that pile of leaves when my bath towel-cape wrapped around my face and I couldn't see a damn thing on the way down. I screamed like a two-year-old and plopped on the ground like an egg out o' Mama's apron. That 'bout ended my flying and baseball careers for the summer. Yup, good old Coach Willis let me sit on the bench with my arm in a cast the rest of the season."

As they caught their breath from laughing, someone suggested they stop for a drink. Randy said, "Why don't we go to the place where my friend, Tom, plays? The band will still be on a little longer."

Frank punched Randy's arm to tease him. "You hear him, guys? His friend, Tom Murphy. Rub it in, why don't ya?"

As they continued the teasing, Sarah laid her hand on his arm for the walk to the car. "Don't pay any attention to them, sweetie. They're fooling with you. They wish they had the same opportunity."

Randy shrugged it off. "Oh, I get it. How have you been? I haven't seen much of you since I started working."

Sarah lifted her arms with palms up. "Same thing, different day for me. I'm feeling like I'm in a rut. I picked up a catalog for classes at the community college the other day. When I went out there, the lady said I should be able to get some financial aid. I need to get serious about something."

Randy's voice rose with excitement. "That's exciting, Sarah. What classes would you take?"

"I'm thinking about the business section. I'd go pretty general at first to ease back into sitting in a classroom and having homework again."

"That's a smart way to get started, and I'll bet you'll do great." She hugged his arm tighter.

They entered the club to the soaring sounds of a steel guitar. Beth and Johnny joined the crowd on the dance floor while the others waited for a large table to be available. Randy waved at Tom, though he knew his friend probably couldn't see him through the stage lights. When the band had their break, he approached the stage to speak to him.

Tom spoke first. "Hi, Randy. How's work going?" They shook hands.

"Whew, I forgot how hard that kind of work can be." Randy made a motion of wiping his brow. "I like being back in the saddle, though. I'm here taking it easy with friends. You guys are on tonight."

As usual, Tom got the talk off himself. "See you Sunday? Jennie sure is enjoying having you around. She's got some new cake recipe she wants to try on you."

"Anything she fixes works for me. Hey, I have a new song I want you to hear, too. I did like you said and got one of those notebook calendars to record all the contacts I've made and gigs I've booked. I guess we'll go over that?" At once Randy realized he was the one with homework.

"Yes, and I'll help you write out goals for yourself. We've got a lot of work to do."

Randy went back to his friends with excitement in his voice, and they listened with the same energy. They stayed until the band quit before heading home. Randy searched the refrigerator for something to help him sleep. He didn't want to face the darkness alone. "Come on, guys, just one more beer."

"Are you kidding, man? I've got to work tomorrow." Frank closed his bedroom door.

"Yeah, Randy, go easy on that stuff," Beth added then batted her eyes at Johnny. "Be a sweetheart, baby, and bring me a water to bed?"

Randy twisted the lid off another beer and drank alone.

Chapter 5

Frank shook Randy's shoulder. "Hey, get up. Your phone's been buzzing forever."

The edge in Frank's voice pulled Randy's eyes open to see his friend standing over him. He rolled his enlarged tongue around the cotton that was his mouth as he tried to move his legs. When he reached an upright sitting position, his hand inched its way up to find his head still attached to his body. "What time is it?"

Frank handed him a cup of coffee. "Ten thirty a.m. Wasn't the sun in your eyes a clue?"

"Give me a break, will ya? Where's my phone?"

"It must be under you. The sound got kinda faint a while ago. You better be glad you don't have to work today. You look like crap. I see you wiped out the beer supply. I'd say that'll piss off Johnny."

Randy moved faster now. "Oh shit, what day is it? Saturday? I'm in so much trouble. Help me find my phone."

Frank's face looked like a man forced to sit through the Gettysburg Address quoted backward. His voice yelled out his frustration. "I've gotta get to work. Here's the damn phone. Get yourself together, Randy, and clean up this mess."

Randy listened to two of the seven voice messages, all from Carrie. He breathed deep, then keyed her cell number. He listened to sounds of carnival games and kids' laughter around her when she answered. The tone of her voice said she wanted to choke him.

"Carrie, I'm sorry. Please let me talk to him. I said I'm sorry."

"No. He's having his party with friends at Chuckie Cheese. Without his dad, who couldn't remember on June 18 he needed to call to wish him happy birthday."

"Damn it, Carrie, put my son on the phone." His hand reached to rub his face.

"Oh, that's funny. He's your son when it's convenient. What? You so busy being a wannabe star you forgot?"

"Carrie, I can't do this right now. I overslept. I want to talk to him, please."

"Oh, I get it. Too much Friday night, huh? Nothing's changed. I thought you were growing up, Randy. You can talk to him later when you're able to make sense."

His head swelled, and his ear echoed with the silence on the phone.

A shower and coffee readied him for the drive to the diner for lunch. Later, he prepared to face the phone again. "Carrie, let me talk to Jimmy."

"Your timing stinks. He's taking a nap."

"Listen, about this morning…"

"Oh, isn't this great? You woke him up."

"Is that Daddy?"

Randy's heart melted as he heard the small voice on the phone. "Hey, little buddy, happy birthday. Did you get my present? I want to hear about your day."

****

Two months later, the men occupied their Sunday places on the porch as Tom reviewed Randy's calendar. "This is what I'm talking about. Why did you call that little hole in the wall way out in Tehachapi? That trip will cost as much in gas as they'll pay you. There's a long-standing, prestigious concert series there. Snagging that one would make the trip worthwhile. I think I have the promoter's number." Tom got out his own notebook and shared the man's contact information. "Think about this stuff, son. Time is valuable. Don't waste it on a gig that does nothing for you."

"I guess I'm still operating on a small scale. I took what I could get." He hated disappointing his friend.

Tom's face became more serious with his impatience. "I have three things I look for in what I call a good gig. Write this down. One, the right audience. Two, a place that might lead to another job. And, number three, it has to pay for my time, effort, and talent. This is no longer a hobby. You're trying to make this your money-making career. Never lose sight of your goal. Doing the occasional benefit you believe in or something for fun, sure. But remember, occasional."

As the evening darkened, Jennie offered them coffee at the dining table, where they made another list. "Randy, what are the goals you have for yourself? Write them all down, no matter how big and far out they seem. We'll work together on the small ones to get you there."

For the next few months, he stuck to the plan he worked out with Tom. Now they spent a portion of their Sundays on performance skills. Tom added an extra guitar passage to enhance a song, or Randy changed lyrics to be more dynamic. Randy's audiences were larger now, and gigs took him as far away as Los Angeles. Word spread about this young singer who could hold and please crowds. He dropped his café job back to one night a week. Joining the gang for open mic when he could, gave him a needed break. Other small gigs moved off his schedule in favor of well-chosen opportunities. He stayed so busy that he only visited the family once more. He thought of Jimmy every time he stepped on stage, but had to keep going.

****

In October, after a successful run of shows and festivals, a feature on local TV, and a reorder of his CD, Randy saw his future come alive.

On a fall Saturday morning, he answered his phone to hear, "Hello, Randy Walters? This is Jake Sims at the Crystal Palace."

"Yes, I'm Randy Walters." He hoped his voice didn't give away too much of his excitement.

"I was hoping maybe you'd be free to come by this afternoon. I've been hearing your name around, and I liked your CD. Two thirty work for you? We'll talk a little, and I want to hear you do a few songs, okay?"

Was it okay? How could he say "yes" any faster? What did this mean? Did Sims have a job for him? Or was he being nice because of Tom? Yeah, Tom must have put in a word for him. This was not an opportunity to waste. He ran through a few songs, then dressed for the meeting. Nervous fingers drummed the steering wheel on the drive. After parking, he gripped the door handle and counted ten long breaths to calm the beating in his chest.

Tom met him at the door, grinning like a Cheshire cat. "Well, look who's here. Jake said he called you. He'll be out here in a minute to meet you."

"I won't let you down, Tom. This is important to me."

Tom grinned. "Remember to be yourself. Your

music is good. Let it do the talking. You've got this."

As Jake walked up, Tom introduced Randy. The band leader guided him to a rear office. As they passed the open door to the theater, Randy's breath caught at the sight. They talked for a half hour before Jake asked, "You ready to show me something?" They headed to the theater, where Randy knew the magic happened. He couldn't allow himself to think about who stood there before that moment.

After two of Randy's songs, Jake left the theater. *What's happening? Does this mean something? Why does it seem I'm naked and alone at this mic?*

When Jake returned, he led a full band to the stage. "Let's hear you sing and play as part of the group. I'll introduce you to the guys later. Let's do a verse and chorus of Pam Tillis's 'Maybe It Was Memphis.' I'll do Pam's part. Can you take the high tenor?"

They knew their parts, and Randy added the right rhythm and harmonies. After a few run-throughs, the others left. Jake stood back to give him a once-over. "Are you familiar with Pam's tunes?"

"Yeah, I like her stuff." Randy wondered what was going on now.

"Great. We're backing Pam here next Saturday night. My rhythm guitar player will be at his brother's wedding. You busy?"

Randy stood taller. "I'll be here and ready with all her songs. Any other music of the band I need to learn?" His mind moved so fast he wasn't sure if he made sense.

"Nothing you can't handle on the fly, I'm sure. We'll get together one night this week. Rehearsal with her is at three on Saturday. The show is at eight o'clock. There'll be a contract for you in the office on Monday.

Stan will talk about money then. Sound okay?"

He sealed the deal with Jake, then walked out to tell Tom he'd gotten the job. His mentor beamed with pride. Randy walked along in a fog of disbelief. He wasn't the main or even opening act, but this Crystal Palace stage was the one he had targeted for years. He couldn't wait to celebrate with his friends.

****

After a successful showing at The Palace, the better gigs started coming. Sometimes it meant travel, come rain or shine. On a Friday night in February, he left work early to drive two hours to Fresno, where he performed at a well-established venue. Headlining the show made the trip well worthwhile. The first sprinkles of rain hit his vehicle as he unloaded his equipment. He introduced himself to the manager, Sheryl. "I hope the weather doesn't affect our crowd tonight."

Her hand waved as if to brush away his fears. "We'll be fine. Most of the regulars are already arriving. They're excited to hear you."

He enjoyed himself from the start. The people danced most of the night. After the show, he sold his stack of CDs before settling back into the green room to unwind. These prime venues had a place where performers could dress, store guitar cases, and enjoy a snack. Much like a dressing room for actors. He finished the plate of cold-cut sandwiches Sheryl provided while they talked.

"I'd better get packed up and out of here. I'll be late getting home in this weather."

Sheryl handed him his check and winked. "We can get you back in here around July if that sounds all right with you. The crowd liked you a lot. I'll be in touch."

Randy stowed his gear in the back seat. As the pickup engine warmed up, he recorded the paid gig and proposed return date in his calendar.

Traffic built as the rain got heavier. A stop for a large coffee did little to keep the drowsiness away. He was halfway home when dense fog enveloped his vehicle. He searched the dial for a radio station to keep him awake. Singing along helped at first, but he found it hard to focus. The steady rhythm of tires on pavement and wipers flapping on the windshield lulled him into a trance.

The truck veered to the right into a guardrail, which jolted him awake. Randy no longer heard the radio over the crashing and screeching sounds. The vehicle bounced off and headed left toward the deep ravine dividing the four lanes of highway 99. A horn blared, and he felt the pull of a car whizzing by him so close he could see the driver shaking his fist. Wide awake now, Randy struggled to right himself and gain control on the slippery pavement. In the glare of headlights, he saw the mud and grass of the ravine coming toward him. The impact took his breath and threw him forward. The mighty force of the air bag pushed him back into the seat, stunned. With slow motion movements, he opened his door. With the first step out, his legs gave way, and knees hit the wet grass and mud.

Randy shaded his eyes as a man ran toward him out of glaring headlights. The stranger shouted to him, "You okay, fella? Sit still, my wife is calling 9-1-1." The man covered him in a welcome jacket.

Randy's head swam as he reached to his forehead. Fingers came back wet with rain and blood. When he could make sense of things, he thought of his guitar. Pain stabbed at his side with each try at getting to his feet. "I've gotta get my stuff out of there."

Again, the Good Samaritan held him in place. "You stay there. I'll take care of it." The man saw the guitar wedged between the front seat and back. He carefully worked it loose and lay it flat, then reported the instrument, Randy's hat, and gig bag appeared to be unharmed. "Best to keep them inside out of the rain for now. You're a lucky one, young man."

An EMT bandaged the cut on his head. Randy refused a trip to the ER. The state trooper who worked the accident site gave him a ride into Tulare where he filled out an accident report and called for help.

Frank made the trip to bring him home. "You're gonna be sore tomorrow. You sure I shouldn't take you to the hospital?"

"No. I just want to get home. Thank you for coming. This is so stupid. I've never fallen asleep at the wheel before tonight."

"Hell, this stuff happens." Frank kept talking to keep Randy awake because of the bump on his head. "As I walked in the door from my gig at Sundowner is when you called. I grabbed a thermos of coffee and headed out. Get yourself a cup. Sure glad your guitar is okay. Did the tow driver say anything regarding your truck?"

"Yeah, he's pretty sure the frame is bent. Someone will look at it tomorrow and call me. He thinks they'll total it, though." Randy's fist slammed against his door. "Damn, I sure don't need this right now. I thought that truck would last me a couple more years at least. How am I gonna get to my job tomorrow night?"

"Hey, calm down now. We'll figure it out. I'm just glad the crash didn't hurt you worse."

They arrived at the duplex around three a.m. Frank carried everything in while Randy got into bed. A successful gig turned into an expensive night.

The next day, Tom introduced Randy to the salesperson who sold him his vehicles. "Art, I want you to take care of my friend here. He needs a road vehicle to get him to gigs. You know what I mean."

Randy chose a low-mileage, four-year-old Ford pickup in nicer condition than he thought he'd find on a used lot. He signed the papers and followed Tom back to his house. Jennie made over the vehicle as if it were the prettiest green machine she had ever seen.

Randy reviewed his plans. "I have to work harder to make these payments. So much for having one paid in full."

"This is a slight bump in the road. Pardon the pun. I've been meaning to suggest you charge more with the success you're having. You've gotten good publicity, and your shows are drawing very well. Signing up for summer festivals is right around the corner, and we can get you in a top spot at one or two of those."

"You're right. What I'm doing now merits more. That'll help."

Chapter 6

Randy was doing well enough to cut back his hours at the livestock sale barn, giving him time and energy to book shows most nights. After he filled in a few more times at The Palace, Jake invited him to open for an established country star on a Saturday night in early July. It was Aaron Franklin, an award-winning artist with six albums out already. He secured tickets near the front of the stage for Sarah and the gang, Tom, and Jennie.

It shaped up to be the greatest night of his career so far. The music from the house band he now knew so well wrapped around him and gave him strength and confidence in his performance. Randy's emotion flowed through the songs and touched the audience enough to require an encore before he could leave the stage. He had dreamed about this for so long. He didn't disappoint the audience or himself.

He stayed in the wings a while to watch Aaron's show before heading back to the green room. The tray of snacks on the table gave him something to do with his shaky hands as he reviewed the night in his mind and vaguely heard the show end. A few minutes later, a heavy voice from a hulk of a man standing in the doorway in a staff tee shirt brought him back to the moment. "Hey, Mr. Walters, the boss wants to see you on his bus. Follow me."

Randy thought he must still be dreaming. "What?

Wait. What did you say?"

The voice came louder now. "Get up if you're coming. Aaron doesn't have all night. We've got to be on the road in a couple of hours." He turned to go, not waiting for Randy to follow.

As Randy stepped into the rolling home of this star, he only hoped his breath would return so he could speak. "Hello, Mr. Franklin. I'm Randy Walters."

"Sit down, Randy, and call me Aaron. Hell, the rest of the world does. Like they know me or something. You don't mind if I eat while we talk? Want a beer, water? I saw a little of your set and liked it a lot, so I wanted to meet you. Where're you from? You play here often?"

They talked for the better part of an hour, and Randy grew more comfortable as the minutes flew past. His heart jumped when he heard, "I already told Jake backstage I was going to steal you. He says you don't have an agent. I'd heard about you from others playing through this area, then tonight, boy, you knocked it out of the park. How would you feel about finishing the summer on the road with us? You can meet us in Memphis. That's about two weeks. I need you on acoustic guitar and vocal harmonies. We'll be recording in Nashville in October. That gives us time to try you for a while before we get there. I'll know before then if you're going to work out. You need to find an agent, too. Are you ready for all this? Everyone can tell you, I run a tight ship and I'll expect you to work hard. You'll have to learn fast. How old are you, Randy?"

Randy was certain he was dreaming, but somehow thought he sounded confident in his response. "I recently turned twenty-five, sir, and I'll work harder than anyone. I appreciate the chance." He jumped up to shake the star's hand.

"Sonny, you met him before, will tell you what you need to know. Don't worry, he's not as grumpy as he comes across. He keeps us all on track. I couldn't do it without him." Aaron grinned as he put his dinner plate in the sink and wiped his hands. "Two weeks will have to be enough time to get yourself in order. You have family, Randy?"

"Yes, sir, my mom will be really proud, and I have a six-year-old son back home."

Aaron pointed over his shoulder at a collection of photos and pictures drawn by little hands. "I have three. Make sure you see him before you leave. We'll be out a few months."

Randy found Tom pacing in the green room as he staggered in to retrieve his guitar. Tom stood straight. "What's happening? Somebody said you were with Aaron." He moved to take Randy's arm. "Sit down. You look like you've seen a ghost."

Randy removed his hat and looked at his friend through moist eyes. Tom patted his back until Randy could form words. "He wants me to join the tour. I might get to record with them."

****

Later, as Jennie put on a pot of coffee, Tom and Randy sat on the couch to talk about what lay ahead. "You sure you don't want to be out celebrating with your friends tonight?" Tom moved magazines off the coffee table to make a work space. "Have you even told them?"

"No, they had already left the theater, and anyway, there's plenty of time. I want to get things settled in my head before I spread it around. I can't believe it." He raised his voice toward the kitchen. "Miss Jennie, do you have some of your chocolate chip cookies in there?"

"I know what you like." She was already beside him with a tray of his favorite treat. "Don't overdose on those now." He smiled back at her with the sweets in each hand.

Tom opened Randy's notebook on the table. "You'll need to give notice at your job right away. Let's see what gigs you'll have to cancel. I wish we had a copy of Aaron's tour schedule. You might fly back to this festival. We'll put a star by it for now. You find out his schedule and let me know."

Jennie brought the coffee in and sat with them. "Get all your performance clothes to the cleaners. On second thought, only the jeans. I can do the shirts to save you money, but I know I don't crease jeans the way you youngsters like. Do you need anything new?"

"I don't think so. Sonny said everyone dresses like they want on stage. Well, come to think of it, yeah, I might get new boots. The job was pretty hard on my everyday boots, and my dress ones are pretty old." He made notes as fast as he could. "Do you think I can get everything ready by the end of the week? I want to spend some time at home. I can leave my extra stuff there. What about my pickup?"

Tom laughed. "You won't have use for it on the road. The first paycheck after you get to Nashville, you'll want to buy a new one, anyway."

"Right away, you'll need to get a place there." Jennie used her Nashville experience. "The hotels are outrageous. The landlords all know how it is, and most of them will work with you on a decent lease. The guys in the band will tell you the places to search. Too many years have passed since we lived there. I can't help too much."

Randy thought for a minute then asked, "Tom, he said I need an agent right away. Can you do that? I mean, I'd hire you."

"Oh, heck no, son. That requires a young spitfire who's up on what's going on in the business today. I've been out of it way too long. I can make some calls, though, and find out who's hot right now. You'll need someone who'll promote your songwriting, too. Might as well work both sides of it. I'll have names for you before you leave town."

The tray sat empty, and the discussion slowed to a stop when Jennie elbowed Tom and motioned to Randy, who had nodded off. "I think our boy has had all the excitement he can handle for one day." Tom convinced Randy to stay in one of their boys' rooms for the night.

****

Time flew by as Randy prepared to leave Bakersfield and all his friends. Tom and Jennie made sure he would hit the road like a professional. Housemates and friends threw a party his last night in town. *Gosh, I'm gonna miss all these folks.*

Sarah was quiet most of the night, even though she danced every dance with Randy at the party. Finally, he had to ask, "What's wrong? You're happy for me, aren't you?"

Her body stiffened in his arms as her eyes shot flames at him when she answered. "How could you even ask me such a thing? Of course I am." She calmed her voice. "I guess I knew you'd have to leave one day, but not so soon. You know I really like you, don't you, Randy?" She laid her head on his chest.

"Let's go outside where we can talk." He led her out

onto the porch, where he leaned against the wall and held her hands before him. "Sarah, you were my first bright spot here. My first friend. I like you a lot, too. I guess we haven't had time to figure it all out, and I know that's on me. I've been so busy and focused on my career, I didn't make time for much else. We should stay in touch, but I can't ask for much more."

"I know, I understand. This is your time, your chance, and I don't want to put pressure on you. I started classes and haven't been around as much either. But tonight, it hit me hard. I can't see you anytime I want anymore."

He put his arm around her and said with a sly grin, "Yeah, and I'll miss helping you with homework. I guess you've got my number if you get stuck on something."

"Oh, sure, I know your favorite thing about those homework sessions was the snacks and libations." Their kidding lightened the air between them. "Randy, I'm so proud of you. Watching how determined you are has inspired me. I probably wouldn't be taking the classes if not for you."

"Then we've been good for each other. Let's hang on to that thought. I'll be back to visit when I can. Now, let's get back inside." Randy pulled her close. They hugged, kissed, then joined the others.

****

Jennie checked off her list. "Have you got everything? You packed those extra shirts, didn't you? Now, call as soon as you get to Memphis. They're sending someone to the airport to pick you up, right?" She hushed long enough to raise a tissue to her eyes.

"Yes, ma'am, I've got all my instructions from you and Sonny both. Don't worry, I'll be fine. I'm sure I'll have more orders from Mom when I get home." She giggled.

"I know you'll do all right, but my nature is to worry about my boys."

Randy locked onto the eyes of his friend and mentor. This part was hard. "Tom, I don't even know what to say. It doesn't feel like thank you is enough. You've gotten me here. Now I have to buckle down and make you proud." He extended his hand to this man who was more than a mentor to him.

Tom clasped his hand, then pulled Randy to him in a bear hug. "You couldn't do anything but make us proud. Go out there and enjoy every minute, but come back home anytime you can."

Randy turned toward his truck and said as he strode away, "Well, I guess I've got everything packed but next Sunday's pot roast, Miss Jennie. I'd better hit the road." As the truck pulled away, he saw Tom in the rearview mirror, a sleeve up to wipe across his face. The couple stood arm in arm, waving as the pickup faded into the early morning light.

When he arrived in his hometown, the people treated him like a homecoming king. His mother had received visitors and phone calls daily from the first announcement of Randy's news. Even the society reporter for the newspaper included his mother's statement in the published interview of the town's musical hero. Randy wanted to spend every minute with Jimmy. The family ate together almost every night.

Their last night together, he and Sherry sat together on the porch swing talking. "Sis, I'll call Mom as often as I can, but you've got to promise to let me know how she's really doing. I hate to put it all off on you and Dan, but I'm glad you're here. You sure you're okay with me sending my checks here and you paying things for me? It establishes a steady address for me, ya know?"

Sherry reached for his hand. "Look, we understand you being gone, Randy. I hope you know, if chasing this dream of yours doesn't work out, we'll be glad to see you come back here. The kids and Dan like hanging out with you."

"Yeah, I couldn't be happier you hooked up with him. He's a great guy. I want you both to know I realize he takes on a lot of the man and daddy stuff around here with me being gone. Someday I'll repay you both."

"Seeing you truly happy will be enough. Don't worry about us, and anyway, Dan enjoys helping Mom. Sometimes he brings our kids and Jimmy over when he's hoeing the garden or working in the yard. It keeps them all close." She gave his thigh a pat as she rose to say, "I'd better get back to the kitchen before Mom thinks I've deserted her." She stopped at the door and faced him. "We've always been proud of you, little brother. I'll always be proud, no matter what."

His mind swirled with her words. *What does that mean? Does she think I'll fail?*

Before leaving town, he made one more visit to his son. "Come on, son, open your door. I want to say goodbye." Randy's knuckles rapped on the door to the little boy's room.

"No, Daddy, I'm never coming out."

Another rattle of the doorknob only frustrated him. "Now, Jimmy, we've talked about this before. I have to go. Please, I'll miss you enough without you keeping one last hug from me." He heard the lock release, and the door slowly opened.

Randy's heart melted as he saw Jimmy's red face covered in tears. He knelt down to catch his son as he ran into his arms. They stayed there until he heard Carrie's voice.

"You'd better get going. You'll miss your flight." Dan honked his horn to remind Randy of the time.

"I hate leaving him like this."

"He'll be okay, but try to remember he jumps every time my phone rings, thinking it's you. Surprise him once in a while."

"Thanks for letting me come by so early. I had to see him one more time." He kidded her. "You know, maybe you should have Dan come take the lock off that door." He could always make her smile.

Dan had the truck in gear before Randy could fasten his seat belt. "You need to tell your boss to fly you out of Ontario airport instead of LAX. Even on Saturday morning, the traffic will be awful."

"I know, Dan, I will. They don't know we live so close to another large airport. When they hear you're anywhere around LA, they automatically think LAX."

"Yeah, even Burbank would be better, though. Don't worry, I'll get you there." Dan wound his way through traffic, finding a few shortcuts, which got Randy to the airport with no time to spare.

Chapter 7

Randy found his way through the terminal and ran with all his might to board the plane before the doors closed. A change of planes in Denver gave him limited time for lunch. A severe case of nerves tipped his stomach over as his plane landed in Memphis. He stopped at a kiosk to buy antacid tablets and downed two. No time to wallow in self-doubt, though, as he saw Sonny waiting for him at baggage claim. *Thank God, a friendly face. Or at least I hope so.*

"Well, hello there, Randy. You made it. Let's get your luggage and get out of this madhouse. My vehicle is right outside." Randy put the tablets in his pocket when he saw Sonny smile.

"Nice. Is this your SUV?"

"No, a rental. Sometimes in a larger city, we need to get around for something. Like picking you up today."

Sonny talked continuously on the ride across town. "The guys are already at tonight's venue to get a preliminary sound check done."

Randy started, "So we'll get right to…"

"You ever been to Memphis, Randy? I love it. Some of us will head down to Leona's BBQ after the show."

"That sounds g—"

"A twenty-four-hour juke joint on the river from way back. Best ribs and pulled pork you'll ever lay your lips around."

Randy finally got a word in. "Sounds great. No, I've never been here." The city sped past them. "Will Aaron be going to dinner?"

Sonny turned his chin up in thought. "Maybe. Usually, he wants to go back to the bus and crash. Can't blame him, he really leaves it all on stage."

"I know. I sure admire the show he puts on." *Be careful, don't sound like a google-eyed fan.* He was part of the show now and had to act like a professional.

When they arrived at the arena, Sonny jumped out of the vehicle and barked orders at the crew. It was such a change from the nice guy on the ride over, it took Randy aback for a moment. *Oh, I get it. He's in working mode now. Hmm, I can go with that.*

While the crew set up multiple speakers, each as large as a refrigerator, the musicians warmed up beside the stage. Aaron laid out a little of the plan for his new band member. "No time to sit and chat much, so I hope you're ready to rock. We'll get a real sound check done this afternoon, but first I want to work on a song I'm adding to the set tonight. Like I told you, Randy, things move fast, and you'll have to learn on your own."

"I'm ready. I won't let you down." His was a voice of confidence.

Aaron turned to glare at him. "I know or you wouldn't be here. You got the contracts Sonny sent you? Everything signed off?" He raised a hand to Randy. "No, don't give them to me. Hand them to Sonny later. He'll mail them to our office. Well, grab your guitar and meet the band. We've only got a few hours to get this thing ready."

The pressure of the moment didn't stop him. Quick introductions over, he joined in the music of Aaron's new song. This was fun and comfortable like being at home. *It's just like I thought it would be.*

Showtime, however, found him shaking at the edge of the stage. He peeked out to see the sold-out house. He had rarely been in a concert hall so enormous, and never to perform. A large hand on his shoulder jolted him. Randy heard Sonny behind him.

"Like Aaron said, if he didn't know you could do it, you wouldn't be here. Try to hang on to that thought and enjoy it all. This is pretty damn special."

Sonny's words proved true. Nerves gave way to the exhilaration of the crowd and the excitement of playing on stage with one of the most accomplished country stars around. Randy relaxed to play and sing with energy he'd never experienced before. He loved every minute. Unfortunately, the fun stopped abruptly when the show ended.

"Hey, don't step on them cables."

"Get that guitar out of here if you want it all in one piece."

"Bring that black tote over here." Shouted orders came at him from all directions from guys he hadn't met yet. He stumbled over stage equipment in his confusion. He didn't know which way to turn first. His feet froze when he heard Sonny's bark.

"Show him what you want. Don't just yell. He's part of the band and not one of you flunkies, anyway." Sonny shifted his head to one side and lowered his voice almost to a whisper. "I'm sorry. I meant road engineers. I sure didn't mean to hurt you sensitive, skillful types." His voice rose again to a roar. "Now, get to it. Time's a wastin'." Sonny's eyes burned into Randy, and he shook his head. "You've got a lot to learn, rookie. Don't let these guys rattle you, but don't get in their way either. You're responsible for your own instrument. Get it off stage as quick as you can. They only have a short time to get all this broken down and loaded into the semi. They pull out ahead of the rest of us. Get your gear stashed in the band's motor home and meet us at my SUV. We'll get some fantastic BBQ in ya."

Food would hit the spot. He had eaten nothing since the hot dog for lunch in the Denver airport. His mind spun with all the excitement of his first day as a touring musician.

At the dimly lit food and music establishment, his nostrils filled with the luscious aroma of smoking meats. A blackboard held the hand scrawled menu above the register. He chose a rack of Leona's ribs. Sonny advised him to add coleslaw, Texas toast, and a piece of sweet potato pie to round out his feast. At the table were three of the band members and Julia Campbell, Aaron's promotional manager. The group included him in the conversation over the loud roadhouse blues coming from the bandstand. They laughed when, after his third beer, he yawned. Later, his first show behind him, happiness put his exhausted body to sleep when he fell into the bunk assigned to him in the motor home.

****

The work could be stressful, but more fun than he could have imagined. For the first two weeks, he found it hard to sleep with his bed directly over the constantly rolling wheels. He learned about laundry on the road and sharing shave cream when someone ran out.

He called home when he could. "Sis, hi. Can you talk a bit?"

"Sure, let me put the baby down." Randy heard his

nephew whine. "Dan, come get your son. I've got Randy on the phone. Where are you, hon? Everything okay?"

"Yeah, great. We're playing Louisville tonight. Hey, when I talked to Mom last week, she sounded kind of off. Is she all right? What's going on?"

"Yes, Doc Phillips said it's part of aging. She gets a little forgetful."

He stood as if to help him take the news better. "You had her to the doctor? Why didn't you let me know?"

Big sister tried to calm him down. "No need to worry you. It was her regular checkup. I asked him to look at a few extra things while we were there. Randy, I told you we'd call you for anything serious. Are you having fun?"

"Oh, sis, so much fun. I love working with the band, and Aaron is a great guy. I mean, he's tough but fair. After all, we drive his career and have to be on all the time." Randy heard his name called over his shoulder and knew he had to get back to rehearsal. "Rest of the family doing all right?"

"We're fine. The kids love the tee shirts you sent. Dan is over here bugging me to tell you hi from him. You don't worry about us. You go out and enjoy yourself. Glad you called."

Her voice trailed off as she hung up the phone. "Yes, Dan, I told him."

****

A few weeks later, Randy was in the groove. Sammy, the drummer, invited him to go out with him after the show.

"I met these girls, and they said they'd wait for us at a club downtown."

"I don't know, Sammy. Aaron said we're leaving

early tomorrow. Anyway, groupies?"

"Come on, man, we'll be back in plenty of time."

It didn't feel right to him. *I don't want to get into trouble, but I need to fit in with the guys.* "All right." Randy grinned. "I guess it couldn't hurt for a little while."

The two young women were indeed at the club when the men arrived. A tall redhead and an energetic blonde. They hadn't waited to start on the drinks. Randy wondered if they giggled as much when they were sober. He and Sammy didn't waste time catching up. Randy's stomach growled, and he took unsteady steps on the dance floor because of alcohol on top of not eating for hours. As they all left the club for the girls' apartment, he grabbed a handful of nuts from the bar. He also caught Sammy's arm. "Maybe we should forget this and get back. Look at the time."

Sammy pulled his arm away. "Will you quit worrying?"

The next morning, the sun beat down on Randy's eyes as he pried them open. He was sure his head was a basketball, and he rolled over to find the object of last night's fun naked beside him in the bed. It was all coming back to him, which didn't help his headache. There was a noise from another room. He held his breath and slid out of the bed to find his clothes. He stumbled to the kitchen where he found Sammy in his underwear, bent over the sink, water running over his head.

Randy's fingers moved like sausages as he tried to button his shirt. "We're late. Aaron will kill us. Get your clothes on. We've got to get out of here. Where are we, anyway?"

Sammy moved away from the sink, slowly rubbing

a cool glass across his forehead. "Stop yelling."

"Yelling? I'm whispering so those girls don't wake up."

"Randy, slow down. I found the address on a piece of mail over there, and I've already got a cab on the way. We'll be fine."

On the cross-town ride to their fate, Sammy started laughing. "Those girls were something, weren't they? Admit it, you had some fun, right?"

"I guess so. I mean, she was, I mean, hey, what was her name again?" Pain stabbed his head as he gently combed his hair with his hand.

Sammy leered at him in disbelief. "Who, your date? Shit, man, her name was Redhead and mine was Big Tits. I don't know, who cares? You gotta chill out some, Randy."

"Hey, now, cut that out. Those girls were nice, and, at the very least, they have feelings."

Sammy shook his head. "I give up on you."

As they arrived, the cab driver asked, "Where do you want me to pull up?"

Randy wiped sweat from his neck as he answered. "The motor home with the extremely large man standing beside it with his arms folded. Damn."

"Sonny, I'm sorry we're late. I can explain." Sonny's look said to shut up.

The big man glared at the two revelers. He yelled in crescendo, "Aaron suggested a $1,000 apiece fine ought to remind you next time, when he says we're leaving early, that's not the night to stay out. Lesson learned?" He turned to walk away. "We roll in five!"

****

"Hey, there, rookie. How's it going?" Julia

68

Campbell was usually all business. Her friendly greeting surprised him.

"I'm fine, but I'd be better if everyone would drop the rookie stuff. Hey, I didn't see you around last week." *Oh, shoot, now she'll know I've been noticing her. But she has to know she's a hard one to miss.*

"I was in Nashville. I'm not on the road all the time. Somebody has to be back at the office setting all this up, you know." She gave a little smile and pushed back her straight brown hair. "I'm working on promotions for the new album already. There's a lot goes on behind the scenes most folks don't know about."

Randy liked her smile. "I'm sure. You're always running around working hard."

"Well, thank you for noticing. Maybe you can tell Aaron I'd like a little of his attention, too. I've been chasing him all day to get him to sign off on photos. 'Yeah, later, babe' is all I get."

"You joining us for eats after the show?" He would have to find out what her story could be. He noticed she only wore a small turquoise ring.

"A girl's gotta eat. See you later, rookie. Oh, I mean Randy."

His heart fluttered when she smiled. He tipped his hat to her.

A voice came from behind him. "You'll get your heart broke with that one." Jackson, the bass player, stood shaking his head. He didn't look up from cleaning his fingernails with a pocket knife.

Randy warmed as the blood rushed to his face. "A little conversation can't hurt. I think she's nice."

Jackson shook his head again as he closed the knife and walked away. "Yep, that's how it starts."

He knew he shouldn't get involved with someone right now, anyway. She could be a fun friend, though. He'd still check her out at dinner. There was an interesting story there, and he was up for the challenge.

As time went on, he discovered some facts, such as they were. She was indeed all business. Others had tried and failed to connect with her. There was someone at home in Nashville, but she kept that part of her life private. A few days later, Randy tried anyway.

"I thought we could grab some coffee or something. We don't get too much time off, and I don't want to think laundry is all a day off is good for. What do you say?"

Julia shuffled from one foot to the other. "Look, Randy, I keep things simple on the road. I'm sure the guys have warned you. Not that I don't think you'd be fun to hang with."

Her cautionary speech didn't deter him. "I don't take much to gossip, never did. Look, only coffee. You can charge it off to work. We'll talk about promoting an album in Nashville, or you can give me some tips on a place to live there. How 'bout it? If the answer is still no, I won't bug you again."

"You're a smooth one. Okay, let's do it. As we rolled in, I saw a little bistro a couple of blocks from here. Are you sure you can take enough time away from your laundry for lunch?"

They laughed together like old friends.

Chapter 8

Aaron had a week-long opening in his schedule in late August, which allowed Randy to keep his commitment to a festival in Southern California, visit family, and make a quick stop in Bakersfield. The crowds for his shows were enthusiastic about his music. He had become used to the large arena crowds Aaron drew, but this was an exciting event and paid him well.

He enjoyed seeing how much Jimmy had grown and spent most of one day alone with him. "You know, I wish I could be here for your school programs and stuff, don't you, son?"

"My friends think the presents you send are pretty cool. I tell everyone my dad is a big country star now."

Randy had to snicker. "Well, right now, I'm only working for a country star. But yeah, exciting is the word, all right." After a day of baseball, snacks, and a movie, Jimmy fell asleep on the way home.

"Carrie, thanks for letting me take him out of school today. I know they just started back. He's sure is a pistol, isn't he?"

Carrie gave him a sideways look. "I wonder where he gets that? He has talked about you coming home for weeks now."

"You're coming to dinner tomorrow night, aren't you? Mom's fixing her peach cobbler to go with the pork roast."

"Oh, she's spoiling you with all your favorites. Yes, I'll come as soon as I get off work around six. I can tell Jimmy's teacher you'll pick him up after school. He'll be glad to get out of the after-school program. I don't have to work the late shift very often, but when I do, it sure helps me out. It makes a long day for him, though."

There was the familiar guilt creeping in. He knew he should be more help in raising their son. "I'd better get going. I'll get an early start tomorrow on the chores Mom has planned for me. Jimmy can help me clean the flower beds. After we stop for ice cream, of course." He gave her his mischievous little-boy grin.

"Don't you ruin his dinner." The corners of her mouth turned up as she said, "Oh, well, you guys have fun."

****

"Mom, you've outdone yourself again." Randy and Dan stood to compare how much tighter their jeans were after dinner.

His mother took charge. "You boys get out of our way so we can clean the kitchen. We'll bring coffee and dessert out in a bit. Sherry, you wash and Carrie can dry." She still gave the orders in her house, though Randy noticed she accepted the help more now.

Later, Randy said to Carrie as they walked to her car, "I'm glad you came. We haven't talked much."

Carrie leaned on the car. "It's good to see you. Jimmy has had a blast. You know, people think the fact we get along so well is strange. I appreciate your family still inviting me to everything."

"Aw, who cares what people say? You're Jimmy's mother, and this family still loves you. Uh, listen." The toe of his boot moved the dirt before him. "Um, Sherry says you're seeing someone."

Her car keys rattled around in her hand as she looked up at him. "Yes, a new guy in town. He works at the bank." She shrugged her shoulders. "We've been out a few times."

Randy nodded in silence a little too long as he watched his toe continue to work until he choked out the words. "That's real good, Carrie. What does Jimmy think of him?"

"Oh, I haven't brought him around. Jimmy knows I'm dating, but I don't want him to like the guy and then he's gone. You know, another man walks out of his life. It wouldn't be fair. But I do like him." She looked up and yelled toward the playing children. "Come on, Jimmy. Let's go."

"You know I want what's best for you, Carrie." He shut the door behind her after she sat down in the car.

Over the purr of the engine, she said out the window, "How about you? Plenty of girls on the road, I imagine."

Randy stood away from the car, hands in his back pockets, staring across the yard at nothing. "Nah, someone to hang with a few times." He turned back to her. "No time for any of that right now." His fist clutched his pounding chest as he watched her back her car around and head out of the gate. *Will the aching ever stop?*

****

The August sun beat down through the trees onto his rental car as Randy made his way down the familiar street to Tom and Jennie's. Tom jumped up from his chair on the porch and yelled into the house as Randy parked in the driveway.

"Mama, he's here."

The screen door swung wide as Jennie ran toward

Randy. "Come here, young man, and give me a hug." Her arms around him were familiar and welcome.

"You'll squeeze all the stuffing out o' me." He kept Jennie in one arm as he clasped Tom's hand. "Hi, Tom."

Jennie made a swipe at her cheek. "Lunch is on the table. Let's get in out of this heat." Randy took her hand to walk inside.

"I tell you one thing, Jennie. I'm sure glad you told me to buy those four extra shirts. Sometimes there's no stop for getting laundry done."

He took his usual seat at the table. "I wish I had more time on this trip. I hope you're okay with me promising tonight to the old gang. Pass those potatoes, Tom."

"This is your time off, son. You kids have a good time."

The food thrilled him, as always, and he treasured the company. Tom talked about the business and hung on Randy's every word. "So, you got hooked up with Neil Farrell? I thought he'd make a smart agent for you."

"Sure did. He actually met me at our stop in Montgomery. We hit it off right away. Thanks for finding him for me."

As Jennie started clearing the table, Randy offered, "Are you going to let me help clean up the kitchen this time, Jennie?" Of course, that didn't happen.

His friends invited him to stay overnight. Bill rented Randy's old room after he moved out, so the couch would be his. Randy thought staying was a safe idea, knowing the night would involve a cold keg. Randy took a long look around the familiar living space. "This is like old times, and I sure have missed you guys. Hey, where's Beth and Johnny tonight?"

Frank and Bill looked at each other before Frank

answered. "Well, if you can believe it, Beth got a job with a country group out of Phoenix and took off. Johnny's still pretty shook up about it. He'll be home from work about seven. He can tell you more."

Randy ran a hand through his hair. "I thought they were tight. Like maybe they'd end up married someday. The gig was that important to her? That is real messed up."

Bill spoke up next. "You might as well know, too, Sarah is dating some accounting student from her school. We don't see much of her."

"Oh, yeah, she told me last time I called. She said she'll be by tonight. Hey, listen, we're all right. There never was much more than special friendship between us, not really. I'm happy for her." He laid his hat on a side table. "Hey, what's a guy got to do for a beer around here?"

Randy enjoyed the laughter, pizza, and music with these friends he missed. He found a moment alone with Sarah to catch up on their lives. "I thought I'd get to meet your new fella."

She laid a blushing cheek on his shoulder. "He thought we'd all like to relive the old days." Sarah gave a nervous giggle. "Anyway, he's studying."

"Sounds like you've found a good one. You getting serious, Sarah?"

"I don't know. I'm trying to take it slow. David is different from the guys I've always dated. He has a plan to open his own financial business someday."

He noticed the sparkle in her eyes as she spoke.

"I like him a lot, Randy. I think I am falling for him."

She took a drink of Randy's beer. "What's new with you? How's your family?"

"They're doing okay. Mom seems kind of lonely, though. Jimmy is growing out of every pair of jeans Carrie puts him in. Sometimes I have to wonder, Sarah. Shouldn't I be back here taking care of everything?" The familiar touch of her hand comforted him.

"Look, they understand. It won't always be so hard. You'll make it, then you can do for them like you want."

"Maybe. I don't want to be just a check in the mail for my son all his life. And we can't talk Mom into moving to town. If I was there..."

"Stop it, Randy. You're a wonderful son and father doing the best you can. You deserve your shot, and I'm sure they want that for you."

His chest rose and dropped. "Maybe you're right."

Chapter 9

Nothing in his contract said he shouldn't get sick on tour. The unspoken expectation was he'd be ready to play as scheduled. As they traveled to a show outside Atlanta, he had a sore throat, stuffy nose, and a persistent cough. He rested most of the afternoon and heeded his mother's rule of drinking lots of liquids. His fever broke by showtime. He packed tissues into his back pocket before the band took the stage. Throughout the show, the drums hammered out the beat on his chest, and the steel guitar screamed in his ears. The pulse of the music filled his head, and a few times only a grab at the microphone stand steadied him. The sweat-soaked shirt clung to him, and his throat yearned for moisture, though a stagehand brought him two extra bottles of water.

Once, during applause between songs, Aaron turned to face him. "You okay, kid? You need to sit down?" That reinforced to Randy that getting off stage was not an option. Stand, sit, or lie down, it would be on stage with guitar in hand. After the show, Sonny took him to a Walgreens for healing supplies. He had to be better for the next show. The entire group depended on him to take care of himself.

****

Two weeks later in Missouri, Randy ran into his new friend. "Julia, when did you get in? I guess you were lounging around home while we slaved away at shows in

Georgia, Alabama, and Arkansas on our way here."

"Hilarious. I was busy keeping the whole Christmas tour from folding on us. We'll talk later. Gotta go see a man about...I forget...something."

"Sure, later." Randy admired the dedication she showed to her job. The tickle in his stomach when he was around her was different now, but he still enjoyed seeing her.

The gang went to Lamar's Back Porch for BBQ after the show. "Do you guys know all the BBQ places across the country?" Randy saw a pattern to their cuisine.

"All the best ones," answered Sammy, wiping sauce from his chin.

"I have to have my fix of blues in these old all-night joints once in a while," Sonny offered.

Julia chimed in, "Why do you think I'm always on the road for this St. Louis stop? I'm no dummy." With mouths full of pulled pork, they all nodded their agreement.

As they finished the meal, the guys turned to watch the band on stage. Julia motioned for Randy to follow her to a corner booth. "We can talk easier here. How've you been?"

"Fine, now. I got sick in Atlanta. Boy, I hope that never happens again."

"It will," she said in a matter-of-fact way. "Welcome to the road, Randy. You had enough of it yet?" She ordered tea for them both.

"Heck no. It sure is harder than I imagined, though. There's only a month left before we hit Nashville. I'll make it."

"Oh, and you think Nashville is going to be easier? You've never made a CD there. You talk about work, and Aaron is a perfectionist. Late nights and a lot of pizzas are in your future, young man."

"Shoot, I told you, I've never even been to Nashville. I'm not sure if Aaron's going to keep me on, anyway. He hasn't said anything."

"You'd know by now. Aaron doesn't keep slackers or untalented around. You must be doing all right. I'll tell him he needs to say something to you." She pulled a Nashville apartments book from the back pocket of her jeans and shoved it across the table. "Here, I picked this up at the airport. On the plane I marked some I think you should check out."

"Hey, this is great. Thanks, Julia. How's things back home?"

"We had to have the cat, Loretta, put down. At fifteen, she'd been a good one, but that's life, I guess. Thank heavens I was there when it happened. Marsha was a mess." She stopped, her face flushed, waiting to see if he had picked up on the clue.

"Your roomie, Marsha?" He kept his eyes on his tumbler of tea.

"Yeah, you might say that. I mean..."

"Listen, Julia." He met her eyes. "I always figured you had someone special, and this isn't the first time you've mentioned her. I'm pretty sharp at two and two."

She focused on her hands around the cold glass. "I did? Oh, man, I'm getting sloppy."

He leaned toward her. "No, you're getting comfortable with me, and I like that. Your friendship means a lot." He sat back again. "Heck, you've kept me sane out here, yelling orders at me like my sister. You remind me of her."

"Gosh, Randy, that's nice. So, this changes nothing

between us?"

"Sure, it does." He watched her smile fade. "It makes us closer than ever. Thanks for trusting me."

Her face beamed with relief, then took on a serious look. "You understand…well…trust is crucial. Deep down I think most of the guys know, and for sure Aaron. But there are some in the business I have to walk on eggshells around because I work in an environment that is still very much a good-old-boys, Bible Belt kind of network."

"All I care about is you're good at your job and a good friend."

****

With three weeks left on the tour, they pulled into Wheeling, West Virginia. Aaron asked Randy to meet in his bus. "Thanks for coming in, Randy. Move those books and take a seat."

Randy's mind slipped back to that first night they met in Bakersfield. He knew he had done well, but what did this meeting mean?

"Afternoon, Aaron. Getting these large vehicles through that last mountain pass was something, huh?"

"Yeah, I'm glad I wasn't in the equipment semi. Can you imagine? I'm glad we found level ground again."

"Real beautiful country, though. I appreciate getting to see so much of it this summer."

"Randy, I hope you've enjoyed it all and learned something. We've had a good run, haven't we? Want a beer?" Aaron took two cans from the fridge.

A hundred thoughts and questions ran through Randy's head at the speed of light. He wondered if this meant it was over for him. Maybe Aaron didn't want to use him on the album. If not, should he stay in Nashville anyway and try it? "I've had a great time and sure learned a lot."

"Tell me, what's the main thing you learned?" Aaron leaned forward, awaiting Randy's answer.

"I know to do this right, it takes a lot of work. A lot of work. But, done right, it's sure rewarding."

Aaron sat back. "Good. Glad to hear it. You've done a great job for me, Randy. I'd be proud to see you move forward with us."

The rush of breath back into his lungs relieved and excited him. Randy didn't know whether to jump up and down or continue to act like he had some sense in front of the man offering him a job. "That sounds fine to me, Aaron."

"Only one thing worries me, Randy."

The unseen fist squeezed his chest again. "What's that, sir?"

"Sonny and I have been listening to your CD some as we traveled. You might have a good chance on your own someday. I know at some point I'm going to lose you. You wrote most of those songs? Out of sight, man. You're a double threat. I won't hold you back, but I hope it doesn't happen too soon." He let Randy see his smile.

As he gathered himself to take in what Aaron had said, Randy straightened in his chair. "Those words mean a lot coming from you."

"I talked to your agent. We discussed bumping up your salary for the recording and the rest of this year. We'll talk later about next year, and I'm thinking a couple of your songs need to be in the show. Whether I'm singing them or you." He flashed a grin at Randy. "Again, we'll talk about it. Neil's sure a good one for you. I spoke up about your songwriting, and he said he's already shopping you around town. That will be important for you. You need any help to get yourself set up when we get there, you can rely on Sonny or Julia. They both think a lot of you, by the way. Two good people to have on your side in a jungle like Nashville."

"I know that for sure. Hey, Aaron?"

"Yeah, something else?"

Randy stopped in the doorway and turned, tipped his hat back. "Did I hear you dip back into the eighties and say out of sight?" He shot Aaron a smile and raised his eyebrows in question.

Aaron threw an empty can at him and yelled, "Okay, so shoot me. I'm a John Denver fan." Randy could still hear Aaron's laughter as he stepped down out of the bus.

Randy's heart jumped as he heard the familiar "hello" on the phone. "Miss Jennie, I sure have missed you. How have you been? Did I call at a good time?" Randy was homesick for more than her cooking.

"We've been busy with the new grandbaby. This one is number three for us. Tom is so cute with him. His first grandson, you know. How are you?"

"I'm great. Mighty good to hear your voice. Hey, where is Tom? I thought he'd be home from work by now."

"He'll be here any minute. Do you need anything out there?"

"I don't think so. We'll be hitting Nashville in a couple of weeks. Did I tell you? My friend Julia said she'll help me find a place?"

"Yes, she sounds like a special lady." The playful tone in Jennie's voice said she thought something more.

"And I told you, she's a friend. Keeping it simple out here. No time for foolishness." He had made her giggle.

"I hear Tom pulling in. I'll go rush him up. Love you, and you take care."

Randy tapped his leg and whistled as he waited.

"Well, is it still wonderful on the road, Randy?" Tom's breathing told Randy his friend had run from the car to the phone.

"Everything is going great. Aaron asked me to stay on. I had to tell you. We have shows in Richmond, a couple in South Carolina, Ashville, then on to Nashville. Neil says he has a couple of things set up for me there. You know, publishers and a few small gigs."

"Sounds like he's working hard. I know everyone will like you. Any time off when you get there?"

"Yes, we'll have three weeks before we start on Aaron's CD. I figure I'll find a place to live, then head home for a visit. You won't be too busy to sit awhile with me, will ya, Grandpa?"

Tom dragged his words out as if he were trying to decide. "Oh, I guess I can work you in. Let us know when you'll be here, so Jennie can start fussing. Can't wait to see ya, son. I'll have your spot on the porch all ready."

Chapter 10

The last leg of the tour, from Raleigh, NC to Nashville, stretched into the cool fall evening. All throughout the day, the guys made phone arrangements for rides home. Everyone packed to leave their rolling home behind. Julia offered to pick Randy up and drive him to a hotel.

The fire in his chest surprised him as the Nashville skyline came into view at sunset. The lights of the city appeared to stretch on forever. Seeing Los Angeles and Disneyland for the first time as a kid couldn't compare to this excitement. This was a new chapter in his life and career. As their trucks and motor homes on Interstate 40 split the town in two, he strained his neck, looking out windows on both sides. He saw the cluster of neon in what he thought must be downtown. He understood the streets were full of iconic bars and venues he'd only read about up to now. Somewhere down there was Music Row, the area where a lot of the music publishers and recording studios were located. Lit up for all the world to see stood the old Ryman Auditorium, the historic home of The Grand Ole Opry since decades before he was born. He couldn't wait to see all the landmarks of the country music industry and find his new place to live in Nashville.

Occupants of the motor home let out one loud cheer as the oversized vehicles lumbered into an empty stadium parking lot for unloading. Headlights from vehicles ready to take band members and crew home filled the night sky. After letting the others exit toward their loved ones, Randy stepped off to survey the crowd in search of Julia. The sea of handmade signs held by kindergarten hands, kids in football jerseys and colorful kitty tee shirts, soon distracted him. There were flowers and bottles of wine offered by welcoming spouses.

Through the glow of the lights, he saw a mountain of a man deluged with kisses from two little girls in Shirley Temple curls and lacy dresses. As the man stood to wrap his arms around their mother, Randy recognized Sonny, the road manager with a gruff demeanor, transformed into the role of father and husband. Randy missed Jimmy more than ever. A trip home had to happen soon.

****

The next day, Randy's agent, Neil, introduced him to a few of the many recording labels and publishers in Nashville. He showed himself to be a good representative.

"Jerry, I'm telling you, this guy is going to be hot. Some of the best lyrics I've heard since Dean Dillon. You need to get in on the front of his career. Randy, give him your CD."

The bald-headed publishing executive shuffled his unlit cigar to one side of his mouth and pointed at the CD. "So, are you going to sing or write?"

Neil jumped in. "Oh, he's a singer for sure, but if you want him as a staff writer, he'll be a good one."

The man glared at the agent, removed the cigar, and laid the CD on his desk. "Does he talk, too?"

Randy took over. "Yes, sir. I enjoy the writing,

which I started as a kid. I can't deny I'd like to make it as a singer, but when I do, it would be good to have a relationship with a good publisher already in place."

The man grinned at the boldness of Randy's answer. He stretched back in his chair. "Well, how about you sing one or two of these songs you're so proud of?"

After listening to a couple of Randy's favorites, the busy man praised the work but didn't offer more than advice. "Look, young man, where'd you say you're from? California? Yeah, you might have something, but I can't use you right now."

Neil tried again. "Listen, he's for sure to be picked up by somebody. You don't want to miss out."

"Neil, you've been at this long enough to know he's not quite ready. Yeah, I like what I heard, but to tell you the truth, I don't think he's right for us. We're moving away from some of the old, classic country sound. These kids nowadays are bringing in something new." He peered back at Randy. "Get some experience here in town. Take it all in and see what's working out there. You'll be okay."

As they returned to Neil's car, Randy let his frustration out. "That's the fourth place we've been today. This is harder than I thought it would be."

"Patience, my boy, patience. The important thing right now is these guys are hearing you. Listen to what they're saying. I invited them all to your show next week at Legends. One night, one of them will walk in and hear something to spark their imagination. You keep making the rounds. I've got you set up to meet with Nancy over at RCA as soon as you get back from your trip to California. Patience."

****

"Julia, I don't think I can look at another apartment or duplex, whatever." Randy slumped in the seat of her car. "I'm so confused with so many good choices."

Julia's nose wrinkled. "Well, don't forget that one awful dump."

"Oh yeah. What was that smell?" They both faked a gag at the same time.

"Listen, Randy, I think a couple of them were keepers, but the one with the covered patio and two bedrooms stood out, and it being partially furnished will help. Don't you think the price is right?"

"I do. And the location is excellent. I guess that's the one. Let's go back and put down the deposit. Hey, I'm starved. We've been at this all day. While I finish the apartment paperwork, you call Marsha to meet us for dinner. We'll let her choose the place. I'm still lost here."

"Give it time. You've only been here three days. You'll get it figured out soon enough. It doesn't take long to make friends either. Be smart, though. Everyone is after the same job, so choose those friends carefully."

"I get it. This is business. On the road, the guys told some wild stories about hardship, lies, and breakups. I guess it can get pretty nasty. Thanks for looking out for me, sis." He cut his eyes over to see her smile.

A few days later he was able to say, "Home sweet home. It looks a little bare, but I can work on decorating when I get back." Randy surveyed his new apartment as he patted the place next to him on the couch. "Sit with me for a bit. I think we've done enough for today."

Julia flopped down hard. "The only thing you need now is a new mattress. That one looks awful. What time is your flight tomorrow?"

"I took an early one. 7:10 I think. You sure you can

get me there?"

"Oh yeah, perfect. I can still get to the office for my nine o'clock appointment. You have all of your visit planned out?"

Randy's sore muscles welcomed the cushions of the sofa, and he answered. "No, other than spending time with family. I'll need to see my friends in Bakersfield, too. It'll be good to not have to work at all. Man, no gigs for two more weeks. I love it."

"Yeah, you'd better get some rest, too. You'll be hitting the studio when you get back. Aaron is The Energizer Bunny when it comes to getting an album out. He won't stop 'til it suits him." Julia shoved his arm. "You'll have fun, though."

"I can't wait. I want to learn all I can from him. I don't want to miss anything."

****

Randy enjoyed the ride to his mother's place from the airport with Dan, who had not stopped talking since Randy got in the pickup. "It is so good to have you home. The kids have talked about nothing else for days. The guys at Carl's are planning a get-together tomorrow night. How long can you stay?"

"A week and a half or so. Then I have plans in Bakersfield. Quick visit, I know. I have to get to work on gigs for myself around Nashville. I'll need some income while we're off tour. I haven't seen much of Nashville yet, but I can tell you, the place is really something else."

"Our oldest thinks you're about the coolest uncle ever. Her friends come over to sing and dance to your CD all the time."

Randy looked out the window to survey the town he still considered home. A shiny new Starbucks stood in place of the Dairy Queen from his childhood. "Things sure change fast. I guess I'll be taking the kids over to Connie's Cones and Cream this time, if she's still there." He turned to his brother-in-law. "You know, Dan, I appreciate all you do with Jimmy and Mom. I couldn't be doing this without your help."

Dan turned the radio up a little. "Don't go there, bro. I love 'em like my own."

Randy believed him.

As they turned onto his mother's property, the rumble of the cattle guard still made music to his ears. The women met him in the driveway.

"Hi, Mom, sis." His arms enveloped his mother. He didn't remember her being so small.

"Mom, that front acreage is overgrown. I worry that's too much for Dan to deal with. I'll ask Mr. Hayes if I can pay him to bring his tractor over to mow it. That dry stuff is a fire hazard."

She shook her head and responded with strength. "We never used to have to worry about this when the cattle were here to eat it down. I don't know why you insisted we sell every bit of the livestock when Dad died."

"Mom, there's no way you could handle it with me gone so much. We've discussed this before."

Sherry added, "Oh, you don't know how many times she's brought it up."

Randy wondered how long his mother could stay on the property she loved. "Well, let's get inside. I'm pooped. After dinner, though, I want us all to sit down and talk about this place."

Of course, the kitchen had been a flurry of activity all day. Sherry helped her mother prepare a feast of ham, sweet potatoes, and green beans for Randy's homecoming. Carrie and Jimmy arrived and parked under the oak tree beside the driveway as Randy and Dan finished repairing the pasture gate.

"Dad! Dad!" Jimmy ran all the way to his father's open arms.

Randy held him at arm's length to look him over. "Oh my gosh, son, how you've grown, and look at those fancy sneakers." He turned to Carrie as she walked up. "I see what you mean about him outgrowing clothes all the time." He removed his hat and bent down to graze her cheek with a kiss as she moved away. *Well, that was awkward.*

"Yes," Carrie answered. "The sneakers were a special treat for his last report card. He swears all his friends have them."

"I'm sure they set you back some. I could have helped had I known."

Carrie looked over at Jimmy. "I worked an extra shift and poof, new sneakers. We manage."

Later, the dreaded discussion brought tears to their mother's eyes. Sherry sat close and tried to comfort her. "Mom, we're not saying you're not the woman you've always been. We know you can still take care of yourself right now."

Randy added. "No, that's not it at all. We want you to think about the future. We'd feel better if you didn't have all this property to worry about, that's all." He could hear in her voice she would not budge, but he kept talking. "Bob Rogers is coming over while I'm here to give us some advice."

The mother's eyes shot arrows at him. "The realtor? What for? I told you; your father and I built this place, and it will be my home, now and forever."

Randy focused on her face. "Dad left Sherry and me to take care of you, Mom. Your welfare concerns us first."

Sherry gave support. "That's right, Mom, and it would be easier for Dan and me to help you. I think you could be happy in town. We'd find you a little two-bedroom house with enough yard for your flowers and a garden. You'd be close to stores and church."

Randy stood his ground. "Bob will be here tomorrow afternoon. I'll walk around with him, and we'll have more information than we have today. Nothing happens until you're ready."

The dark cloud hadn't lifted, but at least she listened.

****

"Jimmy, how's school these days? Mom said you got a real good report card," Randy asked as he drove them downtown for lunch.

Jimmy waved at friends out his window. "Yeah, school is pretty easy. Mom's been talking to people about some different school. Chapter, Cart..."

"You mean a charter school?"

"Yeah, that's it. I don't want to leave my friends, though."

Randy's brow furrowed. "She's really thinking about it, huh? Well, maybe Mom thinks it will be better." *I'll be bringing it up with her later.*

Jimmy brightened. "The good thing is they have music classes there, and the older grades even have a chorus and a band."

"That sounds good. So, you like music, son?" Randy always hoped he would.

"Sure, Dad. Grandma lets me play around with her

piano as long as I don't get too loud. I have that toy guitar you gave me when I was little. It doesn't play right, though. I don't have one like yours." The little face curled into a grin.

Randy checked the rearview mirror, turned the corner fast, and found a parking space in front of Hoover's Music Store. "Come on, let's see if we can fix that." Jimmy jumped out and ran to push open the door to the store. Randy followed him and heard the voice of an old friend.

"Well, look who's here. Come on in, Randy. It's good to see you, as always." Grey hair, a little too long, peeked out from below the man's Taylor Guitars cap.

"Mr. Hoover, it is sure good to be back in here. How have you and the Mrs. been?"

"Oh, you know, we get along. I'm thinking about retiring."

"Your son Tommy is going to take over?"

"No, he's a lawyer now in San Jose. My grandson works here part time while he's going to Cal State over in San Bernardino. I don't think he wants the place. I guess I'll have to sell when the time comes."

The possibility of this store being gone took Randy aback. He loved the familiar sound of his boots on the wood floor as he walked around the room where he had spent so much of his youth. "I can't imagine. You've been here as long as I can remember."

The old man stood from his stool and straightened the basket, holding CDs from local performers like Randy. It took the prime spot on his counter. "Forty-three years. I played in a rock band in the early sixties and did well enough Mary and I could leave San Francisco to buy this place. Things aren't like it used to be, though. What brings you in?" Randy never tired of hearing his story.

"My son is six now and thinks he wants to play." Jimmy had been carefully eyeing all the shiny guitars hanging on the walls around the shop.

Eldon Hoover's eyes lit up as he looked at Jimmy. "Let's get one down and see how it feels. You like that Gibson with the birds on it, eh? Well, it might be a little too much for you right now. Try this smaller one."

Randy had to chuckle. "At least he has good taste, although a little expensive. Son, maybe Mr. Hoover has one better for starting out."

Energy and excitement filled the old master as he showed Jimmy each style. He taught the boy about feeling the wood and listening to how each one sang out with the first strum of the strings. "Grab a chair and let me get a few down. You'll find the one meant for you."

Jimmy hung on his every word. He reached out, running his small fingers along the wood grain of the front, then the back of each one. He closed his eyes to listen to the sound. Randy's heart burst at the sight of his son, so young, finding the same joy in music as he had.

Randy knelt down to face Jimmy where he sat with a guitar in his lap. "Jimmy, are you sure this is what you want? You understand you'll need lessons, and it's a lot of work on top of school and sports. You can't let those suffer."

"I know, Dad. I promise." He wrapped his arms around the instrument. "This is the one."

Randy glanced at the price tag. "Let me call your mom." Jimmy listened to every word from his new friend. They went back to see the classroom area while Randy talked to the boy's mother.

"Carrie, we're down here at Hoover's. Jimmy had been talking to me about some school with music classes, and, well, one thing led to another."

"What have you done?" Her voice gave him pause.

"Now listen, I think it'll be a good thing. He wants a guitar. He knows he'll have to take lessons, and he promises to work hard. I called to make sure you could get him to the lessons on Tuesday nights at five thirty."

"I guess this is kind of like the sneakers?" He heard her almost laugh.

"Maybe so. He's such a good kid, Carrie, and he's convinced me he's serious about this. I think it will be worth a try. How about it?"

"Two musicians in the family. I must be crazy. Fine, I'll see you guys when you get here."

He hesitated. "Uh, it'll be awhile. We got so excited about the guitars; we haven't had lunch yet."

Now Carrie let go the laugh. "Like I said, I must be crazy."

Chapter 11

Tom and Jennie convinced him to stay with them for a few days, which made it easy for the two men to work on music whenever they wanted. Besides, he wouldn't find a better breakfast in town.

"Tom, I have a few new songs, but I found it hard to write on the road with so many people always around. I wanted to talk to you about my style, too. I keep hearing I'm not writing the fresh stuff they're wanting nowadays."

His mentor thought a minute, then asked, "Have you been listening, I mean really listening, when you go out to the clubs? Can you identify what's different?"

"I guess I know what I like and don't pay much attention to the rest. Some I can't get into. I mean, you can't even hear the words."

Tom had a response. "All I know is when I see these concerts on TV, the audience is singing along. They're getting the words. Maybe the stories are what you don't like. You don't write about hanging out on the tailgate getting drunk with girls in Daisy Duke shorts."

"No, and I don't want to."

"So, don't. Stay true to yourself, but change it around to be something anyone can relate to. You can keep writing about the boy getting the girl, but make it fun or upbeat sometimes."

"You'll have to show me."

"After lunch, we'll sit here and listen to the radio to see what we learn."

They spent the afternoon listening to new music and comparing it to Randy's songs. Tom got it first. "Hear it? She's singing about your guy who fell in love with the girl next door. Only she says they met and spent the night at the fair. Hear the music going round and round? They're having fun riding the rides in the midway. And yeah, she mentions the beer and making out behind the tilt-a-whirl. I'm not saying you have to go there. It wouldn't work for you. You're twenty-five, she's maybe sixteen, seventeen?"

"So, what you're telling me, Tom, is I write sappy ballads and they're out. But they've always worked for me up to now."

Tom stood to stretch his legs. They'd been at this for hours. "Heck no, ballads will never go away. First, what works in the honky-tonks and dance halls you've played in differs from where you are now. I'm saying give the folks something livelier sometimes. George Strait does it, Randy Travis, and others. They can throw in something upbeat and still be true to the sound their fans expect."

Randy slumped in his chair. "Why do I feel like I'm starting over?"

"You're not, son. I should have recognized this before. You have to change with the times. From what we've heard today, yes, these kids are bringing in something totally new. Your writing is good, and you'll have a following with it. Some songs may need to change to build your audience. Maybe you only freshen up the arrangements. Get out and listen to these new artists, get into their world. New songs will come, you'll see. We'll work more after supper. Smells like she's got it about ready."

The men spent most of two days working on Randy's music. Tom helped with the musical arrangements. Randy wanted to keep some lyrics as they were, and Tom agreed. Randy had fun finding a new way to express himself.

On the second day, Jennie came back from babysitting the new grandbaby in time to start dinner. "Are you guys going to keep up this work all night?"

Randy raised his arms and stretched. "No, ma'am. I'm ready to eat one more of your gourmet meals, and maybe we could sit and talk tonight. I miss that more than anything. Tomorrow, I'll need to move on."

Jennie surprised him with, "Want to set the table tonight, Randy?"

He jumped up in a flash. "I sure will. I must be at home now."

The visit with his other friends consisted of playing music together for fun, catching up on their lives, and questions about life in Nashville.

"Frank, are you still playing with the same guys, staying busy?"

"About the same. I'm kind of thinking maybe a weekend musician is all I am. They made me a field supervisor on the job, Monday through Friday. I had to take it. I guess I'll always play gigs with a little oil field under my fingernails."

Randy searched for a response. "I hate for you to give up. You're an outstanding player, Frank."

"Yeah, player. A backup guy, sideman. I'll never be more, and I can do my playing anywhere. Might as well stay right here. I've met someone, too. Sue Phillips.

We're getting pretty serious, and I'm happy about how things are working out for me."

"Sounds great. I'm happy for you. She must be nice. Man, old Frank settling down."

Frank grinned. "My dad says he's glad to see me finally grow up."

Randy slapped him on the shoulder. "Let's get the music started again."

He missed seeing Sarah and her David on this trip. Finals had them both studying. He spoke with her on the phone. "I understand, Sarah. It's so good to hear your voice, though. I need to call you more. The emails are not the same. How have you been?"

"Great, Randy. I have a surprise to share."

"What, a ring? It's about time."

"How did you know? We're getting married at the end of the semester. David will graduate this year, and I can finish at Cal State Channel Islands. We'll be moving to Ventura. He wants to set up his own accounting office there. Everything fell into place for us."

"This is such good news. I'll get an invitation, right?" He wondered if he'd be able to come back for the wedding.

As he made his way to his departure gate the next day, he thought of his friends and family. He fought the urge to turn around and go home. Would this ever get easier? He missed them all but wanted his career, too. He had his mind right when the time came to board.

****

The California trip had been short but fun. Now, standing outside baggage claim at the Nashville airport, he searched the sea of cars for his ride.

"Randy, over here." Sonny's voice carried over the

noise of cars and buses at the arrival/pickup area.

Randy waved and maneuvered through the traffic to Sonny's parked car. He said as he slid down into the Lexus, "Am I ever glad to see you? Thanks for coming and on such short notice."

Sonny turned the radio down. "I'm happy to do it. I thought you were going to drive your pickup back."

"Well, my brother-in-law's pickup broke down the other day. I left mine for him to use so he's not borrowing my dad's '73 Ford pickup and putting miles on it because I'd like to restore it someday. I figure I'm doing well enough now to treat myself to a new one, anyway. I'll check out the dealerships around town tomorrow. I've never had a brand-new vehicle. This should be fun." He couldn't hide his grin. "How's things been here?"

Sonny shook his head and laughed. "I got in a little golf, but my girls and Aaron have been keeping me busy. I think there were two, maybe three days Aaron did not need me for something. He's supposed to be relaxing, and he's already so hopped up about the new album he can't stand it."

"So, we show up at the studio on Wednesday, right?"

"Watch your email. Aaron's talking about starting rehearsals before then. Most of the songs are the ones he broke in on tour, but some are totally new. You don't want to pay studio time to learn songs." Sonny gave him a sideways look.

Randy's face heated. "Of course, that makes sense." *Damn, I should have known. I've got a lot to learn.*

They recorded in a studio on Music Row, an area on the southwest edge of downtown, the heart of the entertainment industry in Nashville. Buildings housed record labels, publishing companies, recording studios, and radio stations on both sides of 16th and 17th Avenues. Most buildings were old converted residential houses which kept a vintage look through the area.

After arriving at the studio, he checked in at the front desk to find the exact place where he should report. The photos and gold records along the wall distracted him as he made his way down the hallway. A jolt went through him as his shoulder met another. "I'm sorry. I need to watch where I'm going." he said as he recognized one of his favorite female singers. She didn't even stop to hear his apology or offer her own. As he entered the studio, he said to Sammy, "Guess who I literally ran into in the hall."

Sammy didn't stop rushing around. "Yeah, yeah, yeah. Come on, get set up. Aaron is in a mood today. We're in for a long day of it."

The abruptness of Sammy's answer stopped Randy in his tracks until he remembered this stuff was old hat to all these people. He couldn't imagine it would ever lose any of the excitement for him.

Randy found the first day of recording thrilling but intense. Aaron hired local musicians and singers to enhance the sound of his regular group. Randy now had stories he couldn't wait to share with Tom.

During the second day, he felt more at ease in the studio, but Julia hadn't been kidding when she said Aaron expected perfection. Several times, Randy thought something sounded good, but Aaron wanted another take. Stress overtook the room when Aaron yelled at someone for missing a note or being slightly out of rhythm. So far, Randy eluded his tirades but sensed the tension. While Aaron sat in the sound booth with the engineer to review a recording, the rest of the crew took a quick break. They couldn't go far and knew to be in their places at the next downbeat. The first days lasted until sundown. He rushed straight from the studio to the gigs Neil set up for him.

Aaron surprised Randy by shutting down the recording for the weekend as he told the crew, "This will give everyone a chance to rest and refuel. We need to come back and hit it hard to wrap this thing up next week, for sure." He looked around the room at the weary faces. "You guys and gals are doing a great job. Kick back and have some fun, but…" Everyone said in unison. "Don't be late on Monday."

"You've got it. Now get out of here."

A few of the guys invited him out to see the town. They made one club after another on lower Broadway with a beer at each. Each place had a stage for open mic or scheduled acts. Most performers, like him, were young and trying to break into the business. He enjoyed hearing the talent, but it revealed the magnitude of his competition. Sammy picked up a girl early in the evening, and after a few more stops, they went their own way. Randy stayed close to his group as they led him around. The crowds engulfed him amidst neon lights, and music. Performers were in front of stores and on every corner playing for tips. At midnight, they joined the crowd at The Ernest Tubb Record Shop for more live music. They ended the night at Tootsie's Orchid Lounge. Since 1960, and while they still held the Opry at the Ryman across the alley, the iconic bar had been a late-night home to lots of up-and-coming stars. Artists finished their set on the Opry then went to Tootsie's to drink with friends. He tried to see all the autographed photos covering the walls. The beer flowed freely, and Randy didn't remember how he got home.

****

The following morning, Randy woke to something like the sound of a screaming wild animal. Or could it be a fire engine next to his ear? For sure, a jackhammer pounded his head. In his nightmare-like state, he kept wishing the sound would stop. At last, he recognized it as the ringing of his phone. He almost fell out of bed as he reached for it. His mouth opened to speak, but he coughed dry air instead. Finally, he managed, "Hullo?"

"Oh my. Been run over by a truck, have you?" He heard Julia laugh.

"Hey, *cough, cough*, can you hear me? *cough*. Hang on, I gotta take a piss." He got to his feet and hung on to the wall on his way to the bathroom. He washed his face and staggered back to the phone. Relief filled him when he saw no one else occupied his bed. "Hi, what time is it?"

"Well, let's just say you've missed breakfast. Marsha and I thought we were supposed to take you on a tour of Nashville today. You going to make it?"

Randy couldn't imagine it right then. "Yeah, give me an hour. No, I tell you what, let me have some coffee and a shower, then I'll call you back."

"We'll make it a mini tour. We've got tickets for the Opry tonight. Maybe your head will be cleared by then." Again, her laugh.

"Yeah, great. Hey, if you're gonna laugh at me, could you at least keep it down some?"

On the shortened tour, the women showed him as many landmarks as possible related to the music business. They drove to Music Row and explained the history of studios and publishing houses he drove past each day. The trio spent a rushed hour and a half at the Country Music Hall of Fame Museum, then walked the streets of downtown. In the bright sunlight, the buildings looked older and the streets dirtier than the night before. Some of the neon lights still flickered. Street performers were at strategic points along the sidewalks. Music filled the air.

They took a tour of Ryman Auditorium, the former home of the Grand Ole Opry. The docent told them the building had opened as the Union Gospel Tabernacle in 1892. No wonder the industry now thought of it as the Mother Church of Country Music. Stepping into the hallowed space took Randy's breath away. The tour guide let everyone stand behind the old microphone seen in every photo of performers on that stage since the beginning. He thought of his dad and how much he had wanted to see a performance in this historic building.

Next, the women introduced him to one of the many fried chicken places where he ordered as if he hadn't eaten in days. "Ladies, this is great. We don't have anything like this back home."

"Southern cooking is one perk of this job," Julia said.

Marsha added, "I have to watch myself, or I'll blow up like a balloon. The flavors are so good, it's hard to stop sometimes."

Julia regarded Randy with concern in her eyes. "Randy, maybe it's none of my business, but you don't have a problem knowing when to stop the drinking, do you?"

He put down his fork and asked, "What are you talking about? You mean because of this morning? I'm fine now."

Julia continued with slow, well-thought-out words. "The thing is, I saw it some with you on the road, too. I only bring it up because many people have failed here, not because of their music, but because they couldn't handle everything else. I want you to be careful, is all I'm saying."

Randy stared into his plate. "I don't think I'm any worse than the other guys. I mean, we go out and tie one on once in a while to relax. You know how tough it is on the road." His eyes and smile rose to hers. "Don't worry, I'm okay." He patted her hand as if to end the conversation. She had, however, planted a seed to ponder.

After dinner, they drove to Opryland on the outskirts of town, a resort and convention center with the building that had housed the Grand Ole Opry since 1994. Excited fans filled the auditorium.

Randy looked around in wonder. "Hey, how did you get the tickets? These seats are great."

"Oh, that's not me," Julia answered. "Marsha works at WSM. They're always getting tickets to something." Randy knew WSM as the radio station that broadcasted the Opry around the world.

"Then I owe you one, Marsha. I've dreamed of seeing this all my life. Thanks."

The lights dimmed, and Randy's heart danced with anticipation as the announcer started the show. The music and excitement of what he experienced filled him over the next two hours. He imagined himself on stage. The love from the audience and the roar of their applause warmed his heart. This was where every country artist wanted to be. He vowed someday he would perform there.

****

Randy found it hard to build his own career while supporting Aaron. One late afternoon, Aaron gave them some unexpected direction. "Listen up, guys. I'm sorry, but we'll have to stay until this is right. We only need three more tracks. We knock this one out tonight, and the other two are easy. That way, we finish by Friday afternoon for sure. So, grab some food, call the wives, whatever, and be ready in an hour. There's pizza in the other room."

Randy's heart sank. *Oh my God, I have a gig tonight. What the hell can I do?* This wasn't like canceling a show back home. He tried to get in touch with his agent.

A pleasant voice dripping with southern charm greeted him. "Neil Farrell's office. How can I help you?"

"Can I speak to Neil please, about something important?"

"Who may I say is calling?"

"Randy Walters." Of course, she wouldn't recognize his voice.

"He's got someone in his office right now. Can I take a message?"

At this nerve-wracking moment, he found the sweetness in her voice infuriating. "He scheduled a gig for me tonight, and I can't make it. We're in a recording session, and I've only got maybe forty-five minutes until we start again. Please ask him to hurry." His gut told him this couldn't end right.

He sat with Jackson and Sammy and tried to convince his stomach to accept one slice of pizza. He'd like a beer to go with it. He wondered if even alcohol would soothe his nerves.

Jackson reached for another piece. "Hey, didn't you say you had something tonight? Did you call and cancel yet?"

"I called my agent but had to leave a message. He set up the gig. I wanted to ask him what to do."

Sammy chimed in, "Man, there's only one thing to do, cancel. Aaron's counting on you. We all are."

Randy's whole body shook when his phone rang. He jerked it from his pocket and walked away as he answered. "Hello, Neil? Yeah, what a mess. Aaron is having us work into the night. I can't make my gig tonight. How do I handle this?"

Neil spoke in a gentle, firm voice. "Calm down, Randy. I'll make the call. This one is a small open mic, no big deal. Thing is, I convinced Harry to put you on the list. I thought you might have finished the album by now. You understand, no matter who's at fault, you'd still have to cancel. Your job right now is Aaron."

"But I don't want this Harry mad at me, either." He thought of his future.

Neil let out a half laugh. "Trust me, Randy, there'll be ten to fifteen performers there waiting to take your place."

His point hit Randy's ears and heart with a thud. The brutal competition of Nashville loomed ever at his heels.

****

The following day, he watched the clock in the studio until Aaron called it finished. Randy put his instrument away fast and ran to his vehicle for the drive through busy Nashville streets, often testing the length of a yellow light at an intersection. He burst through the doors of the bar to find another singer on stage in his place. Anger and frustration filled his voice when he approached the manager. "What's the deal? You knew I'd be here. You replaced me?"

"Look, kid, I can't serve up maybe to this mob. You know the rules. You're not here warming up fifteen minutes before your time, you're out."

The man turned his back and walked away. After the set, the performer left the stage and bumped into Randy on his way by. "Too bad, sucker. You snooze, you lose. Ha ha ha."

Randy grabbed the man's arm and drew him around to meet the force of his clinched fist. The fallen singer returned as good as he got until bystanders stopped the fight. The next morning, the studio erupted in laughter when his fellow musicians saw the black eye and cut lip.

Sammy held him at arm's length to look him over. "Man, you look awful. You know, you really need to protect that pretty face. I guess welcome to Nashville is all I can say."

More laughter rang in Randy's ears. His temper had cost him embarrassment and a venue he could never play for again. He couldn't get it off his mind throughout the day. Sleep came late that night and didn't last.

Chapter 12

With Aaron's recording behind him, Randy could concentrate on his own career. Neil continued to introduce him around town. Playing open mics and small gigs for a little money kept him in the loop. The most profitable result was meeting other performers. He listened as they shared the difficulties of trying to make it. A fellow musician he met at a gig invited him to a jam session. It was fun to sit and play with peers, and learn all he could about getting his name and music known.

After he finished a turn in the jam, he went to the kitchen for a drink. He asked his host, "Mack, who is the woman sitting next to Scotty? I have to meet her."

"That's Angie Wilkins. Go up and introduce yourself. We're all friends here. You gotta put yourself out there, or you'll get lost in the crowd."

Randy watched her a little longer. Her curvy blonde hair framed a delicate face and bounced as she stroked her guitar. Blue eyes sparkled and danced as she sang. Her voice captured something in him he couldn't explain.

Randy gathered the nerve to approach her at the snacks table. "Anything good to eat here? I didn't know what to bring, so I grabbed a bag of chips as I left the apartment." His hand rose to his hat as their eyes met. "Hi, I'm Randy."

"Yeah, I know. I asked somebody. Angie is my

name. First time here?"

"Yes, I've only been in town about a month and a half." *She noticed me already. Stay cool and don't make a fool of yourself.* "You have a nice voice. Are you recording?"

She led him to a bench outside where they could talk. "I used to be with a band, Aunt Sara's Penny." She looked at his face for some recognition of the name. She shrugged and continued. "We put out an album with Curb Records last year. Our single charted, but not enough to create much excitement."

"That sounds good, though."

"Yeah, well, they released us last month." She gave a weak smile. "I told the others maybe it was our name. I mean, our initials on tee shirts would be A.S.P. Maybe everyone was afraid of being bitten." *She's funny, too. I like that.*

"Are you thinking of trying it on your own? I think you could." *Don't flatter too much, she'll think you're a goof.*

"Yeah, I've given the band three years. I need to get back to my own dreams. How about you? How are you doing?" She shifted to face him.

"I was lucky enough to tour with Aaron Franklin this year. You know, sideman stuff. We recorded a new album for him when we got back here. I'm still learning my way around all this."

Her eyes lit up. "That's an impressive way to start."

They talked for a while, then joined the others in music again. They exchanged phone numbers. He wanted to see her again.

Angie quickly became part of Randy's life. Most of their time together meant music venues or jam sessions with friends. Their moments alone were unique and intimate. He enjoyed listening to her sing, and his heart still fluttered each time he saw her. Learning from her years in Nashville was a plus.

They sat together in his living room. "You've been here a while. Has it been tough?"

"Yes, but I don't think I would change anything."

"You learned from it all?"

"That's right. See, I came very young. At first, I took jobs as a server, souvenir shop cashier, anything to pay the rent. Hanging out with other musicians and playing small gigs around town eventually led me to the band."

He asked for more. "Did you think the band had what it took? To make it, I mean?"

She pulled her long hair into a ponytail and scooted closer to him. "We had it good at first and got some touring experience with the record deal. The egos started coming out, though, and it got harder. I think we tried to make it happen when, really, we all wanted our own spotlight. Now, I can concentrate on my solo career again."

"Was it fun for you on the road?"

"Fun and tough. I mean the never-ending sameness of night after night. The close quarters of five people on a bus. You know, you did it with Aaron. I'm afraid I didn't handle it the best. We were all drinking too much, and I got into pills, too. I'm okay now, though. My agent, Frances, has been great through it all. I think she knew what was happening, but let me fail to learn. Now I'm back to three roommates and gigging around town as much as I can to keep moving ahead."

Randy took her hand. "You won't quit, though, right?"

"I can't, Randy. You, of all people, know what I mean. Music is more than life to me. It is me."

His kiss said he understood. "You don't go on until ten tonight. Let's stop for a bite on the way. We can still get there for the first shift players."

Angie jumped up. "Sure, let me fix my face." He grabbed her at the end of the couch. "Hey, beautiful lady, you gonna dance with me tonight?"

She fell into his arms. "You bet, cowboy."

****

Randy sat in the office of Josh Baker, assistant to the head of talent development at Carnival Records. The possibilities excited him, but he still had the pangs of frustration. *This routine is getting old. Meet the guy, show him your stuff, leave empty-handed. Go to the next.* He could only hope this time would be different. Josh attended his show the night before and invited him here to talk.

"Randy, your show knocked me out last night. Are the songs all your material?"

"Except for the last one. A friend in California, Frank Harrison, wrote that one. I appreciated you being at my set. I hope I gave you a good idea of what I'm about."

"Oh, yeah. What a damn good mix. Man, that one about Billy Bob and Uncle Jimmy's tractor is a killer. I hope you do something with that one for sure. I'm still laughing. Listen, I asked you to come in so we can talk about the future."

"Fine, Mr. Baker. I respect your opinion and the sounds you get out of here."

"Now, none of that. My name is Josh. We're still small and pretty casual in the office. We get serious in the studio. How do you see the next few years, Randy?"

The impact of being on the spot tightened his throat. He put together some quick thoughts as he squirmed in the chair. "I think I have something the listeners like, and I'm proud of what I've been writing, too. Building my audience is key. To do that, I need a new album with some of my up-to-date material. The next few years? I'll have a record deal, a tour of my own, and I'll work hard to get there."

"You know? I believe you. I'd like to see us as some part of your future. You bring in a demo of a few of the songs you did last night. I'll shop 'em around to some of our talent and see if anyone is interested in recording them. Getting you some songwriting credits will be good, and the publishing side of our company recently lost one of our young writers. I want my boss to hear some of your stuff and maybe see you perform. What have you got coming up?"

"I'll be at Fiddle and Steel next Tuesday night, then I'll be out on Aaron Franklin's Christmas tour for a few shows in the southeast between Thanksgiving and Christmas. We don't tour again until April."

Josh's face wrinkled. "While I appreciate your loyalty, that could make it hard to do business. Are you contracted with him?"

"Through the end of the year, and he mentioned he may give me some solo time on the next tour. He said I might even open for a smaller show or two. He and my agent, Neil Farrell, don't have it all worked out yet."

"Well, it sounds like he thinks a lot of you. You may have some decisions to make. If the boss ever signs you to an album, it will mean a hard six months of promoting the thing. Harder to do when..." He stood and put his hand out. "Well, you get a demo in here, and we'll go from there. Think about what I said, though. I think we would work well together, but the choices you make now can be crucial."

Randy's mind processed everything on his drive home. He dropped into his recliner without spilling his beer and keyed Neil's office number. "Hi, Barb, Randy Walters here. Can I speak to him?"

"Sure, darlin', let me get him. Hey, my mom loved the CD you gave me for her birthday. That was nice of you. Here he is, sweetie."

"What's up, Randy?" His usual enthusiasm carried his voice through the phone. "Did you snag Carnival? Sorry I couldn't get over there with you."

"I'm not sure. Can we meet for lunch or something tomorrow? I have lots of questions."

An Irish pub in Hendersonville was their favorite spot for business, away from the office. Neil overflowed with questions right away. "Fill me in. What happened? Did he make an offer?"

"He seems interested in my songwriting for now. Let's sit down and order." They discussed Randy's meeting over corned beef on rye with Guinness to wash it down.

"So, he said nothing about recording?"

"Not in so many words. He liked my set the other night and wants his boss to see and hear me." Randy reached for another napkin. "He said for me to bring in a demo of a few songs. He wants to see if any of their talent wants to record something. I think he's giving me a test, don't you?"

"Could be. Not a bad idea. You've made a good start, Randy. I'll take it from here. First the songwriting contract, then I'll work on the recording."

Randy pushed away the second half of his sandwich. He steadied his hand to reach for the ale. Trying to stare a window through the dark liquid, he explained his dilemma about Aaron's tour. "I don't know. He seemed upset that I would continue with Aaron."

"Get a real good feeling about all this before you talk to Aaron. As a matter of fact, let me handle that, too. He's a lot of sure money and exposure for next year. I'll set up something with Josh and get things rolling. The possibility of an album deal is the question here."

Randy had a situation that tore at him. His father had taught him to stand by his word. He knew Aaron was counting on him. "Maybe this isn't the right opportunity. I mean, Carnival is a small company and still kinda new. I'll keep trying to get on at places like The Bluebird Café. Maybe someone else will hear me and show interest."

Neil set down his glass to look hard at his client. "It doesn't matter the size of the label, the quality of what they put out is most important. For only being around four or five years, they've been doing some good stuff and making things happen for other singers. You've got your foot in the door. You could be the one that comes in to make them an important voice in town. Listen, this is the big time now. You're going to have to toughen up a little. You can't always please everyone. Aaron should understand you going with a recording deal. Talk with Barbara about getting the demo made, and I'll tackle the rest. This could be the beginning of something, Randy."

****

The crisp weather in the south was perfect for Aaron's Christmas tour. It consisted of twelve shows across Georgia, North Carolina, Virginia, and back through Tennessee. Randy enjoyed playing the smaller venues and seeing families sharing the holiday season. This reminded him of Tom's talk about sometimes doing things because they felt right. No doubt the shows were profitable or Aaron wouldn't do them, but he could see him having fun, and it kept the band sharp.

"Randy, how's it going for you?" Aaron found him tuning before a show at a church in Georgia.

"Oh, you know. I've been making the rounds and playing a few gigs." Randy thought he would get Aaron's opinion on the direction his career was taking. "Maybe you heard it looks like I've landed a staff writer slot at Carnival?"

"Yes, that's great. I want to hear all about it. How about breakfast in the morning?"

"Can we do Cracker Barrel? We don't have those yet in California."

The next day, Aaron said, "Randy, this is on me. You order anything you want. I'm a pancakes guy, myself."

The server recorded Aaron's order while Randy decided on the Smokehouse breakfast of scrambled eggs, biscuits and gravy, bacon, and coffee.

"So, you've been able to get some work around town?" Aaron had a way of making Randy comfortable.

"Yeah, every little bit of money helps. I tried to save from the tour, but I may have to get a roommate. I guess that's why Julia suggested the two bedrooms for me. Anyway, somebody would be there to take care of the place when I'm on the road with you."

Aaron took a drink of his coffee. "Yes, Julia is pretty savvy. About next year, Neil says you may have a chance at a record label."

"I sure wish. I think he's being optimistic, though. Don't you? The songwriting seems all they want for now. They're gonna shop my songs around a little. It'd be cool to have one picked up right away."

"Sounds good. I hope not one I want." Aaron gave him a smile.

"I think I know the ones you like."

The server delivered their breakfast. Aaron poured syrup on his pancakes. "Randy, I told you I thought things would happen for you. I know you want it all right now, but it takes time. You'll get there. When a record deal does come along, we'll have to let the business minds work out the details. Just know, I want to keep you with my show as long as I can."

"I appreciate it, Aaron. Making it on my own is such a dream for me, but I want to stand by my commitment to you, too."

"I know, and your integrity is one reason I want to help you. Someone gave me a leg up years ago, and it's time I start paying back." Aaron shook Randy's hand.

****

In a few days, Neil announced over the phone, "I got you the deal with Carnival. They want you to write with another guy on staff. I think you'll like the contract we worked out. This is exciting, Randy."

"Yeah, sounds great. I've never written that way, but I know that's how they do it here sometimes, so I'll figure it out. How about the recording?" Randy held his breath.

"We'll continue to work on that. Patience, Randy, one step at a time. They want to see you prove yourself a little more, is all. As soon as you get back off this brief tour, dive in to the writing with your partner. We'll talk soon."

Randy sat back and thought as the motor home rolled along. He hated that word patience. *But now I can actually say I'm a Nashville songwriter.* He almost keyed Angie's number to tell her the news, but thought again. He wanted Tom to hear it first.

****

Back from the Christmas tour, Randy went right to work. He met every bar and venue operator he could. He and Neil found enough work to keep him busy through the end of the year. He was making his name known around town, but not much money. The bartenders made sure he was never without a beer at the mic. Driving home with a buzz on seemed a perk, or was it a downside of the gigs?

His writing assignment was with Jeff Myers, a young man from Oklahoma. Jeff also sang and played around town, and they wrote well together. He liked him right away and after a few weeks asked this new friend to share the apartment, which helped with expenses.

Randy smiled when he saw Angie's name on his phone. "Hi, Ang. What time should I pick you up? I go on at eight."

"Here's why I'm calling, babe. Frances let me know a little while ago, I got the call to be on a songwriters' showcase tonight. I've been trying to get into this one for a while."

Randy choked back his disappointment. "That sounds good. I know you'll have fun."

"You're not mad, are you? This is vital for my career."

"No, of course not. I enjoy having you at my shows, is all. But this is about you. We'll talk tomorrow." He took a deep breath and shook his head. *And this is how it goes.* Life in Nashville was exciting, and he was making friends, but he yearned for the closeness of a deeper relationship.

****

"Angie, get up." Randy turned from the mirror, wiping shave cream from his face.

She pulled the covers over her head. "You've got to be kidding."

With one jerk of the bedspread, he left her uncovered and writhing. "I have the same hangover, but I'm up. Work doesn't stop because we tied one on last night. Get up."

Angie rolled over. "Where are you going? Can't I call in today?"

He buttoned his shirt. "Jeff and I are going to try writing with a girl he met a few days ago. And no, you can't flake out today." He sat on the bed and tickled her sides. "Who makes all that fancy coffee for the customers if you don't show?"

After rising up on an elbow, her hand reached for a container from her purse. A swallow from the beer bottle by the bed washed down a capsule.

Randy's brow furrowed. "What's that, Ang? I have Tylenol if you needed some."

"Just a little something to get me going, babe. I obviously don't bounce back as easy as you, and Tylenol would not do it."

"If you say so, but be careful. I saw you taking something last night, too."

She sat on the bedside. "You keeping tabs? Sometimes I can't come down from the excitement of the stage without a little help. I know what I'm doing."

Randy watched her stagger to the shower. "Try to hurry. We'll grab a breakfast biscuit on the way to your car. I hated leaving it in that parking lot."

Randy's heart jumped when he looked at the caller ID on his ringing phone. "Sis, what's wrong, is it Mom?"

Sherry's steady voice didn't calm him. "No, not this time. The kids were playing at Mom's, and Jimmy thought he could fly from one limb to another and fell out of the oak tree out front. Dan took him in the truck, and Carrie met them at the hospital."

His eyes filled as he set the coffeepot down. "How bad? Is he okay?"

"Broken arm. Doc calls it a nice clean break right above the wrist. They're putting the cast on now. He'll be home tonight. Come on, no worse than his dad has done a few times."

"Not funny. I should be there. He needs me. I'll see if I can get away."

"That's unnecessary. He'll be fine. He was being a little boy, and these things happen. Call him later. He'll want to tell you all about his exciting adventure."

"I've gotta go. I want to talk to Carrie. Thanks for letting me know, sis."

He keyed Carrie's number. "Hi, how's it going? What does the doctor say?"

He heard the waver in her voice. "Jimmy's better than me. It scared me at first when Dan called. He's so good with Jimmy."

"Yeah, I'm glad he's around." Another time Dan filled the caretaker role. "I told Sherry I'd fly in, but she said no. What do you think?"

"She's right. You know how these things go. I'll stay home with him tomorrow. He should be able to go back to school the next day. Nothing for you to do here."

Her words cut deep. He swallowed hard. "Tell him we'll talk later."

"Make it tomorrow. He'll be out of it tonight."

"Tomorrow then, and I may be home soon, anyway."

"Thanks for the call, Randy. It means a lot."

He stared at the receiver as the line went dead. *Thanks? It means a lot? I'm his father. Of course, I called.* He finished the coffee and got ready for his day. It would be hard to focus, but he had to make it happen.

Chapter 13

Randy's mother sat at the breakfast table with him. "I'm so glad you're home, honey. I was afraid you'd be too busy for Christmas with family."

"I thought I might be working, but Neil said I needed some time off. He's probably right, and anyway, he knew how much I wanted to be home."

"Is anything wrong?" She reached for his hand.

Her touch sent the warmth and comfort of a mother's love coursing through his whole body and settling in his heart.

"Mom, everything is fine. I don't want you to worry. Hey, I need to do some Christmas shopping. Want to go into town with me?"

"Sherry took me into Riverside last week, so I think I'm finished. I'll stay here and get ready for dinner. I hope you want pot roast."

"Perfect. I can't wait to see everybody tonight. Excuse me while I call my Bakersfield friends."

Randy grinned into his phone. "Hello, Tom. You two ready for Christmas?"

"Oh, you know Jennie is still fussing and decorating. How about you? Will we see you any for the holidays?"

"People are crazy this time of year. I'm thinking the adults get gift cards from me." They laughed together.

Randy sighed. "I won't have time to see you on this trip. I needed to talk with you some, though. Can I pick your brain a little more about Nashville?"

"Sure, kid. I'm free right now. Is everything working out?"

"Seems like it. That's what everyone says, anyway. I wish things would go faster so I wouldn't get frustrated. Everyone says I'm getting ahead, but that record deal doesn't come. I'm afraid I've let it get to me and gone off on a bender more than once."

"Well, I have to say I'm surprised at the alcohol. I didn't know you drank that much."

"Not on any regular basis, but I've sure been guilty. I'm surprised my friends seem worried. Oh, I don't mean anyone is suggesting rehab for me, but they don't want me to get there, ya know? So, anyway, do you think I'm on track like I should be?"

"Of course. I'd say you've had a great start. But it is that, son. A start. I told you there was a lot of work ahead of you. Look, we've all been through this. You think getting to Nashville solves it all, then you get hit with the facts of life. But you can't let it get to you. Stay focused, work hard, listen to those on your side. Don't be one of the many that let their egos run things. That's when the frustration takes over and you're sunk."

Randy paced with the phone to his ear. "Sounds like what I've been hearing from everyone, Neil, Julia, Aaron. Somehow, it means more to hear it from you."

"Is it not working with you and Neil Ferrell? I thought he'd be right for you."

"He is, Tom, and I know I'm impatient. I appreciate you talking straight to me."

"I told you from the beginning I wouldn't pull punches. Now, you get yourself together and stop whining. I believe in you. You're gonna make it."

****

After the holidays, Randy found that between writing with Jeff, performing, and pursuing more opportunities, he grew weary of the grind.

"Come on, man, the crowd here loved me last time. I'm available again Thursday night." Randy followed the club manager around as he worked.

The man dumped ice into a well behind the bar and set the tub down to address Randy's request. "Look, kid, you know how many guys like you want that slot? The people come in here expecting someone, something different every time. There are no regulars working here, and that's what you're asking for. I'll get you in again, maybe six months down the road. You'll have to wait for me to call you."

Randy's neck throbbed, his face crimson with anger. Clenched fists relaxed with each step out into the cool January air. He stopped to watch a young woman singing outside a boot shop. Her head nodded to the couple dropping a dollar into her open guitar case. She looked only seventeen as she closed her jacket tighter around her neck. *I guess I should feel glad I don't have to resort to playing in the streets.*

He drove to the next venue on his list, as was becoming his daily routine. He had to keep trying. Some producer or recording executive might come into one of these places one night and love his set. After all, Carnival hadn't promised a record deal.

Before he left a club, disappointed again, he sat at the bar to down the shot of whiskey the manager offered as a consolation. His frustration called for another to put him back in the mindset of trying the next place. After repeating this at other stops, he made his way to Neil's office.

Neil greeted him as he stumbled in. "Randy, what can I do for you?" He came to the front of the desk to take Randy's arm. "Woah, sit down. You look awful. Man, tuck your shirt in, comb your hair. You smell like a distillery."

"I think I've been to every club and bar in town trying to get work." The chair met Randy's butt hard.

"Did you have to sample their wares as you went?" Neil reached for his intercom. "Barbara, bring us some coffee, please."

"Sure thing, hon."

He took the chair next to Randy. "What were you thinking? You're drunk and in no shape to be talking business with these people. Not to mention driving."

"I can't sit home waiting on Josh and Carnival to decide I'm good enough to record. I left my family and home to come to Nashville on a mission. I'll make things happen on my own if I have to."

Neil slumped back in his chair. "Wow, thanks a lot. So, you think I'm just sitting here on my hands letting a recording deal go by? I told you this takes time, Randy. Even though I do have other clients, I'm talking to people about you every day."

Barbara brought the coffee in, and Neil waved her out of the room. She closed the door as voices rose behind her.

"Hell, I got the songwriting job on my own." Randy reached for a warm mug.

Neil stood to face the accusation. "Oh really? Do you think so? It wasn't me that spent an hour on the phone with Josh and another two in his office getting you a great contract? Man, I can't believe this."

Coffee spilled on the floor when Randy's boot tangled with a chair leg as he tried to get up. "I can handle things. You'll see."

"Sit down, finish the coffee. Or I'll have Barbara call you a ride home, one of the two." The room grew deathly quiet as Randy downed most of the pot of coffee. Neil ran a hand through his hair, then sat at the desk between the two men. "If this is the way it's going to be, Randy, maybe we've both made a mistake in our choice of business partners."

Randy didn't speak as he rose to leave the office.

****

The next morning Randy raised an arm, heavy like a ten-pound salami, to block sunlight streaming across his body, sprawled over the bed. Clothes from the previous day clung to him in a sweaty stranglehold. His mind whirled with troubling thoughts. At first, he recalled bits and pieces of a fight with Neil. After the first cup of coffee, the details became clearer. He reached for the phone but couldn't bring himself to key Neil's number.

He called Julia instead. "Hi, can I see you this morning?"

Julia's voice hesitated. "Uh, I'm guessing you don't realize the clock already struck noon. I'm free about three. Will that work? What's wrong?"

"I need to talk. I think I've made a mess of things. I'll tell you then."

At the appointed time, he entered Julia's office and sank into a chair. "Thanks for seeing me. I've been thinking about this for hours and still don't know what to do."

"Well, maybe if you spell it out, I can help. Your

call earlier frightened me. What's happened?"

He began the retelling while trying to calm his overactive leg. "So, I don't know if I even have an agent anymore."

Julia's eyes grew large. "You haven't called him or anything? Yeah, I'd say you've screwed up."

Randy got up to pace. "I'm too embarrassed to call, but I know I have to fix this."

Julia nodded. "You answered your own question. Talk to him and apologize. You need this guy, Randy. He's done well for you, from what I've seen. You don't seem to believe everyone when we say it takes time. You're moving faster than most. Take it easy on the guy."

"Maybe you're right. I'll call him now. Catch me if I start to say something stupid." Randy already had his phone out.

"You won't. Get it done, and we'll go to dinner where we can really talk. I'm worried about this path you seem to be on."

While he waited for an answer to his call, *here we go again with the drinking sermon.*

He sat up straight when the secretary answered. "Hi, Barbara. Can I speak to Neil, please?"

"I'll see if he's available. You all right today, hon?"

Shame flooded over him again. "Yes, ma'am."

Randy almost didn't recognize the terse voice on the phone. "What is it?"

"Yeah, Neil, I was wondering if we could talk a little."

"I'm on my way out for the day. It'll have to be before lunch tomorrow, maybe ten thirty. I'll tell Barbara to pencil you in a half hour."

Most of the breath left Randy's chest. "Tomorrow. Sure, okay."

Neil ended with, "That should give us both another night to think."

****

The walls of the office seemed closer than he remembered, the room smaller. Everything was pressing in on Randy as he sat down. He watched Neil finish writing on a form, lay his pen down, then lean back, eyes glaring.

Neil broke the silence. "Well, what is it?"

The words wouldn't come until Randy cleared the lump from his throat. "I, uh, wanted to apologize. I know I said some crazy things and was way out of line. I do realize how you've helped me. I didn't know what I was saying."

Neil glared until his client squirmed. "And the midday drunken stupor? That can't happen, Randy."

"I know. I let my frustration get the best of me. I want things to move faster, and after a day of no, no, no, I lost it. I'm sorry."

"I'm going to say this one more time. Listen. Take it in. This machine moves at its own pace. You're doing just fine. Some people never get what you've already achieved. You're touring with a top-name artist, you write for a well-respected publishing house, and their parent company is, are you listening? They *are* looking at you for an album in the future."

Randy's heart pumped faster. "That sounds great."

"You think I'm not working that for you? I don't even have to say who it is anymore. I call so much Josh recognizes my voice. I know you want it all, and I believe you'll have it, but you've got to play the game. If you don't trust me to lead you through that, it will never work. I have to trust you, too. I won't have this conversation again."

"I get it."

"I mean it. No more stunts like yesterday. I don't have time or patience, and it will only hurt your chances and my reputation."

"I'm in all the way." He stood and extended his hand, waiting for what seemed an eternity until, at long last, Neil rose to speak.

"This is it. I'll give it one more try, and if you don't take it seriously, we're done."

Neil's weak handshake said how close Randy came to losing his agent and friend.

A new attitude gave Randy energy and a return to the excitement he experienced at his first view of the Nashville skyline. He dove into writing with Jeff and others. Neil had him on a busy schedule of performances and songwriter circles around town. Networking with peers got him recognized, and he enjoyed meeting stars and newcomers alike.

Angie accompanied him to gigs more often as her performances became fewer. "Randy, that was a great show. You should do more of those fun songs."

"You don't think my ballads are good?" He pulled her close.

"Sure. I wanted you to save those for me." She kissed him and headed to the bedroom.

Randy retrieved two beers from the fridge and followed her. "Hey, Ang, I talked to your friend Robbie tonight." He stopped in his tracks at the sight of her downing pills in the bathroom.

"Cool, is he still starting a band?" She looked up to

see him staring. "What? What is it?"

"What was that, Ang?" He set the drinks on the bedside table.

She shot around and away from him. "Don't start, Randy. I want a decent night's rest, that's all."

A deep breath kept him from getting into another argument. "I think I'll sit out here and write a little. That's what helps me relax after a show." He picked up his beer, kissed her cheek, and left her getting into bed.

Chapter 14

In March, Aaron pulled his group together to start tour rehearsals. "I'm glad everyone is here. Not too many changes this time. I appreciate you guys staying with me. I've got some new songs we'll work through, but first, let's warm up with one of our old standards."

Randy was glad to be back into a routine. On a break, he sat to talk with Aaron. "I'm sure glad to be back with you. I've been knocking around town again, getting my name out there some."

"That's the way to do it, Randy. Keep working on it. I know something is going to happen for you. By the way, how would you like to do a song on some shows on this tour? It'd be more exposure for you."

"That sounds great. I can't believe it. You're sure? I mean, I'll start right away deciding which songs to do."

"Ha ha, whoa, boy. Not every show, you know, when it feels right, I'll bring you to the mic. We'll see how it goes."

By mid-April, Aaron was happy with how the group sounded and ready to start the tour. Randy selected songs to practice with the group. He would be ready whenever his turn came. Two months later, at The Birchmere, an important venue in Alexandria, Virginia, Aaron met Randy in the hallway before the show. "This is it, Randy. When we come back from break tonight, you give 'em your best tune. Then you can bring me back to the stage after."

"I'll do one I'm sure of, like 'Standing Free.' I think it will give them an idea of what I'm about, don't you?"

"That's what you and the guys were noodling around with yesterday? Yeah, I like that one."

In the few minutes he had, Randy hummed along with the guitar chords of his song to prepare for his debut. *Why am I so nervous? My songs are show fillers for this crowd. I have to make it memorable for them.*

Lights dimmed, and the audience returned to their seats. The band took the stage and began Randy's song. He looked across the crowd, smiled, and winked at a woman in the front row as his voice rang true into the mic. His heart drummed, and he wished it would beat in time with the music. A bead of sweat fell from the tip of his nose as his nerves calmed and he found himself at home with the audience. When he finished, they rewarded him with loud applause. With his hat off, he nodded and thanked them. Inwardly, he was three feet off the floor. He recovered to introduce Aaron.

Aaron shook Randy's hand as he stepped to the mic. "Isn't my band great? The young man you just enjoyed is Mr. Randy Walters. I predict right now you'll see this guy topping the charts one day."

Randy's head spun through the rest of the show. He was in a giddy fog about what Aaron said and the crowd's reaction. Yes, he wanted this to last forever.

The next day, Randy called Angie to share his news. The phone rang again and again until a weak and confused voice answered, "Hullo?"

He thought he heard her snore. "Angie, are you there? Angie, c'mon."

"Oh, sorry, who is this?"

He shook his head. "It's me, Ang. What's wrong? Are you still in bed?"

"What a party last night after Jason's show. It was great. Where are you?"

"Virginia, on our way to Kentucky. What about your job?"

"Oh, I quit that. I can't be dipping ice cream for smelly little tourist kids and their parents. Besides, something will break for me soon, and I won't need a silly job like that."

Randy didn't say he was skeptical about that. "I'll let you go. You can call later if you feel like it." He heard the deep breathing of sleep again.

A few weeks later, Randy got up from the poker table on the bus when his phone rang. "Hi, Jeff. Did you get the lyrics I faxed to you? What do you think?"

"I did, and I think we can work with it. I changed a few things, but overall, I like it a lot. I worked on a song with Josh Thompson a couple of weeks ago, and I'll be damned if Trisha Yearwood isn't interested. Wouldn't that be something? How's it on the road?"

"Awesome. Man, you've been busy. That's great. I think I told you Aaron is letting me do a song now and then. I'm having so much fun, and I feel like I'm getting close to something important in my career."

"Sounds like we may both have something to celebrate when you get back."

****

In mid-August, Aaron took a break from the tour. It was enough time for Randy to make a quick visit home. His first call was to make plans with his son.

"Hi, Carrie. Yeah, I got in last night. Hey, I want to take Jimmy to the skate park this afternoon. I'll pick him up about one."

"He's staying with my folks this week. Dad is taking him fishing. Mom fixed them a picnic lunch and everything."

"Oh, well, maybe I could take them all for dinner later." He gave his head a disappointed scratch and shake.

"He's got baseball practice if he's not too tired. Why don't you stop by the field?"

"Yeah, I guess so. I'm only here for three days. I was hoping for some alone time with him, but I don't want to cut in on their time either."

"Talk to them tonight. I'm sure they'll work something out for you."

Great, I have to schedule an appointment with my kid. "I'll do that. Thanks, Carrie. Anything you need?" The old familiar butterflies invaded his stomach.

"Nope, we're fine here. Sorry about the scheduling mix up. I guess I forgot you were coming."

He sat on the porch with his mother. "Mom, I feel so disconnected from what goes on here. How could Carrie forget I was coming? Now, I may not get to spend much time with Jimmy."

"Honey, she has a busy life, and you have to admit she does a wonderful job raising Jimmy. It's only one slip up." She patted his hand next to her on the porch swing. "You still have the lady friend in Nashville?"

He rolled his eyes. "Yes, Mom, and you know her name is Angie. You don't have to remind me I'm supposed to be moving on from Carrie, and I am, but there will always be something there with my first love that I can't erase. I can't explain it."

"I understand. Divorce must be very hard. I only

wish you could let go and enjoy your new life. Carrie and Jimmy will always be a part of it."

"I know. I guess I can't expect them to drop everything when all of a sudden, I get a chance to come home. Thanks, Mom. You always make things better. I set up with her folks to take them all to dinner tomorrow, so I'm a cowboy without a date tonight. How about pizza and a movie? It's been a while since I treated my best girl."

She giggled. "Let me fix my hair and put on something nice."

****

At their next tour stop in Dallas, Aaron approached Randy backstage. "Randy, how was your trip home?"

Randy set his guitar on a stand. "Short, but I'm glad I went."

"I get it. I love being home with my wife and kids, no matter how quick the visit. Listen, I bumped into Josh Baker while I was home. He asked about you."

Randy stopped his work not to miss a word. "Really? What did he have to say?"

"He was pretty impressed that I've been featuring you some on tour. I think Neil had already clued him in, though. I told him you'd do in a pinch. Ha ha. No, I bragged a lot about you. He's intrigued. I would sure act on this, Randy. Get Neil to set up some shows there in Nashville for when we get back. Invite Josh and crew from Carnival to see your performance. It could tip their thinking about that album they've dangled in front of you."

"Oh my God, Aaron, that's fantastic. Thanks for the good words. I'll call him right away." He was already reaching for his phone.

"Neil, hey, man, did you get those gigs set up we talked about? Aaron spoke to Josh, and he thinks they may be close to offering something. Invite that whole gang to one of the better shows."

Neil giggled. "And yes, I'm well. Thanks for asking. Slow down, I have it all handled. Josh says they'll be at Legends on October 23rd. We may want to do some extra advertising to pack the place. I'm glad the excitement is back in your voice. Everything going well out there?"

"Yes, a blast. I have to admit to one slip up in June. I went out with the guys and probably shouldn't have. The next day my poor head felt every bump in the road on that bus."

"I expect you to have a little relaxation once in a while. Don't be going overboard, though, and no little Randys left along the trail."

"I hear ya." He knew his friend was using humor to veil the seriousness of his words.

Neil hesitated. "I saw your girlfriend the other night. What's her name, Angel?"

"Angie Wilkins. What did you think?"

"Not bad. I keep trying to decide what she's missing. And she looked a little rough. But yeah, it was a good show until she had one too many drinks on stage. I'm pretty sure it wasn't water in that sport bottle of hers. I know you like her, but be careful, Randy. You don't need that kind of influence."

Randy took a deep breath. "You know, I might go off on anybody else talking about her that way, but I know you're trying to protect me. I'll talk to her again when I get home. I hate to give up on her."

****

It was BBQ time again in Memphis, which meant Randy would get to see his friend Julia. After the show, the gang went to Leona's, the place where it all began for him well over a year ago. This time he was a pro and ordered for himself with ease. "Julia, sit here with me so we can catch up. How're things back in Nashville?"

Julia set her full plate on the table and slid into the booth next to Randy. "As crazy as ever. Marsha says hello, of course. You eager to get back?"

"You bet. I'm going to concentrate on getting that recording deal. I think we're close."

Her eyebrows rose. "You think so? Wouldn't that be outstanding? What does Angie say?"

His eyes shot down to his hands as he unrolled his napkin and utensils. "I'm not sure. She says nice things, but then every once in a while, there's a little jab from her. I know it must be hard for her with the years she's worked at it herself, with little result."

Julia turned to him. "You can't help that. You stay focused on your future, whether she's a part of it or not."

He met her eyes. "I think she's back into some bad stuff again, and I sure can't seem to help her with that. Keeping watch on myself is a full-time job."

"And that's all you can worry about. You've got some exciting things happening, and you don't want to lose the support you have with Neil or Aaron. You can't screw up."

"Whoa, girl, tell me how you really feel." He smiled at her.

"You want me to go easy on you or be your friend? I only know one way to do that. Straight up."

Randy lifted a saucy rib to her in salute. "That's why we get along so well. Dig in to your food. I'd like to get to bed sometime tonight." *All around me are good friends and business partners. I'd better hold it together.*

Chapter 15

Late September saw Aaron's tour completed and Randy back in Nashville working at the jobs Neil scheduled for him. He also wrote every day with Jeff, which pleased Carnival executives. The two friends celebrated when successful artists picked up one of their songs.

Jeff tried to get him to relax with burgers and a movie. "You haven't stopped laboring since you got home. Surely one night off won't hurt anything."

"I have to be ready to show Josh and his bosses what I can do, how great it would be to record me on their label. The show on the 23rd is only a few weeks away, and I'm practicing all I can." Randy reached for his phone. "I'm going to call Angie before I get back to work."

"How's that going?"

"I don't know. I guess I haven't been too available since I got back, but I keep trying." After no response to his call, the phone went back into his pocket. "On second thought, a movie sounds fun, my friend."

Randy enjoyed jam sessions at a friend's house on Tuesday nights. He liked the camaraderie and networking with his peers. A few times, Angie accompanied him.

One Tuesday night between songs, Randy saw Angie go to the kitchen. When she didn't return in a few minutes, he went to join her. To his surprise, the kitchen was empty. Hearing voices outside, he stepped onto the back porch where she laughed and lounged in the arms of a man Randy didn't know. As he approached them, he saw the man place a small packet in her hand. Her kiss to the man's cheek stopped Randy cold. She turned from the man and bumped into Randy.

"Hi, babe. You know Mark, don't you?" She slipped the parcel into her jeans pocket.

He glared at the stranger. "Can't say as I do. Come on, Angie, we're leaving."

"But I'm having a fun time. Relax, Mark is a friend. He helps me out sometimes."

"So I see. Get your things. I'll meet you at the truck." Randy closed his guitar case and shoved the screen door open on his way out.

On the ride home, Angie made the first move. "What are you so mad about? I have other friends, you know."

"Friends? I thought we were there together, then I find you making out with some guy."

"You're kidding, right? We weren't doing any such thing. Oh, I get it, you're jealous. Well, you can just stop it. You don't own me."

"No, I guess that little bunch of pills or whatever he gave you is what's owning you, huh?" Randy pulled to the curb and slammed on the brakes. "What was that anyway?"

"None of your business. You act so righteous all the time. I believe that was you downing three Coors pretty fast back there."

There it was again. "Everyone is so worried about me having a few drinks. At least I'm not adding drugs to the mix." He watched her staring out the window. "We both need to watch it, I guess. I'm sorry. First, I saw him slip you something, and then you kissed him, Ang."

She jerked around to him. "Are you kidding, babe? A friendly little thank-you peck on the cheek? Seriously, I do what it takes to survive. If that means taking supplements or flirting with a guy, everything is all about trying to get somewhere in my career. The longer you're here, you'll see."

Randy shook his head and looked away.

Angie laid her hand on his thigh. "Wanna come in?"

"I don't think so. It's laundry and errands for me tomorrow. Anyway, I get up earlier than you ever will."

She laughed and kissed him hard on the lips. "Now, that's a kiss for someone more than a friend. Got it?"

****

In early November, Randy waited at Neil's desk for him to get off the telephone with Josh. Something about a serious moment like this always caused his leg to go into action. He stood to walk around the office. Photos and awards lined the walls. Book shelves held volumes about the music business and biographies of its historic stars. He turned as he heard Neil's phone slam down into its cradle.

Neil slapped his hand on the desk. "You ready to record? Cause I've got to tell you, this negotiation about beat me. Both guys were tough. I think we got Aaron and the label both happy, though."

"I am so ready. So, I got it?" Randy pumped his fist and sat again to hear more. "Oh, man, thanks for all your hard work. When do we start?" Both of his legs bounced like pistons in a well-oiled engine.

"Well, they know you and Jeff have an assignment to finish up. By the way, they want those three songs by

Friday. No questions asked. As soon as you get back from Aaron's Christmas tour, you hit the ground running toward a January recording. Things will start in the planning stages. You know, song list, the players, art work. Now, understand those can change as you go along. You won't hit the studio until mid-January. Even if all goes as planned there, we'll only have a short time to promote the album before you hit the road with Aaron in April. It'll need some significant airplay for it to be worth Aaron giving you a slot as an opener on his show. So, make it a hot one."

Randy stood again. "So, this is happening. I have so much to do. I've kind of got a list of songs ready in my head. Will those be my choice?"

"Mostly, but be open to what the producer wants. He knows what he's doing. Guess what? You'll be working with Dave Easton. Not bad, huh?"

"No shit? Oh man, how did you manage that?"

"Your label put it all together. They're taking a chance with an unknown voice, and they want to give this thing every shot possible. Usually, Dave likes to meet with the artist a few days before you get into the studio. He'll be working up his own plan."

The chair met Randy's butt again, hard. "This is a lot to take in. I've wanted it so long, and now it happens. I hardly know what to say."

Neil came around to sit on the corner of the desk. "You know, most performers are at this for a lot of years before they have your success. Some never get it. Believe me, I know this is about your talent and hard work, but never forget the impact of Aaron Franklin on your career. He took a cold, unknown kid on tour with him and spoke highly of you at every turn."

Randy's head moved up and down as he spoke. "I know. He's been great. I can probably never repay the guy."

"Here's how you do it. Make the best damn album ever and promote the hell out of it. You help fill the seats on his tour and prove you've earned a place on stage. Never forget, it's his stage to give this time. Someday you'll have your own. Don't mess this up with him."

On his drive back to the apartment, he reached to lower the volume on the radio. He wanted to call Angie but remembered she had a new day job at the mall. He'd tell her later.

Jeff met him at the door. "What happened? You got the deal, right?"

Randy grabbed a beer from the fridge, then looked at his roomie with a look of defeat. After seeing Jeff's face fall, he let a smile break across his face. "I did. Can you believe it? I'm still trying to wrap my head around it all."

Jeff shook his fists. "You had me worried there." He jumped around the room, then came back to Randy and grabbed his shoulders. "You did it. You did it. I knew it would work out. When do you start?"

Now pacing the room, Randy's words flowed. "Oh man, we've got to hand in all three songs by Friday. Let's get busy. We only have one finished."

Jeff caught him by the arm and pulled him to a chair. "Whoa, sit down. This is Monday, so we've got time. Take a breath, man. Tell me what all he said."

The two friends ordered pizza and talked for the rest of the afternoon. Randy thought about Jeff's trials.

"Jeff? You've been here four years?"

"Yeah, tough ones. I keep plugging away, though.

After all, I left home to make it big. Now, I've got to admit I'm kinda done with working mornings at the car wash. I could do that back in Pauls Valley. Something's got to happen soon."

Randy wished he could share his success with him. "I know I'm lucky. Has nothing gone right for you?"

Jeff opened a package of parmesan to shake onto his pizza. "I think I'd been here about eight months when a guy from BBR Music heard me and made an offer."

"An important label. What happened?"

"I was a kid, fresh out of high school, sleeping on anybody's couch that would have me. I didn't even have an agent and thought I could do it all on my own. Well, I'd never heard of them, so I thought I could do better. You know, it didn't sound like Capital, Decca, or somebody working out of Studio B. Turned him down. Now look who they record. What an idiot."

"Don't feel so bad. I almost did the same thing. I mean, I'd heard of these guys, but I knew they were small and only offering the songwriting at first. Neil convinced me to go for it."

Jeff nodded. "Live and learn, I guess. I wonder sometimes if word got around town I wasn't serious or something. The jobs dried up for a while. I wonder if I'd given them top hits like Craig Morgan has, if I might be on easy street now." He gave a nervous laugh. "I can't complain too much. I mean, I'm writing with some top guys, play pretty regularly, and make a living of sorts doing what I love. Once in a while, after too many beers, I feel like I've given up and sold out, though."

"You shouldn't. You're good, Jeff. Keep after it. Heck, you're younger than me with plenty of time. Stay after your agent. You need a bulldog like Neil. Let me know if you want me to set up a meeting with him."

"Thanks Randy. Right now, this is all about you. I'm proud of you."

"Hang on, man, I've gotta make a call."

Randy tapped his foot as he waited for his mentor to answer. "Tom, you'll never believe it. I got the record deal. Things are going like a roller coaster now."

"Well, son, I'm not surprised. Did Neil get you the right deal?"

"Yeah, but I don't even remember all the details. I'll still be with Aaron, and he has agreed to give me more time on the tour and even open some shows. Of course, I have to make and promote the album first. Hey, let me speak to Jennie. She'll be excited, too."

He heard a sudden gloominess in Tom's voice. "I guess I should have called you. She's in the hospital. She fell in the garden a few days ago and broke her hip."

Randy sat upright in his chair. "What? Is she okay? Did she have surgery already? I wish I could be there."

"The surgery went well. She's as feisty as ever. Heck, they got her up the next day. It will take a lot of physical therapy, of course. You've got your hands full right now. Don't worry about us. I'll give you the number to her room. You're right, she'll be thrilled with your news."

"I can't believe she fell. I thought she was a little unsteady the last time I visited. How are you doing?"

"Oh, for goodness' sake, you sound like our boys. We're getting old. Don't worry, they'll have us put away in a nice place when the time comes." Tom chuckled.

"I know you think that's funny, but I'm counting on you guys to take care of each other. I'll call her when we hang up. Hey, I want you to go over the song list for the album with me. Got time?"

"Of course. You know the producer will have a say in everything on this first one."

"I know, but I want to have a strong list and reasons for it when I get there."

For a while, Randy ran in all directions, juggling his writing work with Jeff, his scheduled gigs, and preparation for the album. He and Angie had little time together. He missed her.

As usual lately, he had to catch her on the phone. "Can I see you tonight? We finished my photo shoot early, and I'm not playing anywhere."

"I am, though. I can get you in if you'd like to come by. I can't remember how long since we even had dinner together, much less any quiet time."

"I've been thinking the same thing. Jeff will be gone tonight. How about we come back here after your show? I'll fix breakfast in the morning." Randy smiled into the phone.

"Oh my gosh, that sounds good. Scrambled eggs and those fluffy little biscuits you make?"

"My grandma's recipe, you bet."

Angie's voice whispered and stirred things inside him. "You're on, cowboy. I'll think of some way to repay you."

Every nerve in his body came alive. "I bet you can. See you at the club."

Chapter 16

The experience in the studio was different for Randy
this time. Never again would he question Aaron's
tension and shortness at a recording session. The
slightest error could throw off what everyone else was
doing. He tried to be patient when the group had to wait
for the lead guitar player to get his part right or the
harmony singers to search for just the right note. Though
his producer made most of the decisions, he still wanted
to be a part of song selection and arrangements. His
entire future hung on what happened with this recording.
Josh and the label were giving him the best chance
possible. From the producer to singers to players, and the
crew was top-notch. Through it all, he had more fun than
even he expected.

On the first morning, Dave Easton's voice came
from the booth with authority. "Randy, let's get a test on
your mic. Today's primary goal is for you to get
comfortable in here. If we get a track down even better.
These high-priced musicians"—behind the glass he
waved his arm across the room at the group as laughter
went back to him—"yeah, they're here to support you.
Get to know them and share what you want. They'll
listen or tell you what works better. Trust each other. Got
it?"

"Sure, Dave. I'm ready."

"Let's warm up with a simple one. Something

everyone will know while I get some levels set. You're a Bakersfield boy. You got something by Merle?"

He'd never had such talented musicians at his disposal. They started the first track before lunch time. They were off and running with creative licks and harmonies after hearing a song only once.

During a break, the non-smokers stayed in out of the January cold. He enjoyed a Coke and snacks with a few of them. The steel player asked, "So you're from Bakersfield? You must know Tom Murphy."

Randy's eyebrows rose as he swallowed a drink of soda. "I sure do. He's a mentor and a good friend for sure. How do you know him?"

"He worked studios when I came here. Me, a wet-behind-the-ears kid who thought he knew everything. He set me straight quick and taught me a lot. A brilliant musician, too. How's Miss Jennie? She still running things?"

"Oh, you know it. They sure have been good to me. I'll tell them you said hello." He shook his head and laughed at the coincidence as they got back to work.

The first day left him tired but excited. His mind relived the day again and again. He thought a few drinks at Layla's Honky Tonk on the way home might help him relax. As he sat at the bar, words of concern about his drinking crowded out the happy thoughts. He couldn't take a chance on not being ready for the next day. He finished the one shot of whiskey, left a tip, and headed home.

****

Three days later, Randy stood at the door to the sound booth. "Dave, I thought we were going to use 'Hometown Hero' as the fourth track." He wanted to stand up for his song choices. "I like that one, and it should connect with a lot of down-to-earth people across the country. They go crazy when I hit that chorus." He sang it for him.

"Hometown heroes, I find to be the best.

They lift you up and stand the test.

The barber, the preacher, and old Coach Benson.

My Aunt Sally, the butcher, and for sure, my dad.

Hometown heroes are the very best."

Dave shook his head. "The song is not ready. I mean, it has got a nice hook, but I'm not sure the melody is right. I tell you what, if we have time at the end, you might let these guys see what they can do with it. That costs money though, Randy. Trust me, not for this album."

Randy looked from Dave to the engineer at the console, to Neil sitting in the corner. He remembered Tom telling him to pick his battles. "Yeah, sure, Dave. Let's get started."

The days lasted into the early evening, and he shared more song discussions with Dave. Through it all, he wanted to create a product from his heart. After one of those full days, he set down his guitar and flopped onto his bed as soon as he got home. Jeff came into his room and wanted to hear all the details. "So, how is it going?"

"Hard, frustrating, exhausting." He sat up and grinned from ear to ear. "Man, it is the greatest ever."

He shared everything with his friend, reliving every high and low of the day. After, he went to his bedroom and laid his head back on his pillow to key Julia's number. "Hey, Julia. What are you two up to?"

"Hi. We want to hear everything. Too tired to come over? We'll toss an extra steak on the grill. See you in fifteen?"

As he arrived, he gave them both a hug. "I've sure missed you, ladies. I know I need to do better. There's been so much going on."

Marsha understood. "Look, we haven't exactly been knocking down your door, either. We've all got stuff. I always think when she's in town, it will be different."

"Are you complaining about me being home?" Julia reached to tickle Marsha's side as if she knew the answer.

Randy smiled at their playfulness. "You two are lucky. I have to admit, I miss having that one special person to share it all with."

Julia's face darkened as she sat at the table. "Are you and Angie having a rough spot?"

Marsha brought the food and stopped to hear his answer.

Randy didn't look up. "I guess so. Heck, we're both so caught up in trying to be somebody, we seldom see each other. Unless, of course, we're at some bar with a hundred people around 'cause one of us is playing there. I know I feel something for her, and I'm sure she does me. I'd like to be somebody's number one, you know? Neither of us can offer that. The music is always first."

The women's silence made a strong point. There was no answer.

****

Randy took an afternoon break from recording to talk to his mother. "Hi, Mom. How are you? Sorry I haven't called sooner."

"I'm glad to hear your voice. When can you come home, Randy?"

"I'll try soon. There's a lot happening here with my

149

recording and all. Is everything okay?" He heard something in her voice he did not like.

"Of course. I know you're busy."

"Mom, something is wrong. Talk to me." As he listened, he planned the call to his sister for the real scoop.

"I guess I'm feeling sorry for myself. A lot of my friends are leaving one by one."

"Leaving, Mom?"

"Either dying or their kids move them somewhere. I miss your dad."

His heart broke for her. The guilt of not being there to support her grief washed over him. "I've still got a few days in the studio, then maybe I can get a week off. After that, things are going to get crazy for me. You hang in there. We'll go do something, just you and me. I'll let Sherry know my flight details."

She sounded brighter as she said, "Oh, that's wonderful. We're going to the store tomorrow. I'll get all your favorites. We can have family dinner one night."

"Slow down, Mom. Don't get yourself into too much work. Anyway, I'll be ready for some rest. The important thing is I get to be with you."

He took a few extra minutes to call his sister. "I just got off the phone with Mom. What's going on, sis?"

"I guess you picked up on her being down lately. Everything is changing for her, Randy. She's healthy, and either outliving friends or they retire somewhere else. Again, her time of life, I guess. I try to keep her busy. I take her shopping, to bible class, to get her hair done."

"Has she stopped driving? What a surprise."

"No, but she doesn't argue when I offer, and it gives

us an outing together. Dan and I have gone to a movie a few times, which gives her time with the kids. I think she gets lonely."

"I told her I'd come home as soon as I finish this recording. I can't stay long, though."

"Thank you. I'm running out of ideas to help her. I know we promised Dad to always be there for her, but you know, Dan and I still miss him, too."

Randy wiped his hand down his face. "I know, sis. I know."

He went back into the studio with extra reason to finish on time. Neil needed to change a few things on his schedule, but it would all work out.

He called to announce his plans. "Neil, I can't help it. I'm only asking you to rearrange this one week. I can do the interviews over the phone, and I can do the songwriters' circle another time. Please, I have to do this. After that, I'm all yours."

****

After the week and a half of intense work, the last day in the studio was exhilaration and relief. Randy hadn't worked so hard since helping his dad at branding time. He thanked the crew, and they promised to stay in touch.

A call to Angie on his drive home, "Hi, we're finished and I'm beat. You want to come over? We can send out for something."

"Actually, what if I told you Jeff let me in your apartment to cook this afternoon? His girlfriend and Julia and Marsha are coming over tonight, so we can celebrate your album."

It sounded nothing like the quiet night he wanted, but he knew everyone meant well. The thought of her setting it all up for him was nice. "Now, that sounds like a party I don't want to miss. I'll be there soon."

Angie met him at the door with open arms. "Kiss me, cowboy. I've missed you."

Randy could have folded into her arms the minute he saw her, but the guests were all there. "Hi, everybody. I hope you can give me a minute. I've got to get the studio dust and sweat off me. Angie, can you bring me a beer to the shower?"

The night turned out to be what he needed. He hadn't allowed himself much fun in weeks. Angie's lasagna, salad, and Italian bread hit the spot. Marsha's pecan pie topped it off. During dinner, Jeff stood to make a toast.

"Does everybody have a glass?" He opened a bottle of Jack Daniels Single Barrel and shared it around. "Henry gave me this in payment for a gig a few weeks back. I can't think of a better reason to crack it open." He poured a healthy shot into each glass. "We're all real proud of you. I hope you remember us when you get too big for your britches. Back in Oklahoma, we say you're gettin' above your raising." They all laughed. "Here's to you, my friend."

Julia asked, "How are promotions going? I wish I could help."

"I know they have a lot planned. Interviews, shows around town. I don't care. I'll do a Kroger opening if I have to. We've already got commitments from some of the best radio stations around the country. I hope I don't faint the first time I hear it on the radio."

Jeff asked as he gave Randy a refill, "Are you going to be there for the mastering and all?"

"No, Dave said I could sit in, but it sounded like he

had final say, anyway. I get it. Besides, I have to sneak in a trip home for a few days to check on my mom."

Plain-thinking Julia said, "Yeah, this may be your last chance for months. When do you leave out on tour with Aaron?"

"I think April 20th. Of course, there'll be a lot of rehearsal before we leave. While I'm doing some shows for the album, too. I'm not sure when I get to sleep. Jeff, how about another slug of that JD to help lay my head down? If you guys don't mind, I'm pooped. I hope you know how much I appreciate all of you."

Angie followed him to the bedroom to say good night. "You sleep well, and I'll see you later tomorrow."

Randy set the glass of whiskey on the nightstand. "Can you stay, please?"

She took his face in her hands. "Aw, baby, you're exhausted, and I have an early morning interview on The Big 98. We'll find time before your California trip. I promise." Their passionate kiss would have to do.

Chapter 17

Randy looked across the parking lot at California's Ontario airport to see his green truck with Dan beaming from ear to ear and waving for Randy to get in.

"I thought you'd enjoy a ride in your old truck. I'm surprised you didn't rent a car, though."

"Thanks for picking me up, Dan. This will be fun. How's your truck running?"

"The poor old thing is on its last legs."

"You still owe on it?"

"Paid it off last year."

Randy spent the flight thinking up a plan. "How about we go right now and trade this one in? I'll add enough down to get a payment you can handle. You can sell your old heap later. What do you say?"

Dan's eyes grew enormous, and his words came slowly. "You'd do that for us?"

"Sure, what's family for? Besides, I have the new one in Nashville. I'm making good money now, and I owe you a little something for all you do here."

They completed the business and made the drive home in a shiny new pickup. "Randy, I can't believe this. When I called to let Sherry know we'd be late, I almost spilled the beans."

"Glad you didn't. I can't wait to see her face. You know, you have all supported me with all my crazy dreams. This is such a small payback."

He sat in the kitchen with his mother while Dan took his family for a ride. He downed a piece of her fresh bread with lots of butter while they waited.

"Well, Mom, you look great. I can't tell you how glad I am to be home."

"I've been looking forward to this so much. Son, I know you were too busy to come, but it sure means a lot. So, tell me about your record."

"Well, first, now they're CDs, not vinyl records. We still say album cause, I don't know, habit, I guess. But anyway, I think you'll like it. There's a couple of your favorites on there but a lot of new stuff, too. I've been writing."

"How exciting. I've been keeping the ladies updated about you. Have you talked to Jimmy yet?"

"No, I'll call when he gets home from school. You talk to Aunt Sylvia and tell her we'll be over for lunch on Wednesday. How long since you saw your sister, anyway?"

"Too long. I wish she didn't live all the way over in Glendale. Talking on the phone once a week isn't the same. No matter how famous you get, son, don't lose touch with your family. That's the most important thing you have."

Randy nodded. Her words rang true.

As she promised, the family gathered for dinner. He loved having his nephew and nieces around him. His mother rushed from kitchen to table, making sure everyone had plenty of roast beef and potatoes on their plates. After dinner, Jimmy treated them with a few simple songs on his guitar.

Impressed with his son's new skill, Randy said to Carrie, "He's come so far in such a short time. He must like it."

For a moment, Carrie placed the back of her hand on her forehead in mock frustration. "We've created a musical monster." She smiled. "Most afternoons he comes home from school, does his homework, then heads to his room. The rest of the night, all I hear is plink, plink, plunk on the strings."

Randy laughed. "I was the same way. He's keeping his grades up, then?"

"Oh yeah, he knows the deal. Mr. Hoover says he's got some natural talent."

"So, where's your friend? Still not bringing him around?" He nudged her arm.

She pushed the hair back from her face. "We kind of cooled off. I guess it wasn't happening for me. He's a nice guy, though."

The corner of his mouth turned up.

The next day, Randy met his sister at Miss Millie's café for lunch. "Sis, be honest. How do you think Mom is doing? Every time I come home, she seems a little, I don't know, older."

Sherry took a drink of her raspberry tea before answering. "Doc says her health is good. I agree, but she goes through these times of depression. Doc says that's normal, too, but I don't like it. For her age and after what she's been through, is what everyone always says."

Randy wondered what that meant. "Explain, sis. She's not like elderly or something. I know they had us later. She was maybe forty, but that only makes her in her sixties. I wonder why they waited? I always wondered why they were so much older than our friends' parents."

Sherry took a deep breath. "She broke down and told

me a little while back. At first, they thought they'd wait until the cattle business got going. Then, when they tried, she had two miscarriages. It took a few years for them to even try again."

Randy's voice shook. "I never knew. No wonder Dad was so protective of us."

She grinned. "Like he wouldn't have been, anyway. With Dad's heart attack and death so sudden, she wasn't ready. She hasn't said anything, but I know it's been hard."

Randy's phone rang. "Excuse me, sis. Hello, Neil."

"Hi. I've got you set up to interview in the morning at six your time. A spot on the early drive-time radio here is hard to come by. Jack wants you ready thirty minutes early, so set an alarm and sit by the phone. When will you be back?"

"I fly in on Sunday."

Neil shared, "Good, you're on Monday night at The Bluebird. Took some doing to get you in there again."

"Thanks for the hard work. As soon as I'm finished here, ready to get back to it."

"Oh, yeah. How's your mom?"

"We're figuring out some things. Don't worry, Neil, I won't let you down."

"I know you won't let yourself down. See you when you get back."

Randy stepped up the conversation with his sister. "You know, Bob Rogers contacted me a few weeks ago. He thought he had someone interested in the property. I told him we still weren't ready. Was I right?"

Sherry didn't hesitate. "You sure were. I've decided as long as her health is good, it has to be when she's ready to move. The place is the one constant she has, and her memories with Dad are there."

"I thought so. That puts a lot on you and Dan for upkeep on the place. Maybe we can lease some of the acreage to keep the grass down, and it might do her good to look out and see cows grazing like old times."

"What a good idea. There's no problem for us to look after her otherwise."

"I'm glad we've made this decision. I'll see if Bob can help us with the leasing. I'll be the one to tell her what we have planned. I think she'll go for it. I'll try to let her hear my voice more often, too. Family comes first." After what he learned about his mother, he wished he could put his arms around her more often.

While Randy was in California, the producer had the CD mastered and sent it off to the printer to be ready by the first week of February. Neil sent promotional copies off to radio stations for pre-play. The record label pulled out all the stops for a release party at the company's building on February 25th. Newspaper, magazine, and TV reporters filled the offices and hallways. Randy bounced from one interview to another. Cameras flashed at him on the front steps as the President of Artist Development officially introduced him and invited everyone to a small venue for a kickoff concert that night. The way he described Randy and the album, you'd think he had discovered the greatest new artist since Hank Williams, only better looking. Randy scanned the crowd for his friends and waved when he spotted them. They couldn't get through to him, but at least they were there.

This was the beginning of a whirlwind of activity. Album promotion filled his days and nights. He played songs on early morning TV and radio and performed at upscale venues around the area. With the album playing on the radio, he toured states close by, which put him back into the old routine of performing, travelling, and struggling to sleep alone in motel rooms after too much to drink.

Chapter 18

In mid-March, Aaron's group met in his new home studio. "Let's get going, everybody." Aaron controlled their lives again. "New stuff first. We're lucky to have Clay Henry on steel. Most of you know him. You guys heard we'll be using Randy more this year. He'll open for us about a quarter of the time. Now, I know it means more work for everyone. The contracts we sent you should reflect a bump in pay. You're here, so I guess that's all agreeable. You all got a copy of the schedule? If not, see Sonny after. Questions?" They made no response.

"Charts are on your music stands. All of them are my songs today. Remember, I'd like to be at my son's soccer game at six thirty."

Randy thought, *and I have a gig at eight*. Rushing from the studio to his own gigs was the way it went for those two weeks. On the Saturday night before they left for the tour, Aaron invited the crew and their families to his home for a cookout. Angie went with Randy, and they enjoyed talking with Julia and Marsha there.

"Marsha, thanks for helping me at the station the other day. I still get lost there."

"No problem, Randy. I didn't want you to be late for your interview. Are you ready to head out?"

"I think so. I can't believe I'm looking forward to sleeping in a motor home again."

Julia heard Marsha laugh and joined them. "What's so funny?"

Marsha held her laugh to say, "He's worried about his beauty sleep on the road."

Julia, always the concerned friend, gave advice. "Listen to me, Randy, you stay on that bus as much as possible. No all-night partying."

He pulled her to the side. "You're still worried about my drinking? Come on, Julia."

She looked deep into his eyes. "This should be a fantastic time for you. Fun, travel, excitement, girls even. Be careful, that's all."

He put an arm around her. "First, I'm not stupid. And anyway, Aaron won't stand for foolishness."

"Yeah, something to remember. You know where we are if you need anything."

The morning he left, he yelled, "Jeff, come on, let's go."

His roommate came out of the kitchen, two coffee cups in hand.

Randy ran through the apartment, packing last-minute items. "You've got all my information, right? Anything about paying rent or something, you call my sister. I'll try to stay in touch."

Jeff handed a full travel mug to Randy. "I've got it, man. You've drilled it into me for days. Everything will be fine here. Get in the car."

Randy moved an empty McDonald's bag and cup so he could sit down in Jeff's Honda. "Thanks for getting up so early to get me there."

When Jeff started the engine, the radio came on right away. Randy's song blared out of the speakers.

Time stood still for him. "It still shakes me every

time."

Jeff grinned. "Everybody talked about you at the club last night. Man, this album will explode for you."

"Yeah. Hey, pull up by the huge brown motor home. Thanks again for the ride. I appreciate you, Jeff."

Randy spent most of the first day catching up on sleep as they traveled toward Cincinnati. It was a free night for them, and he hoped for a decent dinner and more sleep.

He and Sammy walked to a restaurant where he drank two beers with his rib eye steak. On the way back to the bus, they stopped at a convenience store for two six packs each. He didn't even finish one can before he fell asleep.

An enthusiastic crowd made the first show sold out and fun. He agreed with Aaron earlier not to do his usual solos. Aaron wanted the band to get even more comfortable with his own songs.

The next night in Indianapolis, Aaron brought him up to the mic. More applause flooded over him than he expected. He could only see a few front rows of the audience because of the spotlights, but most of the people were singing along with him. That had to mean his song played on the radio there, too. Promotion was working.

After the show, he joined fans at the merchandise table. They waited in line patiently for him to sign CDs, which sold well. He stood for photos, then went back inside the auditorium where he saw Aaron still signing for hundreds of people. *Someday it will be the same for me.*

****

A month later, his phone rang. "Hi, Neil. What's

happening back in Nashville?" Randy covered his free ear to hear over the Keith Urban CD rocking the bus.

"I know you're out in the middle of nowhere, but do you not get any news? Is your phone not ringing like crazy?"

"I'm lucky if I hear from my sister or Angie. What's up?"

"Man, the second single is on fire."

"Really? It only came out last Tuesday."

"Can't argue with the numbers. You're already charting at twelve this week. Kid, you've got to get rid of that piece of crap you talk on for a smart phone. Get on the internet."

"I can't believe it. This is awesome news."

Sammy passed him on the way to the fridge. "You win the lottery or something?"

Randy clipped his arm as he brushed him off with a smile. "Get outta here." He turned back to the phone. "Neil, what's next?"

"I've got calls in to TV, radio, the works. What's your next city? I wanna do a hookup between a local station and like *Good Morning America* or one of those. They love the small-town-boy-makes-good stories."

"We're headed to Oklahoma City for tomorrow night."

"Yeah, I see it on the schedule now. Probably too quick, but I'll work out something soon. I'll let you know. And get your old phone traded in. We need email, text, the works."

Randy sat with the silent phone at his ear as he tried to absorb all Neil had told him.

The flip phone snapped closed and went into Randy's pocket. "Sammy? Can you teach me the internet on your phone? I gotta look up something."

****

A week back in Nashville gave them all a chance to catch their breaths. Aaron had commitments with his kids, and Randy looked forward to time with Angie. Neil had a few other things on his mind, however.

"Be at WSM TV at six. That's a.m., Randy. These morning shows have lots of viewers. Your segment is supposed to be six forty-five, right before they go to the weather. They may ask for a second song later in the show."

Texting with Angie took his attention right then. "Yeah, yeah, I got it. Hang on, let me finish this." After a few more clicks, he put the phone down. "So much for tomorrow. What else?"

Neil checked his notes. "You have a meeting with Carnival on Wednesday at three. They've been talking about another album. *Country Magazine* on Thursday. I think that's it, so far. Randy, things are going to go faster now. Aaron is through the roof about what you're bringing to the tour."

"Yeah, lots of fun." He picked up the phone again when it buzzed.

"Fun? You have nothing else to say? You act like there's nothing to it. I don't think you realize how extraordinary it is to have a hit on your first time out. You are hot right now."

Randy looked at his manager and friend.

"Of course, I do. I follow on the internet. Fans keep telling me I should have my own tour instead of being an opening act. I've been thinking maybe they're right."

Neil's voice revealed his shock. "Wow, got yourself a big head there, mister. Listen, you have a good thing with Aaron. You need to continue to build, then make another album. If that one takes off, maybe. You can do some solo shows around the country when you finish with Aaron in late September. Then you're on your own time. Let me handle this, Randy."

"Sure, you do that." He picked up the phone again. Randy left Neil looking stunned at the uncharacteristic arrogance of his client.

****

He invited Julia and Marsha to go with him to see Angie perform at Fiddle and Steel. When they arrived, Angie was about to go on. "Let's head up front, ladies. She saved us a table." As they crossed the room, the place burst into applause. He looked at the empty stage, then around the room. "What's happening?"

Julia clarified things for him. "You, Randy. The applause is for you."

It surprised him, but he went into waving his hat and thanking the crowd as he did at one of his own shows.

Julia looked around for Angie, who stood at the side of the stage with confusion and hurt on her face. He continued to enjoy the crowd and sign autographs.

Julia caught his arm to pull him down in his chair. "You need to put a stop to this. This is her night, Randy."

"Oh, c'mon, she's proud of me." He looked around to wave at her on stage. Angie turned away.

After the show, they arrived back at her apartment. Angie set her guitar down in the living room. She tossed her gig bag into the corner as Randy walked in and closed the door. He watched her stomp around the room and slam the refrigerator door.

He ventured forward. "Okay, I give. What's wrong? You've hardly said a word to me all night. I've only been home one day. How bad can it be?" He winked and slipped his arm around her waist. She slapped it away and spun around to stare at him.

"You really don't know, do you? You float into the room, and suddenly everything is all about you."

"A few fans went crazy. No harm done."

Her face showed her amazement. "Unbelievable. You didn't think the applause, the autographs, throughout my show weren't a bit much? My show, Randy. My time."

"Oh, you gotta be kidding. What was I supposed to do? They recognized me." He tried to reach for her hand.

"Stop it, I'm mad. No, I'm hurt."

"Aw, Ang, I guess I let it go to my head. I'm still not used to all this. I don't want to hurt you. What should I do?"

Her body stiffened as he reached for her again. "I don't know, Randy. It hasn't been as easy for me, you know. I've been here all these years and still trying. Do you know how hard it is for me to even get a gig in a sharp place like Fiddle and Steel? They want fresh voices all the time."

"I get it, and I don't want this between us. Next time will be better."

She stepped away. "Maybe we should say good night."

"No, baby, listen…"

"Not this time, Randy. I'll call you. Leave now, please."

A few mornings later, "Hey, Randy, you up?" Jeff yelled from the living room as he filled a trash bag with empty bottles and pizza boxes. "Randy, no kidding, get up." He walked to Randy's room and jerked the covers off his sleeping friend. When he still didn't move, Jeff opened the blinds.

Randy covered his head with a pillow. "Get out of my room. Leave me be."

"Okay by me, if you want to miss your interview. But I need help cleaning up your mess." Jeff stood at the end of the bed with his arms folded.

Randy slid the pillow off his face. "What time is it?" The contents of the glass on the bedside table burned his throat.

"Ten o'clock. Sherry Abrams and the photographer will be here at two thirty. Friend, I'm trying to help you here, and I've got to get to work." He took Randy's arm and pulled him to a sitting position on the bed.

Gradually, the blood stopped rushing around behind his eyes. Randy grabbed his head in both hands. "What happened?"

"You tell me. I came home around two a.m. to find the place a disaster. It smells like a pigpen in here. You let your sleazy friends smoke in here? You know I can't be around that wacky stuff, either."

Randy looked around the room. "My room doesn't look so bad." His smile only increased Jeff's frustration.

"I suggest you finish this and get in the shower. I've got to get to work." Jeff threw the trash bag at him on his way to the door.

His head still pounded, but he tried to get up, one leg on the floor at a time. Every inch of his body hurt. The reality of his plan for the day set in. He drifted around the apartment, picking up the lingering garbage. He checked each bottle for the remaining drops and downed them as he went. It took two trips to the dumpster to dispose of the revelry from the previous night. A quick swipe with the dishrag took care of the spills. The air freshener he aimed at the stench.

Finally pleased with the results, he headed to the shower. Standing under the hot water pelting his body brought his tight muscles to life. It did not remove more than dirt and grime, however. The memory of last night ending in another fight with Angie remained. He'd have to deal with that later.

After the interview, he brushed the glass back and forth on his nightstand, then tried to calm his leg as he waited for her to answer. "Hi, Angie. I'm sorry about another fight last night."

"Yeah, me, too. I hate to see this becoming a regular thing."

"Not what I want, either. I hope I wasn't too much of an ass."

She gave him silence for a minute before responding. "You don't even remember what it was about."

He hesitated, then decided on the right response. "Well, honestly I don't. But I know I'm sorry. It had to be my fault. You going to tell me?"

"Let's say I'd like a little respect for how hard I'm working. I don't begrudge you any of your success, but sometimes it feels like you think my career isn't as important. It couldn't be more serious to me."

He felt two inches tall. "Honey, whatever I did, you know it was the liquor talking. I believe in you. You'll find the right break soon."

"Let's drop it. We're not going to solve it this way. How did your interview with the magazine go today?"

It was unfinished in his mind, but he didn't know what else to do. "It went okay. They posed some pictures of me playing guitar in here and writing out on the patio. She wanted to talk a lot about home, family, my influences, you know."

Angie's voice brightened. "Sounds like a good article. I'll watch for it when it comes out. Are you coming to my show tonight?"

"If you want me to. You know I want to be there."

"Of course, I want you with me. We'll be okay."

Chapter 19

Aaron's tour lasted another four months. Randy's contract with him finished with the year's end. Then he could work on his own album and tour. He was itching to be out on his own. He didn't feel like anybody's sideman anymore.

Aaron stopped him in the hallway of an arena in Atlanta. "Hey, Randy, we have an off day tomorrow. How about lunch?"

"Great. I have some ideas for the show I wanted to run by you."

"Yeah, we can toss 'em around. You're the opener tonight. Have a good set."

The next day, Sonny drove them to The Varsity in Athens for hot dogs and fries. "You ever been here, Randy? The place is a mainstay with the college fans around here." Sonny sat down with his three slaw dogs, fries, and a large Coke.

"No, I was sick when we came through here before."

"You said you have some ideas, Randy?" Aaron didn't waste time.

Randy took a drink of his Coke and wiped the chili from his mouth. "Yeah, I've been thinking, there's such a short time left on the tour, anyway. I might add another song or two on the nights I'm not opening. The crowd is into me. I've got a few new things they haven't heard." He saw Sonny look at Aaron, who stopped eating.

Aaron calmly wiped his mouth and laid his napkin down. "Randy, you think that's how this works? Don't get me wrong, you're bringing folks to the shows. My name is on the marquee as headliner. Most come to hear me."

"Oh, I know, but I thought a change might be good for all of us. Give the audience and the band something different."

The stony silence at the table urged Sonny to leave the two musicians alone to talk. "I need a drink refill."

Aaron sat straight in his chair. "Listen, Randy, this is why I wanted to see you today. The guys are having some trouble working with your new holier-than-thou attitude. And you miss another of your own rehearsals with them, and I don't know they'll do anything for you at all. They're trying to support you. Your day will come, but for now, you need to know your place."

Randy's insides were churning with a mixture of embarrassment and anger. "I thought maybe we were more partners than that."

"We are, and you have the contract to show for it. It spells it out pretty plain. Like I said, you're bringing a lot to the tour, but it's still mine. Be careful."

Randy sat as quietly as a little boy scolded for spilling his milk. Sonny returned to the table and broke the silence with talk of southern heat and the Atlanta Braves.

Later, Randy got his agent's take on the lunch conversation. "We need to talk."

The silence on Neil's end of the line was deafening until he said, "You did what? Are you crazy? What have you done with my Randy? I don't even know you anymore."

"I do think I deserve more. Maybe I go out on my own now, not wait for another CD. I've been number eight and number one on the charts already."

Neil's breath quickened, and his voice tightened. "And remember, Aaron Franklin still puts out nothing but gold and platinum. You break a contract with him, and you'll be blackballed in Nashville."

"How much slower can this go? I'm better than this."

"You still don't get it. Next year, Randy, that's all I'm saying. The label is ready to back another album like crazy. You're on your way. Aaron's right. You're not there yet. Do I need to come out there so we can talk?"

"No, I hear what you're saying. I guess I get it." He didn't like it, but at least he could be happy Neil didn't say the word patience for the hundredth time.

****

While the driver refueled the motor home outside Ashville, NC, Randy caught a minute to make a call. "Hi, Mom. How are you?"

"Oh, my," she squealed into the phone. "How long has it been? I thought you'd forgotten me."

"Of course not, Mom. I know you haven't heard from me enough. The tour keeps me busy. But, see, I called to say hello."

"I'm fine. You know, Jimmy is keeping us busy with baseball again."

"Yes, I talked to him last week. Anything you need around the place?"

"No, son. Dan came over last night. He brings the kids to help me with the garden. They're all getting so big it keeps me baking cookies all the time."

"Some of your oatmeal cookies sound good right

now."

"Can you make it home soon?"

Randy hated this part. Most times, he couldn't avoid disappointing her. "We have a short break again in August. Maybe I can work something out then. I have to go now, or they'll go off and leave me. Love you, Mom."

He'd talk to Neil about setting up a show or two in California while he made that trip home. It would be good to see everyone, and maybe his friends could come to a show. He wanted to talk to Tom.

"Hi, Jennie. Tom around? How have you been?"

"We've been busy with the grandkids, as usual. Tom is thinking of retiring before long. Maybe you can talk to him. I've never had him around the house much before." Her laugh was so welcome to him.

"Well, yeah, I can't imagine him not being at The Palace."

"Don't tell him I said anything about retirement. He sure misses talking to you more often. Here he is."

"Hi, boy. How's it going out there?"

"Great. It sure is good to hear your voice."

"Yeah, I enjoy talking to you. We hear your songs on the radio all the time. We're so proud of you." Randy beamed at Tom's familiar support.

He started to tell his friend about the Atlanta conversation with Aaron but thought better of it. Somehow, he knew Tom would agree he needed to wait for his time.

"I think I may be there in August. If I do some shows, I hope you can be there."

"Well, hopefully close by, son. I'm thinking of retiring, you know."

Randy kept his promise to Jennie. "No kidding?

From The Palace, playing, and everything? What will you do?"

"Yep, we think it may be time to slow it all down. I might give a few lessons, so I don't go stir crazy."

"That sounds like a plan. I've got to go now. You two take care, and I hope to see you soon."

****

In early August, Randy opened the show in Houston to a sold-out arena. The crowd liked his new songs. Most in the full arena sang along with his well-known hits. After his talk with Aaron, he enjoyed the tour, though the thoughts of his own tour lingered. He regained his connection with the band, and the shows were fun again.

Sammy stayed a loyal friend through it all. "Hey, I contacted some girls I met here last year. Let's go out after the show. You haven't been out since Louisville."

"No, thanks. I'm catching a plane home for a few days. You have fun for me. Anyway, you know I have Angie."

"Man, how is that going? I tried a long-distance relationship once. It didn't work for me."

Randy shook his head. "Yeah, it is rough. We text every day and talk as much as we can. I feel bad. She's still struggling to play every night, and my career is taking off."

Sammy cleared his throat and asked, "Can I be honest? She's a good singer and all, but I don't know if she'll ever make it to stardom. Maybe she's missing something distinctive to set her apart, ya know? I'm sorry, I don't want to be mean."

"I know what you're saying. All I can do is keep supporting her."

"You're a better man than me. Guess I'll see you

when we pick up in Baton Rouge."

****

After getting off the plane at the Burbank airport, he drove his rental car to the Marriott hotel across the street to finish the sleep he started on the flight. He woke early, showered, and ate the complimentary breakfast.

The drive to his mom's place gave him time to think. An act canceled, which made it possible for Neil to schedule a performance for him at the Crystal Palace. It was special to him, but he was even more excited to see family.

As he drove into town, Main Street looked different again. Wilson's hardware and Fulton's Furniture were gone from the town square. A Dollar General stood in their place. *When did that happen?*

One thing never changed. The clatter of the cattle guard welcomed him home. The place looked good. It had been a good idea to lease out some of the acreage for cattle grazing. Dan did a good job with the other landscaping.

He bounded onto the porch and yelled inside the house. "Mom? Where are you? Your wandering son is home."

She ran screeching all the way from the back bedroom. "Ahhhhh. I'm getting the guest room ready for Jimmy. He wants to stay with you this time."

"That'll be fun." He swept her up in his arms for a hug. "You're just as pretty as ever, Mom."

They spent the morning catching up and discussing her plans for his visit. At noon, she got tomatoes from her garden and made BLT sandwiches and potato salad for their lunch like old times.

"I always love this lunch, Mom."

"This will be the last of the tomatoes this year, so eat up."

They spent the afternoon on errands, including buying groceries, and showing him off to her friends. "Mom, have you given up driving all together? You're so young," he teased her.

"Oh, yeah, right," she teased back. "I still get myself around just fine. Sherry acts like I need her to drive me to errands. It gives us some good time together, though." She giggled. "Maybe I'm getting lazy."

"You deserve to kick back a little, Mom. I sure appreciate everything you've done for me. I know I must have been a handful growing up, and it has to be tough with me being away so much now. If you don't mind, let's stop up here at the convenience store a minute."

"Son, do you and Dan really have to have all the beer? It worries me."

"Come on, Mom, we have to have a cold one with our burgers."

"You're a grown man, I know. I notice he drinks more when you're here, though. I hope you don't overdo it out on the road."

"Now, you know Dad drank one once in a while. I'll take it easy, though." *Another reminder.*

Randy sat in the car listening to the radio as he waited for Jimmy at his summer day camp. When the young boy ran out, Randy thought he must have grown a foot.

"Hi, Dad." He waved his arms as he ran. One toss of his backpack to the back seat and he jumped into the car. "You're finally here."

"I sure am. I'm awful glad to see you." He reached to hug his son.

"Not here, Dad. My friends are watching."

He hadn't seen this before. "Okay. So, I guess we'll head out then. How have you been?"

"Great, Dad. My camp group is doing a play on Thursday night. You'll come, right?"

"Of course. How are the guitar lessons going?"

"Great. I have to be there tonight. Can you take me? Mr. Hoover sure talks about you a lot."

"Sure, you want to grab a snack or eat after? We need to go by the house, right?"

"Duh, yeah, Dad. I have to have the guitar. I'll grab a yogurt or something."

Randy pulled the sun visor down. *I sure miss this.*

Their stop at the house included an uncooked wiener and a juice box for a snack.

"That's it?"

"Don't want to mess up dinner later." The energetic boy ran back to the car.

Randy parked in front of Hoover's Music, and Jimmy jumped out, running to the store. Randy hollered at Mr. Hoover as he entered. "You have any control over this kid? How are you, Mr. Hoover?"

"You go on back and set up, Jimmy. Well, hello, Randy. Listen, he's a good kid. And more talent than you at his age." He smiled as they shook hands.

"Oh, goodness, don't brag on him too much."

"Heck no, he's got all the ego he needs. You home for a stretch?"

"A short visit again. We're still on tour. Everything going okay here?"

"Same. Business is kind of slow. The city says the changes they're making will bring in traffic. We'll see if it happens while I'm still here."

"You still thinking of selling?" Randy hated to hear it.

"I'll stick it out a while to see what my grandson does after college. I'm pretty sure he doesn't want it, though. I can't complain too much. I've had a good run here."

Randy watched the old man walk to the classroom and tried to imagine what the town would be like without this business.

As he waited for Jimmy, he went out to the sidewalk, where he tried Angie's number. At first, he didn't think she was going to answer. "Angie? Hi, I wanted to say good luck for your show tonight."

"I'm about to go on."

The rush in her voice hurried him along. "I forgot about the time difference. Okay, well, we'll talk another time, then. Knock 'em dead, baby."

"Yeah, thanks. Later." The phone went silent.

Randy stood looking up and down the street, feeling exposed and alone.

That night, as usual, the men grilled the burgers and hot dogs while the women spread a feast of sides and desserts. After dinner, the kids played while the adults talked a mile a minute. Randy caught up on business with Sherry. His mother shared happenings around town. Sherry told him their mother led the committee for the Vacation Bible School at church in July.

"Wow, Mom. How impressive. It must have been a lot of work."

"I had plenty of help in a labor of love. Carrie has news."

Randy's heart jumped. "Really? What's new with you?"

"Nothing much. I got on at the new Dollar General." Carrie blushed.

Sherry took over. "They've only been open a month, and she's already made assistant manager."

He thought he should have known by now. "A month. That's great. I'm proud of you."

"The money is better, I get benefits, and they work with me on my schedule with Jimmy." She looked at him with a smile.

"I always knew you could do well."

After the others left, Jimmy wanted to show his dad what he had learned on the guitar. "I've been working on this for a while. I watch it on YouTube, then Mr. Hoover helps me."

"Sure, let's hear it." Randy expected more "Twinkle, Twinkle Little Star" like last time. He sat in amazement when Jimmy so easily started the intro to "Stairway to Heaven."

"That's as far as I've gotten. What do you think, Dad?"

Randy recovered his breath. "Son, you're better than I was at your age, for sure."

Chapter 20

Randy pulled into the familiar driveway and saw Tom waiting on the porch. Jennie braced herself at the edge of the stairs as he got out of the car. His heart stopped at the sight of the cane at her side. He loved these people like his own family.

"Hi, folks. I wish I could tell you how good it is to be home."

Tom helped him with his luggage and guitar. "We are so happy to see you. Mama has been watching the driveway all morning."

Jennie hugged him as they walked into the house. "I've got your bedroom ready. You get comfy while I set the table."

He and Tom sat after lunch to go over his set list. "I have a bunch of new stuff you haven't heard. I want this show to be special. A mix of the new and old. There'll be lots of old friends there, and folks who knew me back in the day."

"I know you've looked forward to returning to the Crystal Palace as a star. Make it fun for yourself. Do songs you like. Be yourself. That always works." Tom always knew what to say.

Jennie asked, "Your family is coming, right? I'm looking forward to meeting them."

His heart sank. "Not this time. Carrie and Dan have to work tomorrow. It disappointed Mom and Jimmy.

They'll see me another time."

He excused himself as he stood and reached for his phone to make a call. "Frank? Hi, Randy here. I know you're at work, so I'll make it quick. Remember, I told you I have tickets for you at will call. You can be there, right?"

"Of course, we'll be there. I think Sarah and David are coming, too."

"Great. I'll leave plenty of tickets. We'll go for a beer after. See you then."

He grinned as he returned to Tom and Jennie. "I sure wish I had more time with you, but I need to be there at four to rehearse with the band."

****

The night was magical for him as soon as he walked into the theater. The band was setting up on stage. Jake turned toward him.

"Hi, old stranger. Get up here and let's talk charts."

"Good to see you, Jake. This will be like old times."

"We didn't always have a star in our midst back then. We have a couple of fresh faces. The entire group will be here soon. You'll like them."

Tom, Jennie, and other friends were front row to see him back where it all began. Simply playing with and for friends made him happy. The show gave him a more natural feeling than any he had done since leaving.

The after-show routine took longer than he expected. Fans were buying CDs and tee shirts. Of course, they wanted photos and autographs. He looked up to see Frank holding a baby, a beautiful woman beside him. He broke away from the fans to embrace his old friend.

"Gosh, Frank, I loved seeing you in that audience

tonight. I'll finish here soon, I promise."

"Randy, this is my wife, Sue, and our baby, Randall."

His mouth gaped open as he looked at the little one in Sue's arms. "I didn't know I'd get to see the baby. Wha... What did you say? You named him..."

"Yeah, we call him Randy."

"Awesome. Can I hold my namesake?" Randy cradled the infant with tenderness. "Hey, little fellow. You're something, aren't you? And a music lover, too. He didn't even act up in the show," he said as he handed the baby to his mother.

Frank spoke. "Listen, we have to get him home. You know how it is."

"Oh, man, I have to leave tomorrow. I miss talking to you, Frank." He put his hand out to Sue. "I'm sure glad to meet the one who tamed this guy. He's a good one."

Frank gave him a hug before they turned to leave. "I hope you get to pay me that beer you owe me soon."

He heard Sarah's voice in the background.

"We've got to get back to Ventura, too." She ran to throw her arms around his neck.

"Are you kidding? I finally get to meet this guy, and you're going to rush off? Hi, I'm Randy."

"I'm David. I've heard a lot about you."

He looked back at Sarah. "So, how are you? Sorry I couldn't make the wedding."

"Thanks for the gift card. You were much too extravagant. We're doing well. I'm still in classes, and the business is taking off."

"Yeah, I look forward to your emails. Wish I answered better."

"I get it. Things are finally happening for you. It

must be exciting. Someday you'll have to share it all with us."

David touched her arm to remind her of the late hour. She embraced her special friend. "We've got to go, sweetie. You were amazing tonight, as always."

"Thanks, Sarah. I'm so glad you came."

Later, Randy found Tom waiting. "Good, you're still up. I wanted to get your take on the show."

"We enjoyed it so much, son." They talked until Jennie came in to remind them of the time.

"The old man needs to go to bed. We'll see you at breakfast."

****

In the muggy August heat of Baton Rouge, Randy stood outside the baggage claim area waiting for Sonny to pick him up. He used a sleeve to wipe away sweat as the rental SUV pulled up.

Sonny yelled out to him. "Get in. Don't let all the cold air out. How was your trip?"

"Good. I saw family and friends and played the Crystal Palace."

"Now, there's a trip down memory lane, huh? You're back to reality now. Aaron wants to rehearse and kind of regroup to get back in the swing of it this afternoon. We're on at eight tonight."

Randy was glad a local group opened for them. He needed time to get back in the right mindset. He did his usual two songs during Aaron's set. The crowd screamed and yelled his name. Stepping back into his place on stage as Aaron took the mic again, Randy knew the autographs after the show would take forever. After, he got back to the motor home and downed a beer in one gulp, then opened another.

The next day, the buses made the long drive to the Chicago area, where they had a free night. On the edge of town, they pulled into a BBQ place for dinner. Julia met them there and sat at Randy's table.

"Hi, stranger. How have you been?"

"I have missed you, for sure. How's Marsha?"

"As crazy as ever. She said to say hello. Only a couple more months on the road, right?"

"Yeah, I guess so. I'm doing some travelling on my own then. Neil has it set up. Did I tell you I'm doing another album, too?"

"Yeah, you told us. So, you'll have a tour of your own next year?"

"I hope so. I'm feeling caged in."

"Hey, don't bite the hand that feeds you."

"I know. Everyone says the same thing. Can you understand? I want to be on my own tour. I feel ready." Randy waved at the server to fill his glass again.

Julia looked at him. "You need to treasure this with Aaron. Your time is coming soon. Be thankful you've had it as easy as you have. What do you hear from Angie?"

"Not much. Every time we talk, she's on her way somewhere, burning the candle at both ends. She's frustrated, and I don't know how to help her."

"Listen to her, I guess. We go to see her perform once in a while. She looks tired."

"We've talked about it. We've fought about it. I know how bad she wants to make it. I want to help her, but I'm gone all the time. Sometimes I think my good fortune makes it worse."

"You can't stop her being insecure around your success. Look, I've seen this happen before, where both are performers. Hang in there. I'll try to check on her some."

"Thanks, I appreciate that."

Being busy helped Randy stay focused on the last two months of the tour. They crammed as many shows in as possible. Chicago, Philadelphia, San Diego, Albuquerque, Dallas, and on and on. After each performance, he fell into his bunk but still couldn't sleep without at least one beer. Sometimes, when they stopped for gas, he and Sammy ran inside the truck stop for a bottle of Jack Daniels, which didn't last long.

Songwriting on the motor home presented its own problems. Someone was always talking, playing guitar, or cards. The radio blared constantly. He needed some quiet time to create the right songs for the next album. The crowds liked the ones he tried on stage, but he wanted more available as a cushion.

Clay, the steel player, interrupted his work. "Come on, Randy. I haven't taken any of your money in a while. Jacks or better tonight."

"No, thanks. You have half my kid's college fund already. I have to finish this, anyway." He heard the guys laughing and the chips falling as he tried to get some writing done.

When the nightly card game broke up, Sammy stopped by Randy's bunk. "You gonna have your light on all night again?"

Randy finished writing a sentence. "Maybe. I have to get this stuff down right when it comes to me."

"Yeah, I guess things are different when you have to be the creative one. I sit back and do what Aaron wants. Suits me fine."

Randy smiled up at his friend. "Maybe you have the

right idea. Go away. I'll turn the light out soon."

The work stopped with the light, but long before his eyes closed in sleep. He couldn't turn off the thoughts and pressures so quickly. Leaving Jimmy behind never got easier. Could Neil get him the deal he wanted on the next album? Where did Angie fit into it all? The dream was right there in front of him, but he was tired of chasing after it all the time.

The humming of the tires and the radio playing low for the driver finally eased Randy off to sleep. Tomorrow was another day, just like the last.

****

The show in Charlottesville came during a thunderstorm. The audience didn't mind, and they filled the John Paul Jones Arena. After the show, Sonny drove a group to dinner. Of course, Julia had business with Aaron at this stop. *She knows all the BBQ stops, after all.*

"What are you working on now, Julia?" Randy downed his second helping of slaw.

"I'm trying to get Aaron to commit to some photos for Farm Aid next summer. I sometimes think I should decide for him. How's your writing going?"

"Pretty tough. I envy those people who say they go off to a cabin somewhere to write. Angie gave me an idea for a song the other day. I think it'll be a good one."

"We went to see her the other night doing backup for some new kid. She was much better than him, but you know how it goes. She got a paycheck."

Randy leaned in to ask. "How do you think she is? I can't get her to talk much."

Julia lowered her voice. "Now, I don't want you worrying about anything but this tour right now."

Randy kept after her. "She sounds beat up on the

phone. What do you think?"

Julia gave in to his persistence. "She seemed a little thin. Don't get upset. She may like being a size or two down."

He thought differently. "I think she's hanging at the bars too much."

Julia paused before she spoke. "Marsha thinks she's on something. I sure hope not."

Randy didn't show surprise. "What can I do? Like I said, she won't talk much."

"Randy, I wish you wouldn't involve yourself. But if you think you're interested in her, I'll see what I can find out. Please don't worry, though."

"I miss her when I'm gone. We fight when we're together. There's only six more shows on this tour. I can't give up on her. Thanks for your help."

She laid her hand on his as he pushed his unfinished plate away.

****

Randy was happy to be back in Nashville after the tour ended. He wanted to spend time with Angie and catch up on some writing with Jeff and others. Neil had him booked for a quick tour around the area right away. Sales on the album were still good. As much as Randy appreciated success, time demands were wearing on him. But having chosen this life, he couldn't complain.

"Sonny, burgers on the grill at your house sounds great. I'll be in Memphis that night. Tell your wife hello for me and thanks for the invite. Next time."

"No, Sammy, I can't. Of course, a jam at your place is always fun. Actually, I'm in Huntsville, Alabama for a show with Joe Diffie. I'll see you when I get back."

"Cookeville isn't far, Angie. I'll drive back tonight.

You leave the light on, okay?"

Could he ever have more control of his time? Seeing the balance he craved in Tom and now Aaron, he dreamed of having their lifestyle. Of course, he watched it through the amber-colored liquid of a bottle. *I thought drinking would make things easier.*

Randy and Aaron sat in a breakfast diner in Knoxville. "Randy, thanks for finishing the Christmas tour with me. I know you're ready for some rest before you start your album."

"No problem, Aaron. These are fun shows."

"So, Neil is setting up a national tour for you next year? I know you'll do great, and I sure appreciate everything you've done for me."

"Are you kidding? I can never repay what you've meant to my career. Even if I got a little antsy about moving on. Sorry."

"Wanting it all as fast as possible is human nature. I'm glad you stuck it out, though. It was the right thing to do."

Randy smiled. "So everyone told me. Over and over." He downed his coffee, then watched the server fill their cups again. He had a question for Aaron. "Can I ask you something kind of personal?"

"Sure, we're friends, always."

"How do you do it? I mean, you have the career, family, everything."

Aaron sat back in his chair. "Nothing's easy, that's for sure. Having the right support system is key. From Sonny to my agent and don't forget my wife. She's a gem. And believe me, it hasn't always been roses for us."

"Yeah, I like Sandy a lot. Were you together before?"

"We were both playing the scene in Memphis when we met. We had plenty of time to talk and plan. She knew what she was getting into. No way I would have made it without her."

Randy shifted his hat. "Reminds me of some good friends of mine in Bakersfield."

"Tom Murphy? Yeah, I've met Jennie. You know, some make it alone or acting the playboy, but I can't imagine they're happy." He shrugged. "Could happen, I guess."

On the final bus ride back to Nashville, Randy made an early New Year's resolution to put happy on his list of goals.

Chapter 21

In January, he pushed the crew hard to get his new album completed on time. Dave Easton produced again. They worked well together, and Randy had a little more say on things this time. He didn't do as many gigs around town anymore. Now he had time to support Angie and other friends.

Hiring musicians for the tour took time. Aaron advised him to find compatible team players. Living crammed together in a bus for most of eight months was tough enough without personality issues. Randy couldn't have been happier with his choices. They all agreed to a per-show agreement at first.

Neil negotiated with Miller Beer and Lee Jeans to sponsor the tour. They provided a bus to serve as home on the road for Randy and his crew. He also hired a business manager to handle the promotional details. Randy posed for photos again and again. Most with his butt sticking out, so the brand on the back pocket displayed prominently. Then there were the ones with a Miller in his hand and the label turned just so. He'd have to be careful not to say it out loud, but neither was a favorite brand for him.

As Randy walked out of the WSM TV studios one day, his phone rang. "Hi, Tom. I'm glad you called. What's up?"

Tom laughed. "Sure, can't I want to talk to my

friend once in a while? I figure things are heating up for you."

"You said it. I have to thank you again for finding Neil. Man, he is on top of everything. I could never have guessed how much work goes into getting out on tour. How's Jennie?"

"She's fine. Babysitting, of course. She'll be mad I did this without her."

"Ha ha! I'll make a point to call her some time you're at work."

"Better make it fast. I retire the end of next month."

"Well, I guess you're happy. They'll sure miss you at The Palace."

"Gary, at the music store, is letting me give lessons there for a small cut. I'll stay busy enough. But I want to hear about you. I got the promo copy of the CD. I thought it was cracker jack. Dave did another good job for you."

"Yeah, he's great. He said to say hi to you both, by the way. I think we're about ready to roll next Thursday. Our first show is in St. Louis. This is really happening, Tom. With all the hard work and stress, I love it. Crazy, huh?"

"Heck no, son. Sounds about right."

"We have Sacramento and the Buckboard Festival on the schedule this year in California. I'd sure love to see you while I'm around. Forgive me, I have to go for another meeting at four before I join friends for a jam later. Good to talk to you. Tell Jennie hello."

He awoke the next morning to a voice he didn't recognize on his phone. "Randy? This is Paula, one of Angie's roommates, remember?"

"Sure, what's up?" He sat up in bed like the spring on a mousetrap as his stomach knotted. His voice got louder. "Is everything okay?"

"I don't think so. We can't get Angie up. She's passed out. Can you come over?"

He tore around the room, grabbing his clothes as he ran to the door. "I'll be right there."

He was afraid of something like this. Angie was drinking more, and he now knew she was taking something, too. He pounded his fist on the steering wheel and demanded the truck dart between cars and dodge red lights in his haste. His departure from the pickup at the curb of Angie's apartment resembled a bronc rider's frantic dismount from an angry, wild one. He scaled the three flights of stairs to the apartment two at a time. The door flew back when he burst in past the disheveled young woman.

"Where is she?" He didn't wait for an answer and ran to Angie's bedroom. He found her sprawled across the bed, half naked. "Get some cold water and a washcloth."

Paula brought them and stepped back. "We tried everything."

Randy looked with disgust at her and the other two girls hovering in the corner. "Is this only alcohol?" He rolled Angie over and rubbed her face, a little rougher than he should with the cold cloth.

Paula made a feeble attempt at answering. "Well, see, we had a little party last night, and when she got home, she joined in. She hit the whiskey pretty hard, but…"

His eyes shot around at her as he screamed, "What did she take?"

"We're not sure. Sorry," she cried. "I'm so sorry, Randy. She's not going to die or anything, is she?"

He turned Angie on her side as she vomited. "Call 9-1-1, you idiot. Now."

Julia found Randy sitting on the floor outside a hospital room when she arrived. He continued to stare at an invisible spot as she reached down to brush a shock of unruly hair from his eyes. He didn't move.

She breathed her words close to his face. "I got here as fast as I could. How is she? They have her in a room already?"

His stare didn't change. "Sure, it seems they see a lot of this. Step one, pump stomach, step two, stabilize, step three, if still breathing, assign a room. Next."

Julia slumped down beside him and wiped a tear from his cheek. "So, they'll keep her overnight?"

"Yeah, they'll probably send her home as soon as the doctor sees her again in the morning. I don't know what to do. She doesn't want to see me."

He turned toward the sound of a nurse and attendant coming out of the room. "Mr. Walters, you can go in now."

Julia grabbed his arm to hold him down. "Let me go in first. She'll see you."

Through the afternoon, Randy sat beside Angie's hospital bed. "I wish you'd let me get you something. I'm sure the nurse can find some Jell-O, crackers, or something."

Angie still didn't face him. "Maybe later. You don't have to stay, Randy. You've done enough."

"I want to stay. You gave me a real scare." He took her hand, and she met his eyes. "I'll take you home when they let you out of here."

"They notified my folks. They're flying in to pick me up. I'm sure they'll want to take me home with them."

Randy's heart skipped. "Well, maybe that will be good for a while."

"Oh, you don't know. All we'll do is fight about me wanting to waste my life on music." She looked at him and gripped his hand. "I think I need help. I can't keep on like this. Missing jobs, showing up late. Now I can't do the gig tonight. I've cooked my goose for a while around here because I've done it too often."

"I didn't realize how bad it was. I'll support whatever you decide."

At last, a smile, "Well, I think I say I'd like some ice cream. Can you handle that, cowboy?"

****

The next day, Randy met Angie and her parents for lunch. "Good to meet you, sir. I'm Randy Walters."

The father shook his hand, but gave him a stern stare. "So, you're part of this crazy music thing, too?"

Angie answered for him. "Dad, he had a number one song on the charts this summer. And, no, none of this was his fault. He's a good friend."

"Must not be a very good friend. You didn't see this coming, boy?"

Her mother spoke nicely. "Ray, stop it. Give the young man a chance. Hi, I'm Shirley. How long have you known our daughter?"

Randy's collar got tighter. "Over a year, ma'am. But I'm on the road quite a bit. I've racked my brain to find what I might have done to help her before now." Angie moved her leg under the table to rub against Randy's in silent affection.

Ray spoke again, "When we get her home where she belongs, she'll be just fine. All she needs is some good

Texas air and stop all this foolishness and get back in school."

Angie tried to answer his proposal respectfully but would not hide her resolve. "Not going to happen, Dad. My life is music, and this is where I want to be. I got off track, that's all."

Shirley expressed her own ideas. "Can't you come home for even a couple of weeks? You need rest and regular meals."

"No, Mom, I've decided." She looked at Randy, who held her hand for support. "I need to get myself straightened out. Get off all the stuff that's been controlling me. I know a place outside of town I can go for help."

Her father banged his fist on the table. "You mean a rehab place? Is that what you want to drag this family through now? I won't have it."

Randy put his arm around Angie as she cried under the roar of her father.

Shirley took over. "You hush, Ray. This isn't about us. Our daughter is asking for help, and I think that is a big step, don't you, Randy?"

"Well, yes, ma'am. I do think she needs to get away from all the pressure for a while." He looked at her father. "All the pressure, sir. I care about her, too, but I couldn't help her. Out there, she can get the help she needs." He sat staring at the man, waiting for the next eruption.

After some uncomfortable silence, the father's face softened. "Let's finish lunch, then we'll visit this place. The costs will all come to us, of course. You don't have to worry about anything, puddin'."

Her mother used a napkin to wipe her eyes and took

Angie's hand. "That's right, honey, you focus on getting better."

Their visit to the Cumberland Heights facility after lunch gave them all the time to get to know each other. Randy made a bond with Angie's father he hadn't expected.

Ray asked, "Will you have dinner with us, Randy? Our flight is right after we get her signed in tomorrow morning."

Randy winked at Angie. "That's tempting, sir. I guess I'd better leave you all some time together. I've got a lot of packing, anyway."

After he said goodbye to her parents outside their hotel, Angie walked him to his truck.

She broke the silence. "They're a hoot, aren't they?"

"They love you very much. He's scared about his little girl, is all."

They shared a long kiss. Then she looked deeply into his eyes. "Thanks for everything. Can you ever forgive me?"

"I'm just glad the girls found my number. Hey, when you get back…"

"I know, new roommates. A lot of things will be different, I promise. There will be some rebuilding of the career to do, too."

"You'll be fine. Maybe a little refocus is what we all need once in a while. You can think about the future when you get back. It didn't sound like you could have visitors before I have to leave, but let me know when I can call you."

"This is your time, Randy. Your tour is all that matters. I'll be fine here. I'm so proud of you."

They embraced for a long time, leaning on his

pickup, tears mingling on their cheeks. After a while, he whispered in her ear, "Puddin'?" She slapped his arm playfully.

****

"Julia, thanks for bringing me to the bus this morning. I'm as nervous as can be today."

"I don't know why you'd worry about the biggest event of your career so far." Julia laughed.

"Thanks, pal. I feel so much better. Hey, you haven't lectured me on anything yet. You're slipping."

"No, I wanted to make sure you'd hear me. Last night's send-off wasn't the place."

Randy shuffled his hat. "Okay, let's have it. I've promised I won't drink so much, especially after Angie. Oh, that's it, isn't it? Look, I'm not giving up on her."

Julia parked the car next to the tour bus and turned to him. "Concentrate on your tour. She's getting the help she needs. Stay focused is all I'm saying."

"I know. What the future holds I can't say, but I know right now I can't abandon her."

"You're too good for your own good sometimes. Let up and enjoy yourself. Okay, I'm done lecturing. Grab your stuff and get out of my car. I have to get to work." She kissed his cheek. "That's from Marsha. Stay in touch."

As her car pulled away, he began barking orders to the crew. And so, his tour began.

Chapter 22

Three weeks into the tour, Randy still found it hard to sleep. At least his room in the back of the bus was private this time. Fatigue and lack of sleep kept him on edge and irritable.

"Uh, excuse me. Cliff, right?" Randy's boot tapped as he went on. "Listen, we gave you the set list and stage plot for tonight, right? Well, we didn't spend all that time, paper and ink, for you to ignore it. I need the solo mic on point and my harmony singers' volume up only when needed. Too hard for you?"

A man in a suit and tie walked up to him. "Mr. Walters, can I help you? I'm Ralph Ellis, the manager of your auditorium tonight. Is there a problem?"

"Yes, Ralph. Do I need to go hire my own sound man tonight? Or can we get this guy in line?"

Ralph's even voice continued. "Let's all calm down. This is a city-run performing arts center, Mr. Walters, operating mostly on volunteer labor. Cliff is a sound performance professor at the university who has been with us for over five years. I'm sure his aim is to give you exactly what you want. You return to the stage, and he'll be happy to take it from the top again."

When Randy got back to the stage, Steve, the bass player, whispered, "Really, dude? They'll never have you back here."

He almost jumped at him but knew the guy was

right. Flying off the handle had embarrassed him. Later, he would have to apologize. Some quiet rest had to come soon.

Two weeks later, Randy awoke to the ringing of his phone. He moved the beer cans strewn on his bed to find it. "Hello?"

"Neil Farrell, here. Remember me? Your agent? The guy who works day and night, misses his daughter's piano recital, and forgets his wife's birthday trying to set all this up for you? We need to talk."

"What's wrong?" Randy sat up in bed.

"Today, I received the check for your show in Little Rock. Remember that night? The sound man fiasco? They sure do. It included a terse little handwritten note in the envelope. Have you lost your mind?"

"Hold on, I can explain. I apologized to everyone after the show. I even gave his daughter a CD and took a picture with her."

"Randy, you don't get it. You're in the spotlight at all times. If this were to leak to the press, well, you don't want to know. This isn't like you. What's going on out there?"

"I'm not sleeping much, and being in charge is all extra pressure for me. An excuse I know. Settling into life on the road this time is taking longer than I'd like. I haven't heard from Angie, and my sister has been sick, so I'm worried about all she does for me. A show almost every night. I lost it for a minute that night."

Neil sat in silence before responding. "Like I said, this isn't like you. You had a dream and would do anything to reach it. Has something changed? Because I need to know now."

"No. I'm finally making it, and I want it all. I'll try

not to be on edge so much. We have a three-week break in June. I'll get some rest then."

"You'd better. Be careful, though. We need every return engagement we can get."

"Should I call the guy?" Randy wanted to make it right.

"No, no. That's my job. You keep smiling at the girls, Randy, and try to have some fun."

****

As the bus rolled along the next day, Randy took a break from writing and walked to the kitchen area for something to eat.

The drummer, Roger, asked, "Want us to deal you in, Randy?"

"I don't think so. I came to get a snack. Who's winning?" He walked over to the table to see.

Jack threw up both hands in victory. "Me, as usual. I play cards as well as I play rhythm guitar, boss. I've heard you're good, too. How about a hand? We're literally playing for peanuts."

"Well, maybe I will. Hopefully, I won't eat the pot. I'm starved."

They all laughed together. He enjoyed their company, and after an hour, the muscles in his back and neck relaxed for the first time in a while.

"I wonder if I could get some windows put in my room? I forgot what the sunshine looks like up here." Randy looked from one side window of the bus to the other as the landscape flowed by.

Roger looked around at the other men. "You're sure welcome out here anytime. We thought you wanted to be alone."

"I'm sorry. I've been doing a lot of writing. You

guys are a lot more fun, though. Listen, I know I've been a little tough to live with. I'm gonna do better. And if I'm in there too much, you come roust me out, okay? Whose deal is it? Give me some more of those peanuts. Mine mysteriously disappeared." The group roared with laughter.

****

Angie was allowed one call each week. Randy missed talking to her during the weeks she contacted her parents. Each time she spoke to Randy, her voice sounded stronger, and he knew she was getting better.

"Hi, cowboy. I hope you're having fun."

"I am. You sound great. How's it going?"

"They say I'm doing good. I might get to go home soon. They want to make sure, I guess. I don't mind. The surroundings out here are inspiring. I sit for hours, writing in the garden."

"Amazing, Angie. Want me to see if Julia can help with finding you a place or anything?"

"No, she and Marsha have already been so nice. They've visited me twice. A counselor here will help me rent a place online. There'll be a roommate or two later. I'll have to get a job until I can get some gigs booked so I don't keep letting my folks pay."

Randy's throat tightened. "So, you'll jump right back in?"

Angie didn't hesitate. Randy heard strong words flow from the deepest part of her. "I will. Things will be different this time."

"I know they will. We have two more weeks, then I'll be off the road for three. I can't wait to see you. Maybe I can help you set up a new place."

"I'll tell them that's my goal. See you then, Randy."

When they hung up, he called his sister. "Sherry? Are you feeling better?"

"I'm fine now. Where are you?"

"Birmingham tonight. Is everything else going okay?"

"Yes, but Randy, taking care of things for you has changed."

"Do you need me to find someone else? I thought a job might help you, but it sounds like it may be too much."

"I do hate to give up the extra money, but it's not a small job anymore. You need an accountant."

"If you can hang on a little longer, I'll take care of it. For some reason, I've been thinking about Mom a lot lately. How's she doing?"

"She's fine. She still gets blue sometimes. But then you finally call, and she's on top of the world again." Sherry always got her digs in.

Later, Randy finished writing a new song, then headed to the front of the bus. "Jack, turn that radio off. You guys get instruments out and look over these lyrics. I want to try a new song." They listened while Randy sang it with his guitar chords behind.

Roger spoke up first. "Real nice, Randy." Everyone expressed like comments.

They worked out an arrangement by the time they reached their next city. He liked it a lot. "Feel like trying it tonight?"

They all agreed. "Sure. I'll go for it. Might as well. Hell yeah, let's do it."

It excited him to have something new in the set. The band didn't let him down. The audience loved the song, and after the show, a few people asked which CD the song was on. He told them, "Maybe on the next one."

They kept the bus parked behind the arena, with security provided by the promoter. He went to bed with a good feeling. Two band members went out with local girls. He remembered those few overnighters on Aaron's tour when he and his friends could have some fun. He told his guys the story about staying out too late, thinking the proposed fine would get them back on time.

A few days later, he and the crew enjoyed bags of fast food as the bus rolled along. Randy announced, "Okay, Memphis tonight, then the bus will leave right after the show. So, kiss the girls quick and load up. We'll hit Nashville in the wee hours, but it'll be worth it. Get your calls made for rides home. The first part of the tour went well. I can't wait to see you all back in three weeks. You'll get an email with all the details about departure. I think everyone owes Tony a big hand for not wrecking this monster along the way." They all clapped and kidded the driver.

Randy now managed the tour well. It had been a good experience for him to watch Aaron in action. His band got along well and gave excellent performances on stage. He couldn't ask for better his first time out. He'd ask Neil about an end-of-tour bonus for them.

****

"Angie is supposed to be home the day after tomorrow." Randy sat with Julia while Marsha flipped the steaks. "She got an apartment over a shoe store downtown. I worry about her safety." He endured their quiet before continuing. "What else?"

Julia waited for Marsha to sit down. "Look, we like Angie. You know we've backed her music in the past and even visited her in rehab. Think about what I'm about to say. Remember, she's going to have a hard time. She'll be right back in the middle of what knocked her down. We can support her, but, Randy, she has to do it on her own. Don't get mixed up in anything."

Marsha nodded her agreement.

He looked down at the napkin he twisted and rolled on the table. "I've given it a lot of thought. I know you're right." He found their eyes before saying, "I want to help, but I can't do it for her. You know, the whole mess has been an eye opener for me. I've cut back my drinking, and I probably won't drink around her at all until she's comfortable with it. Supporting her like that is all I can do."

Marsha added, "I've offered to get her an application at the station, but I told her I won't be responsible for her work performance. She said she got it."

"Thanks, Marsha. Is dinner ready? I'm starved."

Julia smiled. "So tell us about the tour, other than you didn't have time to call us much."

"Yeah, my mom gives me heck about it, too. At least you get a text or email sometimes. How'd you like the picture of the BBQ joint we found in Waynesboro, Virginia? Best we ate out there."

"Yeah, I showed it to Sonny. We'll have to try it next time we're in the area. How were the crowds at your shows?"

Randy talked throughout dinner about the ups and downs of touring.

Julia let him finish before asking, "But did you have fun?"

"I did." He thought a moment about how to continue. "Funny thing is, I get the same rush from the songwriting as performing on stage. You know, Jeff and I are still collaborating, and now I'm working with others, too. I know it might not make sense to a lot of people. I mean, here I am on top of everything I ever wanted, right on track, and I'm seeing that a large part of what I enjoy, I can do anywhere. Then I wouldn't be on the road all the time."

Marsha asked, "Are you wanting to quit touring to write and sell your songs?"

He didn't have to think about his answer. "No. No, I still have more I want to do out there. It is more stressful being the guy in charge than I expected. I'm all right, though. I get on stage, and all the stress goes away."

"Take care of yourself." Her words said he hadn't convinced her.

"I'm trying."

****

Randy juggled a small bouquet from hand to hand as he paced at the front desk of Cumberland Heights Rehab Center until he saw Angie walk up the hall toward him. Her blonde curls framed a face with rosy cheeks. He traded the bouquet for the small suitcase and guitar she carried. They walked outside without a word. As the sunshine hit their faces, they looked at each other and laughed, while letting out a celebratory yell.

She whispered as he picked her up and held on tight. "Thank you for coming. I'm ready to get away from here."

He put her down and held her out in front of him. "You look good. You're beautiful."

"Oh, I don't know about that. But I know I'm ready for lunch. Can we stop somewhere? Someplace new?"

Randy got it. "Sure, there's a new place right on the

way. We'll try it." He kissed her cheek.

At the steak house, they looked over the large menu, which included seafood, steaks, and a nice salad bar. After they ordered, Angie asked, "Don't you want a draft with your steak?"

"No, I've cut down a lot. Are you sure the salad bar is all you want?"

"Yes, I'll be fine. Look at all the variety over there. I've been eating a lot healthier, and I want to stick with it. I feel so much more energized. You don't realize what junk and fried food do to you."

"I know. I can do better, too, even on the road." He watched her as she walked over to fill her plate. He fought to deny a difference in her, but it was there. It was like getting to know someone new. She had accomplished something important making him proud.

They talked long after finishing lunch. She wanted to hear all about the tour. He thought it best not to ask too much about what she experienced. He let her share what she wanted him to hear.

She reached for her purse. "I'm eager to get to the apartment. I've only seen pictures. Here's the address. Can you spend the day with me?"

"Of course. I cleared everything as soon as I got your call."

She slid out of the booth. "Great. I'll go to the ladies' room and be right with you."

He read the address she handed him and wondered what they might find there.

As they parked in front of the shoe store, she looked up at the windows with one curtain panel hanging crooked and squealed, "Isn't it cute? Kind of bohemian, don't you think?" She jumped out of the truck, sidestepped the bum perched on the sidewalk, and went inside the store to get the key. He looked around the area and shook his head. He double-checked the lock on his truck.

She burst onto the sidewalk, waving the key. "I got it. C'mon, isn't this exciting?" He didn't quite feel the same.

The stairs at the side of the store were steep, dusty, and, to him, never ending. Her feet were swift to the top, where she opened the door to her new life.

He stood in the doorway, taking in the sight. She moved from room to room, planning and describing what she could do to decorate. He only saw a small, dirty place. The stains on the furniture scared him, and he dreaded the bags of trash on the kitchen counter. He held his hand below his nose to filter the odor.

"Ang, Angie, slow down."

"Come look at the view from this enormous window. At night I can see the neon from lower Broadway. Isn't it great?"

He wiped the window once with his sleeve to give a nearly clear view. His hand turned her face to him. "Baby, are you sure about this? Is this like the pictures?"

She pulled herself up to her full height to answer him. "No, but maybe the landlord thought the last people cleaned. I hope he didn't give them a deposit back." She flew around the room again. "A little elbow grease, and it will be fine."

"And maybe vagrants have been flopping here. The neighborhood, Angie."

She turned to the window again, her voice soft. "Please don't spoil this for me. I need to do this on my own, and it's what I could afford right now. I need time to get on my feet." She looked at him. "Please?"

He nearly choked on his heart. He wanted to sweep her up and run away fast. Instead, he took a deep breath, grabbed onto her positive attitude, and moved forward. "I'll call the cleaning company we use once in a while. You'll stay with me tonight. Your car is at my place, anyway. That will give us time to do some shopping." Now he circled through the small space, too. "New curtains, maybe a rug for the living room, a little paint, and a new lock on the door. We can drop those two bed pillows in the dumpster on the way out."

Dust flew as she dropped into a chair. "I can't do all that yet."

"Then accept what I offer as a housewarming gift." He took her hand. "Let me do this, at least."

She vaulted into his arms. They kissed for the first time all day.

****

Neil wanted Randy busy with interviews and meetings every day. But to Randy, a quick trip to visit family was essential for his peace of mind. He spent a week with Angie, then flew out. He picked up Jimmy from baseball practice, where some of the other parents asked him for autographs and photos. Remembering his agent explaining the need to be on all the time, he still thought that rude but remained polite.

He asked as Jimmy jumped into the car, "So, you have guitar lessons right after this?"

"Yeah, Mr. Hoover lets me use one of his guitars on these days so we don't have to rush home. You're playing a lot of places, aren't you, Dad?"

"Uh, I think twenty something and a couple festivals so far. You want a copy of my schedule?"

"Mom printed one for me. I put a pin on my wall map each time you do a show. You'll see when we get home."

"I'm impressed. Now I'll think of your map in each place we play." *Maybe I can feel more connected to him as I travel.*

He found a parking space down the street from the music store. Jimmy, of course, ran to the practice room before Randy could get inside to greet Mr. Hoover. "What are they putting in next door? What happened to the dress shop? I remember my sister and all her friends bought their prom dresses there."

"Heck, Randy, everything is changing. Mrs. Jones sold her shop, and some salon with a coffee shop is going in. I don't know what will happen when I sell."

"You're sure you'll sell, then?" Randy went into deep thought.

"Seems the thing to do. Probably on my birthday next May. Happy Birthday to me." He shook his head and grabbed at his lower back as he got off his stool. "You ready back there, Jimmy? You tune up. I'm on my way."

Randy shouted after him, "I'll be back before he's finished, Mr. Hoover. I'm gonna walk around a bit."

Randy took an eye-opening look in the windows of shops he knew and those he didn't. As he rounded the corner, he saw the Chamber of Commerce office and went inside.

"Hi, Margaret, I haven't seen you since we graduated. I didn't know you worked here."

"Well, this isn't an office many visit often. What brings you in? I hear you're doing well."

"Yeah, I've been pretty lucky, and I'm killing time

while my son is in Hoover's. Listen, do you have a printed plan on what's happening downtown? I want to keep up. Still have family taxpayers and landowners here, ya know." They shared a smile. *Maybe something here is in my future, after all.*

At dinner, he listened as his family talked of town business and gossip. He watched Carrie with his son. He knew Jimmy loved him, but Carrie had a special closeness with the boy from being there every day.

"Earth to Randy," Sherry said, waving her hand in his face. "What's with you tonight? Are we boring you?"

He regained his posture in his chair. "Not at all. I'm thinking about how I miss this. A few times a year isn't enough."

His mom offered, "You can always come home."

The room burst into laughter. Dan caught his breath. "Oh, yeah, he for sure can't do that. He's hot on the charts."

Carrie gazed at him across the table. "Is something wrong?"

"No, I guess not. Everything is great, as a matter of fact." He squirmed in his chair and waved his hands in the air like a kid waiting for ice cream. "Are you guys ready for this? The call I took right before dinner? My agent, saying the Country Music Association nominated me for New Artist of the Year. Can you believe it?"

They all jumped up from the table at once and surrounded him with hugs. As he watched his mother's tears of pride slip down her cheeks, he thought to himself, *the award I want most has been here all along.*

Chapter 23

Randy got up early the next morning and took his coffee outside to walk around some of the property.

His mother met him at the pasture fence. "You still find it awfully pretty, don't you?"

"How could I forget how nice it is? I can see why you don't want to leave, Mom."

"I still look out there and see James riding the herd. Sometimes I thought he rode out there playing cowboy when there wasn't anything much to do. He loved the life, that's for sure. I'm glad you leased enough for Mr. Furman's cows. Makes it like old times."

"What's in the old barn now, Mom?"

"Storage mostly. Tools and machinery. Of course, your dad's welding outfit and the workbench for his leather work. Mr. Furman stores feed for his cows."

"I think I'll walk over for a look. Remember, Mom, I did a lot of guitar practicing in there? I liked the way it sounded."

"Yes, I remember. Why do you think your dad made the dinner bell? It was the only way to get you in for meals. I've got to go check on my cake. I have the ladies here this afternoon."

The barn door squeaked on its wheels as he pushed it as far open as possible, then reached for the light switch. With the smell of hay and leather, memories flooded his heart and mind as he stepped inside to explore. The barrel and scoop he used to feed the horses for so many years sat in the corner of the front stall. He ran his hand over the leather-working tools his dad used to make and repair tack. He still used the guitar strap his dad made for him one Christmas. Randy remembered all the times he turned over an empty five-gallon bucket to sit playing and singing for hours. He looked to the ceiling as he broke into song. The acoustics of the old building sent chills up his spine as they always had. A cat startled him when she scampered from the darkness and out of the open door. *There is still something for me here. I have to figure out what.*

****

As his tour hit the road again, the single from his album continued to get good air play. His nomination brought requests from artists to work with him. Somewhere between Roanoke and Charlotte, Neil called with more exciting news.

"Randy, are you sitting down? Guess what."

Randy rolled his eyes. "Get on with it, will you? I'm right in the middle of writing."

"Well, maybe you won't be so excited after all. I mean, it's not too impressive that you'll be on the Grand Ole Opry in October."

Randy jumped to his feet. "What? You mean it? You're amazing. Best agent ever."

"Oh, now you want to suck up? I can't take too much credit, though. I mean, I've kept your name before them since you got to town, but this time they called me. The nomination is bringing this on, kiddo. Everyone will take you seriously now."

"I think you're right. We played a show with Sugarland last week and Kristian Bush talked to me after.

He wants to write some with me. And I heard from Dierks Bentley, too. Pretty good, huh?"

He held his hand on the phone and said to his crew, "The Opry in October." The bus came alive with celebration.

"Thanks, Neil. I've got people to talk to."

After congratulations from his guys, he ran to his room and paced the small area while Tom's home phone rang. "Tom, you'll never believe it."

"Whoa, son. Take a breath. Is everything all right? Get on the phone, Mama, it's Randy."

"Couldn't be better. Look at me, I'm shaking. Is she on the extension yet?"

"Yes, I'm here. What is it?"

"I got the nod. I am playing the Grand Ole Opry in October."

Tom and Jennie both screamed and started asking questions over each other.

"I know nothing more right now, except this is it. I've made it. Anything else is icing on the cake."

Tom spoke from experience. "Your first time on the Opry is something you'll never forget, Randy. What will you sing?"

"I can't even imagine right now. I guess the latest hit. They're releasing another one off this album about then. Listen, both of you. Thank you for all you've done to get me here. Is there anything I can do for you guys?"

He could hear the tears as Jennie spoke. "Everything here is right as rain. This is all about you, young man. Enjoy every minute."

"I know I will. We'll talk soon. I have to call the family."

****

At first, he and Angie talked often. She sounded positive, and he wanted to hear all of her news. "Great, Ang, I knew you could get in to play there. You still have the appointment with BBR for a record deal, right?"

"Yes, I can't wait. I have the songs all picked out. I'm going to knock their socks off."

"That's good. If you don't believe it, who will, right?"

After the record deal fell through, he heard from her less frequently. He sometimes woke her mid-afternoon. "Hey, sleepyhead. You better get up. You have a gig tonight."

"Yeah, I'll make it. Whoa, what a party at Benny's last night. They kept asking me to sing another one."

"What happened to the part-time job at the radio station? Angie? Hey, wake up."

"Yeah, yeah, I'm here. A few more minutes, okay? Wake me in an hour or so."

Randy sat staring at his phone. *What is happening? When I can't even keep her awake on the phone, something must be wrong.* He called her back, like she asked, but he had his own show to worry about.

****

Randy enjoyed his dream life now and didn't even mind sleeping on the bus anymore or eating fast food along the road. The people at each place they played treated him like a king. *Somehow there's still something missing.*

Every radio station wanted interviews, and he satisfied as many as he could. The album sold better than anyone expected.

"Neil, you gotta get them to send more CDs again, and tee shirts, too." He shifted his phone to his other hand. "That Buckboard Festival in California next week is huge. We'll never make it with what we have."

In a calming voice Neil said, "I got a call from Tony already. There's a reason I have him run the merch table along with driving the bus. He's right there and keeps me informed. I've already placed the orders. Are you stressing again?"

"Sorry. I guess all this has never been so real. Like I said, this festival is big around there and growing every year. They hold it maybe an hour from where I grew up. This is like the pinnacle for me."

Neil's next statement should have brought Randy back to reality. "You remember you're playing the Grand Ole Opry in Nashville a few weeks later?"

"Of course, I do. All I'm saying is, as a star-struck kid I stood out in that sun and dust watching musicians live a life I could only dream of, and now I'm going to be right there with friends and family from all over the state seeing me on the same stage."

"I get it, Randy. Don't worry, we'll make sure everything is like you imagined. How's the writing going?"

"Great. Kristian and I have emailed some ideas around. We may have something before I get back. Then we'll only need to polish it off."

"I'm not surprised. I always knew the songwriting would help put you on the map. I'll see you in a few weeks."

"Thanks, Neil. See ya then."

The Buckboard Festival proved to be everything he remembered. Music played constantly. Pop-up vendor booths and restaurants stood everywhere he looked. The sun beat down on the dusty desert of the Coachella

Valley. Randy walked the grounds to take in all the fun and excitement of thousands of people gathered to hear music. Maybe some drove to hear him. He stopped at a tent to buy a cold drink, and the girl taking his money recognized him.

"You're Randy Walters, aren't you?" She squealed. "Mary, look who it is. Can I get a picture with you?"

A crowd gathered, and he obliged them all. Then he fast-walked back to his bus. He enjoyed little privacy now. Fans recognized him everywhere.

As he stepped up on the bus, "Oh, man. I didn't even get my cold drink." He pulled a canned Coke from the refrigerator, then heard a knock on the door. When he got up to look out the window, he saw his family standing there, Jimmy jumping up and down. He rushed out to their arms.

"Well, will you look at this? I'm so glad you guys came early. Mom, don't squeeze too tight. In a couple of hours, I have to sing. Dan, thanks for driving everybody down." Jimmy grabbed his father's leg and held on tight. Randy teased him. "Son, I swear if you get any taller, they're gonna toss you right out of third grade."

"Aw, Dad. You know I'm gonna be in fourth."

"Come on in out of the heat. The guys are all out on the grounds somewhere. We've got the air cranked up in here. Sit right there, Mom. Sherry, you sure look good. New hairdo?"

"My goodness, thank you. With the money you've been paying me, I splurge at the salon once in a while."

Jimmy explored and came upon a guitar in one bunk. "Can I play, Dad?"

"That one is Jack's. Why don't you go back to my room and get mine? I want to hear what you've been learning."

Dan spoke up. "He's good beyond his years. He'll be working for you before you know it."

Randy looked back at his son, opening the case with care. "I don't know about that. If this life is what he wants, maybe. I guess Carrie had to work today."

His mother answered, "Yes. You know, honey, someday—"

He cut her off. "I know, Mom. I just thought she might."

Sherry spoke with the voice of reason. "She made sure Jimmy got to come, and she wants a tee shirt, by the way. Randy, she knows how important it is, but with the new job and all. You know, she has her own life now."

He reached into a box behind him and tossed a shirt at her. "Here, make sure she gets this. They give us plenty. I know what you're saying, sis. I guess I'm feeling nostalgic, being in my old stomping grounds."

Dan chattered like a kid on Christmas morning. "This place is crazy. I've never seen so many people in one place, and these VIP badges are cool. The music never stops, does it?"

Randy liked to see him having fun. He tossed a shirt to him, too. "Did you see the line-up? I mean everyone from Sugarland to Toby Keith to Brooks and Dunn. So outstanding."

"And Randy Walters, don't forget." Dan, ever the loyal fan.

"Yeah, my time slots aren't the best, but at least I'm on the main stage."

Jimmy played and sang a few songs, then Randy took them on a tour of the bus. "The guys will be back to get ready for our first set soon. Here's some cash. Get something to eat and enjoy the day. I'll see you at the three o'clock show. Mom, one more hug?" He wrapped his arms around her and squeezed her a little too tightly before they departed.

When his time came to perform, Randy's head swam as the announcer praised him and his hits. At the sound of his name, the shouts of the crowd mingled with the thunder of applause until he almost missed his cue to take the stage. The band began the introduction of the first song while he plugged in and waved at the crowd. His voice flew out across the sea of thousands of people, all standing and singing along with him. His eyes scanned the crowd in the sunlight, then he found his family up front, and shared this proudest moment with them.

After a few songs, he stopped to talk to the audience as he drank from a water bottle. "Hello, California." The roar came up again. "Yes, I am a Cali boy from Lakeview. I attended the very first Buckboard as a fan, so it's special for me to be here with you today."

He looked back at his band, smiled, then said to the crowd, "Our next song is important to me because it was my dad's favorite. You California folks up for a little of Merle Haggard's 'Mama's Eyes'?" Again, the deafening roar. "Listen, my family is here today, so I'd like to dedicate this one to my mom. They're right here in the front row. Mom, wave at everybody." The security guards immediately surrounded the family. "Hey, officer. Yeah you, what's your name? Ben? Okay, Ben, you're in charge of making sure my mom has a good time. Can you do that? A chair, umbrella, water, whatever she wants, got it?" The crowd went wild at his sweet gesture.

He played to the crowd and held them captivated through to the last song. After the show, the autograph table kept him busy. He stopped long enough to tell the family goodbye and hear their excitement for him. "Mom, I'm so glad you came. Did you have a good time?"

"Oh, yes, I loved every minute. Dan took pictures for me to show my friends. I'm so proud."

"That means everything." He shook Dan's hand. "You're the best, Dan. Drive safe. You're carrying some pretty special cargo. Jimmy, give me another one of those third-grade hugs."

"Aw, Dad. I still love you, though." Jimmy threw his arms around Randy's neck.

He finally got away from the fans and returned to the comfort of the bus. After lying across the bed, he fell asleep almost immediately. An hour later, Steve woke him with a shake.

"Hey, man, there's some folks out here to see you. They have your VIP tickets, so I thought it might be okay."

He thought he knew who it might be. "Give me a minute to hit the head and comb my hair. I'll be right there."

When he saw Sarah and David, then Frank and Sue, his heart sent out his greeting. "This is so great. Glad you made it."

David spoke up. "We caught a little of your show."

Sue laughed. "Yeah, after we finally got hooked up with each other, we missed half of it. This place is enormous."

Sarah held his arm tight. "We'll be here for the next show. You sounded great up there."

Randy looked over at Frank. "You gonna stay long enough this time to let me buy you the beer I owe you?"

"You bet. We did like you said and got a motel close by. We're all yours tonight."

Randy shot a look at Sue and Frank. "So, where's little Randall?"

"He's at her mother's. We don't get out often, even for a date night. This is a real treat." Frank put his arm around Sue. "This is our first full night away from the baby. She's already called her mom three times. Funny thing, her mom knows how to raise kids. Who knew?" Sue shoved his arm away in pretend anger. Randy enjoyed their laughter.

He was even more excited about the seven o'clock show. With his friends there to support him and the crowd grew louder and noisier. Randy watched Frank's face as he performed the song Frank wrote for him. One of his favorites off the first album.

He spent less time after the show with the fans in favor of being with his friends. "There's some great food here. Everything from hot dogs to rib eye. Actual restaurants in pop-up tents. Probably easier to stay on the grounds. Does that sound okay?"

When the server brought menus, Randy made it plain he would pay the check. "We'll start with your best on tap all around. Now we're even for a while, Frank."

"Shoot, Randy, I feel like I owe you for putting that song on your album. What a thrill to hear you do it live, and here."

"Hey, we paid you, didn't we?" Randy cocked his head.

Frank chuckled. "Yes, I framed a picture of the ninety-one dollar check." They all laughed. "No, I really did."

"Listen, I hope you guys had a good time. I can't tell you what it means to me you're here."

They all answered with accolades and stories of fun from the day. They ate their meal and talked of old times.

Randy liked David. "You must do pretty well. Sarah sent pictures of your house right on the beach."

David took Sarah's hand. "We're comfortable. Who knew playing with other people's money was so lucrative?"

Sue sat her drink down to say, "You should see their amazing place."

Randy listened in silence while they talked about their lives and plans. His life was right where it should be. *Mine doesn't seem as meaningful as theirs.*

Frank ordered more chips and salsa, then asked, "Randy, you haven't told us much about life in Nashville, and don't you have a lady friend there?" They all sat up to hear his answer.

"Life in Nashville. Well, first, I'm not there much. You saw my home this afternoon. But yeah, I have a nice apartment with a good roommate. He's a singer/songwriter, and we've written some good stuff together. You remember Vince Gill's hit last summer? Yep, that was us. I have a small group of close friends."

Sarah wanted more. "And your girlfriend? Come on, don't hold out."

Randy wondered how much to say. "Angie is also a performer. She came to Nashville at eighteen and has gone through some real difficulties. I'm afraid she might be in a hard spot right now. I'm not sure. She's great, though. We've had a lot of fun."

Sarah kept after him. "Are you thinking of settling

down?"

Randy set his glass down a little too hard. "Marriage? No way, but I sure envy what you guys all have. I'd like to know what time I'd be in bed every night and see the same person waiting for me with kids running around me. As much as I'm enjoying the fun parts, there're hard days, too. Lonesome is the word."

No one knew what to say. Frank tried.

"We all have trade-offs in life, Randy. Nothing is going to be a picnic all the time. Sue can tell you about it."

Sarah spoke instead. "That's right. You talk about us doing so good, but you don't realize how many hours David works. I have classes and then rush over to help him at the office. We can't even think about starting a family until I'm out of school. But no, we don't want to trade it for anything. I guess we want the same happiness for you." They all spoke up to support him.

"I miss you guys. I'll figure this out sometime. There's got to be a way to balance it. Hey, you see what time it is? We head east to Phoenix in a few hours. Four more shows before we hit Nashville again."

"Yeah, and then you play the Opry. We'll be listening that night, for sure." Frank grinned.

Randy counted on his fingers. "Let's see, four more shows on the road, then the Opry, and then the CMA Awards. I'll get some sleep in there somewhere."

Frank sat forward to ask, "Will they have you do a song on the awards show?"

"Nah, our category is low on the totem pole. They'll probably play a song clip while they flash our pictures or something."

Sarah shook his arm. "Oh, like that's nothing."

David said as they walked back to Randy's bus, "Are we allowed to tell people we're your best friends or something? I've never known a star before."

Randy patted his shoulder. "You sure can. You guys are my best friends."

Chapter 24

Two nights later, Randy played a show in Fort Worth. When he got back to the bus, his phone flashed, showing a message from Neil. He couldn't bear talking business at that late hour. He plugged in the phone to charge and went to bed. As he fell asleep, he thought of the two last shows in Kansas City and Louisville. He looked forward to getting back to Nashville in a few days.

The phone woke him early the next morning. "Hello" was all he could muster. He barely heard the voice on the phone, but then recognized Neil.

"Randy, get up. I have something to tell you."

"I can't believe you, of all people, would wake me at this hour. Whatever it is can wait. Catch me later."

"No, Randy, don't hang up." He hesitated. "It's Angie. I'm sorry, man, I hate making this call."

He sat up wide awake on the side of the bed. He knew his lips were moving, but he heard nothing coming out. Then finally, "What? What is it?"

"Randy, I don't know any other way to say this. She's dead. Friends found her at home last night after she didn't show for a gig. They got hold of me to tell you. I'll be in Kansas City tonight in case you need me."

"Need you? I don't understand. I talked to her a couple of days ago. What happened?" His mind raced with all the possible answers to his question, but he feared what he heard next.

"An overdose. The investigation will determine if it was accidental. Maybe we should wait to talk until I get there."

Randy's breath caught in his throat, and the phone shook in his hand as he paced the room. "No, this can't be right. She was clean. Wasn't she?"

Neil continued. "I'll catch a flight right away."

He raised his voice. "What will that solve? Oh, I see. You're worried I'll scrap the shows. The business is so important. You don't care that just maybe the business is what killed her."

Neil paused before responding. "I get it, friend. You're upset. Barbara is handing me my flight info. I'll see you tonight."

Randy drew back to throw the phone at the wall, but Roger ran in to grab his arm. "Whoa, whoa, whoa. What's all the yelling? Sit down, man. What's wrong?"

Randy sat on the bed. Speechless.

He pulled himself together to explain to Roger and the others, then dialed Julia's number.

She answered right away. "We heard a few minutes ago, Randy. It's all over the news here this morning."

He gave a half-hearted laugh. "So, she finally gets the fame she wanted."

"What can I do for you? How can I help?"

"I don't have any idea. Find out what happened. I can't get there for two, maybe three days at the earliest."

"Marsha is on her phone trying to get something from the news crew at the station. So far, nothing new. Angie didn't let on to you something was wrong?"

"So, you think she did it? Why? I knew it had to be rough on her, but she sounded so positive."

"Well, the last time we saw her, she didn't look good. Of course, she played it off to being tired. You know, Frances dropped her. She was working without an agent, and she'd lost her job at the station."

"No, I didn't know. I wanted so much to believe her rosy outlook. I guess I wasn't listening close enough."

"This is not your fault. I know you're devastated right now, but you've got to keep it together. Do you need me to do anything here?"

"I can't think of anything. Oh, yes. Get her guitar. It was her grandfather's. Make sure you secure it until her parents get there. Oh, man, poor Ray and Shirley."

"Don't call them. Not until you settle down some."

"Yeah, probably smart. Thanks, Julia. Promise you'll let me know if you hear anything."

Randy stayed in his room for the rest of the trip to Kansas City. Memories of Angie and questions about what had happened filled his mind. He relived their recent phone conversations. How could he have missed the signs? He wondered if this was how you became another casualty of Nashville. You lose yourself in a dream gone bad. He had no answers, only tears.

He gathered himself to do what he knew he must as the bus lumbered into the arena parking lot in Kansas City. The first person he saw when he stepped down was Neil. "I can't believe you came after the way I talked to you."

"I told you I understood, and I meant it. I'm here to support you, more than the tour. Yes, the show must go on, and I know you know that, but after, we can stay up and talk as late as you like. You are why I'm here."

"Thanks. Have you heard anything else?"

Neil pulled him over to sit down on some boxes.

"Not much. You know, they'll do an autopsy and everything. Red tape out the wazoo." He changed the subject before the discussion got too deep. "Listen, Charlene Sampson is your go-to here tonight. Real class act. This one sold out and should be a breeze."

"Sounds good. We'll set up for sound check in a half hour." He stared into Neil's questioning eyes. "I'll be fine, ya know. Feels wrong, but I know it's what I have to do. Don't worry."

For two hours, including three encores, he channeled all his hurt and frustration into the music. Every rejection on music row and all the dark bars and street corners that held and crushed the dreams of young people like Angie. The pain of the backbiting, lying, and broken promises he knew she had experienced flowed out of him and sailed across the crowd with his songs. He could hear her laughter in the shrill tones of the lead guitar. He saw her smile on the faces of a hundred girls at the edge of the stage. The band members kept looking at each other in disbelief after songs they thought never sounded so good. When at last he stumbled off stage, sweat soaked his shirt and hair, matted down under his hat. He left every emotion out there, and the audience paid him back with ear-shattering applause. The one thing he could not do was spend another hour signing autographs and smiling for photos.

Neil understood. "Hey, guys, I know you're disappointed, but Randy is sick and needs to get to bed. He gave you the show of his career tonight despite not feeling well. You can forgive him this one time, right? If you'll leave your name and address, he'd love to send you a signed 8x10 photo. How does that sound?" Neil had worked his magic again.

****

Randy rushed to pick up newspapers, old fast-food wrappers, and empties around Angie's apartment before her parents arrived. They agreed to meet him there to pick up her few belongings.

Julia accompanied him for support. "You're good to help them with this."

"Yeah, well, dinner with them the other night was hard enough. Now that the coroner has ruled it suicide, it doesn't make it any easier." He heard their footsteps on the stairs and went to greet them at the door. "Ray, Shirley, good to see you again. Come on in."

Shirley grabbed him and held on tight while he shook Ray's hand.

Randy explained, "This is our friend, Julia. She offered to help. I didn't know what you'd want to take, so we haven't packed anything yet."

Julia took Shirley's hand. "I can't say how sorry we all are. Angie was a sweet girl and such a talent."

Ray got down to business. "We'd better get to it. Our flight is at one. Shirley, I don't know what you could want from this dump."

Julia tried to help. "I thought maybe her jewelry, photo albums, and the like. I found some things in her bedroom. Right this way."

Randy squirmed and moved around the living room. "I know it doesn't look like much, but she was trying to do everything on her own. I guess you know about her stubborn streak."

Ray let the threadbare easy chair engulf him, put his face in his hands, and spoke. "I know you think I was too hard on her." His eyes rose to Randy's. "But this is what I feared."

Randy stepped over to put his hand on Ray's shoulder. "She knew it was because you loved her. I'm sorry I couldn't be here to look after her."

Ray moved forward to the edge of the chair. "Don't blame yourself. Whatever happened was her own doing. Sure, you can blame the business. We've heard that since we got here. I'll always wonder if I did enough to support her. Did I make it too hard for her to come home?" He stood and took Randy by the shoulders. "I know you're having the success my baby never did, but don't let it eat you up. Focus on what's important in life."

Randy nodded and turned away. As he gazed at the view of Nashville Angie loved, he pointed to the item at his feet. "Julia made sure her guitar stayed safe until you got here."

Ray teared up. "I'm not sure I can look at it ever again. Maybe you should keep it."

Randy turned back to him. "No, I couldn't. She was so proud it was her grandfather's. She always told the story from the stage."

Shirley spoke from the bedroom door. "It was your dad's, Ray. You know Ashton is playing now. He'd love to have it." She smiled as she looked at Randy. "He's Angie's nephew."

Randy picked up the guitar to hand it to Ray. "That's it, then. The family tradition continues. Now, let's see if there's anything else you want. Julia and I will handle the rest. You don't want to miss your flight."

After the tearful goodbye with Ray and Shirley Wilkins, he and Julia spent the afternoon packing, throwing away, and crying over a closed chapter in his life. But he would never forget the words of Angie's father.

****

Randy stared across the desk at his manager. "No more interviews, Neil. I can't do it. My life is no longer my own since being back in Nashville."

"You have to. You're nominated, and they know you're playing the Opry this weekend."

"And if that's all they wanted to talk about, maybe I could manage it. They all bring up my connection with Angie. Why can't they let her rest?"

"You know that's not how it works, Randy. It won't last long. Something new, and thus more exciting, will catch their fancy. Bear with it. You've been doing a great job and honoring her as you go. I know how tough it is."

"I'll try. Can we talk about everything else another time? I can't focus on all this right now. Remember, I want to get home to California right after the awards show. I promised Jimmy this Christmas. Thanksgiving would be nice."

"That depends. If you win, the carousel keeps turning, only faster. You think you've been in the limelight up to now? You can't imagine."

"What I can't imagine is winning. You've seen the list. Either Hunter Hayes or Thompson Square will be a shoo-in. The rest of us will give the after-speech about being honored to be nominated in such good company as they say. I guess I'll admit I'm looking forward to attending with all the glitz and glamour, but how could I win?"

Neil's forehead rippled with deep furrows. "Hey, you keep the humble talk for the interviews. You've got a good chance. We need to build this up and use it for all it's worth. Are you wanting some time off before the awards? That'll be tough."

"I don't see how I can keep going, but I guess I have to. I can't sleep, eat, anything. My gut wrenches every time I try to sing. Everything reminds me of Angie. I'm writing with Mary Chapin Carpenter this week. It should be so much fun, but I don't feel creative. Mary thinks we have something good together, but I can't deny she's carrying the bigger load."

"Maybe that explains you looking rough lately. You're not drinking too much again, are you?"

"Don't bust my chops, Neil. At least it numbs the pain so I can rest at all."

"I'm only saying be careful. Have you given any more thought to another album next year?"

"I guess. Let's talk about it later, okay?" He left the office with a wave.

Neil yelled after him, "Dammit, Randy, what can I tell your label?"

Chapter 25

The morning of Saturday, October 20, 2012, was like any other. Until he woke up. He turned off his alarm and threw his legs off the bed, feet on the floor. Then it hit him. *This is the night I play the Grand Ole Opry.* His heart raced as he made his way to the kitchen. He hoped the years of work and planning had made him ready for this night. A coffee cup slipped to the floor from his shaky hand.

Jeff came from his bedroom to see Randy picking up the pieces. "What's going on in here so early?"

"I broke a cup, is all. Man, do you know what I did with my blue shirt? I have to have it tonight."

"The one you picked up from the cleaners two days ago? The one still hanging on your door? You need me to help with something before I go to work?"

"No, I have to be at the Opry at ten to work with the house band." He moved to pour his coffee. "You want a cup? I'm meeting Neil for lunch, then I'll go back for the show."

"This is your day, Randy. You need to calm down some if you can. Enjoy it."

Randy wished his friend could experience heading to the dream night of his career. *Too bad Angie can't be here to enjoy it with me.* "Everything in my life has led me here. It all comes together on that stage tonight. I'll be ready when the time comes. I'll have two tickets for you at will call."

Jeff grinned at him. "I know. I'll be the one screaming loudest out there."

When he walked up to the performer's entrance at the Opry House, Randy introduced himself to the guard. The man found his name on the list and told him where to meet the band. He located the room and saw it full of musicians finishing a song for another singer. He noticed a couple of guitar players he knew from working on Aaron's CD. One nodded to him and kept playing.

The man in charge was saying, "I think that'll do it. You guys all have your charts updated like you want them? Last chance. Then we'll see you tonight, Ethan. Thanks for coming in. We know you're busy."

The artist rose to wave at the group and say, "No. Thank you. I knew I was throwing something new at you tonight. Thanks for working with me."

Randy recognized Ethan Briggs who had two hits on the charts. Their eyes met, and Ethan said, "You're Randy Walters. Good to meet you. You're on tonight?"

Randy welcomed his friendliness. "I am. First time."

"Well, Randy, soak it all up. You won't forget your first time. See you tonight."

This day gets better all the time. He played his song choices right from his CD for the band. He wanted them to hear the sound fans would expect. Then they put their own touches on them and made the songs even better. The quality of musicians and singers everywhere he went in this town continued to amaze him. They worked about an hour before he left to meet Neil for lunch. As he walked by the security guard, the man gave him a parking sticker for the night.

****

Randy pulled into the restaurant parking lot and parked away from the entrance. As he entered the place, Neil waved him to a booth by the window.

"Sit down. How did it go?"

"Remarkable is all I can say. They jumped on my songs like we'd been playing together for years. Have you ordered?"

"Yes, I got you the black and blue burger you like. It comes with fries, too."

"Sure, that's fine. This my tea?"

"Yes. Listen, we need to talk about next year. We're booking shows. I don't want to do too much until we know if you're an award winner or not. That affects negotiations, of course."

Randy squirmed. "Makes sense. And the CD?"

"They want to be in the studio in early January like last time. How's the writing going?"

"Good. I'll have plenty of songs after a day writing with Verlon Thompson out at his place. I'd like to record what we came up with. We both thought it was good."

"Well, you sound more positive than the last time we talked. I don't mind saying you had me a little worried."

"I'm still trying to figure it all out. A day at a time about Angie and I mean, you know I don't mind the work. I love what I'm doing, but I want it to stay fun. You get it?"

Neil took a drink of his tea. "I wish I had a nickel for every time I've heard that. You knew it was a hard life from the start, didn't you, Randy? You understand my job is to keep you in front of your audience. Period. The balance thing you have to work out. I don't plan on slowing down."

"I know what I pay you for." He grinned at his agent. "Family is everything to me. I told you I'm going to be in California for Christmas at least. Block out as much time as you can."

"I got it loud and clear. I haven't been booking anything in December. So, what songs are you doing tonight?"

They talked beyond lunch as friends were apt to do.

Back at the Opry House, Randy sat in his vehicle watching the stream of people going to the performer's entrance and recognized most of the artists. Was he ready to accompany them on this historic stage? *Well, I won't find out sitting here.* Besides, the three glasses of tea from lunch made his bladder scream. He got out and walked toward the building.

On the walk, a soft voice came from behind him. "Aren't you Randy Walters?"

He turned to see Lester Ashford, one of his childhood heroes who had performed at The Opry since the sixties. Randy struggled to make his mouth form words in answer. He thought maybe he responded, "Yes, sir, Mr. Ashford."

"Oh, hey now, I'm Les. I think you're scheduled on my set tonight."

The Grand Ole Opry operated as a live radio show with different stars hosting the night's segments. They reached the entrance, where the veteran star spoke to the security guard.

"Good evening, Joe. This is my friend Randy." He ushered Randy inside. "I've got to check on some things in the office. You'll be in The Circle Room tonight. Why don't I meet you there later? We'll go over how everything will work." He turned and disappeared into the crowd.

Randy must have looked like a scared kid to the mature voice he heard next.

"Hi, I'm Mary Beth. I'm a hostess here. Can I help you find your way?"

Relieved by her friendly smile, he said, "Uh, I guess somebody better."

"This is your first night here? You'll be in The Circle Room then." She acknowledged his confusion. "Your dressing room. Come on, I'll take you there."

His face reddened as he remembered the other pressing business. "Uh, yes, ma'am. First, could you direct me to the men's room?"

That relief allowed him to enjoy the small tour Mary Beth took him on as they walked down the hall. Artifacts from the Opry's long history lined the walls. Each dressing room bore the name of a hall of fame star. Room number one honored Roy Acuff, one of the longest performing members before his death in 1992. Many of the room's furnishings came from the old Ryman Auditorium.

Mary Beth advised, "Randy, you'll want to come another time to see everything. The guard will let you in. Well, here we are. Do you know why they call this The Circle Room?"

He shook his head. "I'm afraid I don't."

Mary Beth explained. "When you get out there tonight, you'll notice the circle of wood floor where you stand at the mic is different from the rest of the stage. When they moved into this new building, they wanted to bring the feeling of the Ryman here. They cut a circle from that old stage floor and implanted it into this one. When you stand at the mic, you're actually standing on the same piece of stage as every star since The Opry moved to the Ryman in 1943. So, they put the first timers in here and call it The Circle Room. See?"

Randy's pulse quickened. "Thanks." He laughed and said in a humorously shaky little voice, "Now I'm not nervous at all."

She giggled again. "You'll be fine. I'll come check on you again later."

Now he was alone, walking around the room to survey the photos of other singers who had spent their first night there. He opened his guitar case. Touching the instrument comforted him.

In a little while, a man with a clipboard stopped at his door. "Randy Walters?"

Randy stood like a soldier. "Yes, sir. That's me."

The man never looked up from his papers. "You're on with Lester Ashford. He'll take the stage at 8:20. You be ready right off stage. Your hostess will come get you," he said as he disappeared down the hall.

Randy ran to the door to watch him go and thought, *why, no, sir, I don't have questions at all. Thanks for stopping by. You've been a big help.* He chuckled. *A simple routine for these folks.*

Randy sat on a bench with his guitar to run through his songs. People stopped by to introduce themselves. He was a fan of most. Shortly before eight, Lester stopped in. "I didn't forget you. So, here's what will happen. I go on at 8:20 for two songs. Then a commercial. I'll bring you on right after. Tell me a little about yourself."

His words tumbled out with ease. "So anyway, that's how I got here. I've been a fan of yours forever. My mom will faint when she hears me on with Lester Ashford tonight."

As he rose to leave, Lester patted Randy's shoulder. "I bet she's proud of you, no matter what. See you out there."

The minutes ticked by faster. His leg went into action. He tried to drink water, though his throat tightened.

Mary Beth stuck her head into the room. "Your time to get up there. Got everything you need?"

"Except maybe a set of steady legs. Let me hit the restroom quick."

"Okay, but hurry."

After, she walked him to the backstage area. "You stay here until he introduces you. Good luck. Relax, Randy, you'll be fine."

He stood there listening to Lester perform. Though he had seen the show a few times since moving to Nashville, sitting in the audience in no way compared to being this close to the stage. Everything leading up to this moment raced through his head again. The hours of practice, the gigs in bars, Bakersfield and Tom, even Angie, all pointed to that distinct circle on this stage. Lester finished his two songs, then the commercial for the radio audience played. The vein on Randy's neck grew and pulsed with each beat of his thumping heart. He wanted to find the nearest restroom to throw up, but there was no time. Then he heard the great Lester Ashford introducing him. He believed this was happening. Performance mode took over and banished his nerves. His blood cooled. His muscles relaxed. A smile spread across his face at this special moment.

The crowd clapped and yelled as Lester finally said, "Here he is. Welcome a new star, Randy Walters."

With one hand Randy gripped the neck of his guitar.

The other made a fist hanging at his side. One step forward and the spotlight bathed across him. He continued to the circle as he looked up. "Come on, Dad. We made it here."

He completed two songs with ease. The audience responded to every word and note. He knew he belonged there. Another commercial started as he walked off the stage to congratulations from artists and stagehands alike. He stood to watch Lester finish his part of the show, then exit the stage.

Randy said, "You sounded great out there. Thanks for having me on your set tonight."

The veteran performer shook Randy's hand. "I was glad to have you, Randy. You have a nice voice. Those lyrics impressed me, too. They're yours?"

Randy knew Lester to be one of the most respected songwriters in Nashville. "Yes, sir, I wrote them both."

Lester raised his eyebrows and grinned. "We may have to get together sometime. Listen, my night is over. This old man is heading home. You'll find a pretty good jam session downstairs in the dressing room at the end of the hall. Get to know folks and have some fun."

"I sure appreciate you helping to make this special for me, Mr. Ashford."

His new friend turned to him. "Les. See ya, Randy."

He joined the others to jam until the security guard ran them out so he could shut the building down. Randy got into his truck to drive home but found himself at a Waffle House, greedily wolfing down a plate of bacon and eggs. Watching the morning sun break over the Cumberland River, he contemplated what the future held.

Chapter 26

Three weeks later, Randy watched his mother rushing around a hotel room getting ready for her son's extraordinary night at the Country Music Association Awards. Julia had taken her to a salon where the stylist cut and curled her hair. She thought the artificial nails and color were pretty, but maybe a bit much.

"Son, you're spending too much on me. The plane ticket, the beauty parlor, this fancy hotel. Where am I ever going to wear this gown again?"

He kissed her cheek. "All those things are about tonight, Mom. I want the world to see I have the prettiest date at the CMA Awards. Does Dad's bolo tie go with my new jacket?"

"It does. Where are your dress pants?" She began digging through the collection of shopping bags from their trip to the mall the day before.

He giggled. "I'm wearing my new jeans. Come on, Mom, we've been watching these award shows on TV together for years. You know this is what most of the guys do."

"James and I didn't raise you to be like most of the guys." Before he could respond, "Oh all right, all right. What do I know?"

His arm wrapped around her. "Grab your fancy little beaded purse, and let's head out. They texted the limo is here."

She stopped and beamed up at him. "Limo? You mean like prom night?"

He threw his head back and gave a belly laugh.

Arriving at the venue that night was all he wanted it to be for her. The aerial spotlights lit up the sky as their limo took its turn at the curb outside the Bridgestone Auditorium. A uniformed greeter helped Randy and his mother from the car. A crowd of fans screamed Randy's name from behind the ropes. Camera flashes came from every direction. He saw his mother marveling at the red carpet they walked on. He guided her to the area, prepared for photos and interviews.

"Son, you go ahead. I'll wait right here. This is for the important people tonight."

"Oh, no you don't. Get over here and smile for the TV cameras. You're the most important person here."

Photographers and reporters shouted his name. "Over here, Randy. Turn this way a little, Randy. Do you think you'll win, Randy? One more, Randy. Who's your date, Randy?"

He stood a little straighter to say, "I'm sure someone has already said it tonight, but I am so proud to be nominated alongside these talented artists. This is my best girl, my mom."

The reporters' questions turned to her. "What's it like seeing your son become a star?"

She shocked him by being at ease with it all. "We've always been proud of him." She fielded their questions and posed for photos until someone moved them toward the entrance. As an usher took them to their seats, she poked Randy every time she recognized a star. He knew he introduced her to more people than she could ever remember.

He watched her enjoy the bright lights and loud music of the show. She sat on the edge of her seat to applaud all the winners. When it came time for the New Artist category, he thought he saw her saying a quick prayer. The announcer read out the names of the nominees slowly while the artist's photo filled the backdrop and their music played. His mother reached over to calm his bouncing knee. He placed his hand over hers.

At last, the time came. The stars presenting the award joked as one tore the envelope open and the other read the words, "The New Artist of the Year for 2012 is Hunter Hayes." The crowd erupted. Randy clutched his chest. He expected the cameras to search for his reaction, and his prepared smile filled his face as he looked around for the winner. He stood and high-fived Hunter's hand as the winner ran to the stage. When he took his seat again, the hand patting his thigh held that special power only mothers have to make everything okay.

After the show, the reporters deluged him with interviews and photos. His mother wandered off on her own to greet more people. She met up with Julia, who introduced her to Marsha. Aaron and his wife Sandy invited them all to their house for dinner the next night. "We have to go relieve the babysitter. You'll come tomorrow night, Mrs. Walters?"

"I sure hope so. I'll have Randy call you."

Randy came to take her arm. "Are you having fun?"

Julia spoke up. "She's been telling us all your secrets."

He gave a shiver. "Sounds like you, Mom. Come on, let's get you back to the hotel before you get us both in trouble."

On the drive, she asked, "Are you very disappointed, son?"

He considered how to answer. "Maybe a little. I can't argue with who won, though. I'm even a fan of his. This wasn't my time, I guess. I didn't want to disappoint you, is all."

"The ladies won't believe when I tell them about this entire trip. I'm so proud of you. I wish your dad could have been here."

"Don't worry, Mom, he's always close by."

After he got her back to her hotel, he drove to his apartment. Jeff planned to be out all night. Award nights always meant parties in Nashville. The after festivities were like a command performance for the nominees and winners, but somehow, a cold beer on his patio, surveying the lights of the city, suited him better.

****

Randy signaled as he turned onto Aaron's street. "Mom, you let me know when you're ready to leave tonight. Your flight tomorrow is at 10:20."

His mother showed fresh energy. "Are you kidding? I'm living it up while I can. They were so nice to invite us."

"I'm glad you like my friends. You say Julia and Marsha are coming, too?"

She turned toward him. "Yes, both of them. They're…"

He jumped in to fill in the blanks. "Together. Yes, ma'am. They've been good friends for me here."

She adjusted her purse on her lap. "I'm glad someone is taking care of you."

Randy relaxed his hands on the steering wheel and turned another corner.

"Is this the house?" She bounced in the seat like a child seeing her first puppy.

"Yes, pretty nice spread, huh? Maybe we can have something like this one day."

She didn't hesitate with her response. "I like my place just fine. I bet she has it fixed up real nice inside."

Sandy took her on a tour of the house while everyone else relived the previous night over cocktails. Aaron asked, "Well, Randy, how did you like your first dress-up Nashville event?"

"Only amazing is all. It's sure an ego boost, even if you don't win."

"Sure, certainly more fun to win, though. This is the first year in five I didn't win at least one."

Julia offered, "I'd say being nominated in three categories stands for something."

Aaron chuckled. "Always my promo manager. But, yes, you're right."

Randy took it all in. Could it slip away as fast as it came?

The women helped get the meal to the table while Aaron and Randy rounded up the kids from the backyard. All of them wanted to sit by Randy.

Sandy took charge. "You kids have your own table in here. You can visit with him after we eat."

Later, the men walked around the property while the women prepared dessert.

Aaron asked, "Randy, are you doing another CD soon?"

"Supposed to be in January. I've been working on songs."

"Good idea to be ready. You happy with your same band?"

"I think so. We worked together well, and they came up with good ideas on the last tour. I haven't talked to them yet. They may have other offers, and I get that."

As a supportive mentor, Aaron said, "You probably need to find out pretty quick. This is the time to start rehearsals. January will be here before you know it."

"I know, and I'm going to California for Christmas. You're right, I'd better have it all decided before I go."

"Hey, you gonna let me hear the new songs? I need a couple for my own CD."

Randy still felt a rush every time someone liked his songwriting. "Sure, let's see if we can spend some time together this week. Mom will go home tomorrow, and then I think I'm free for a bit."

"Sounds good. Your mom's a treat, isn't she? We're so glad to meet her."

Randy looked over at the woman of the hour. "She sure is. She has had a good time this week. Thank you for being so nice."

Aaron nodded. "I think we talked about family the first time we met, didn't we? Remember, they'll be there beside you when all this fame and glamour is fading or gone."

Randy recognized the recurring theme.

****

A week later, he was again in Neil's office. "What do you have planned for me? I've got the band question solved, and we're working on the new songs."

"Randy, I'm glad to hear it. How was your Thanksgiving?"

"I stayed in town. Sonny and his wife invited a bunch of us poor single folks over. You know, those who are a long way from family. It was nice."

Neil got down to business. "This morning I emailed you what tour schedule I have so far. Some of the repeat places and a few new ones that requested you. Have you seen it?"

Randy moved forward in his chair. "No, do you have a copy here?"

"Yes, see what you think. I'll fill in the blank spots soon."

Randy sat back with the printout. "A few blank spots might be good. I want to work on the songwriting more this year."

"You're scaring me again. Anything you want to tell me?"

Randy faced him squarely. "I just did. I want more time to write. You know, artists are calling me for songs to record all the time."

Neil stiffened. "You know a limited schedule is not how you support an album. The label will expect filled arenas and sales like the last CD."

"Relax. Everyone will get their bank accounts filled. I'm not saying I won't be out there hawking the goods. I want time to follow another side of my passion. I've thought about this a lot. It can work."

"While you're on your little Christmas trip, I suggest you do some more thinking. There are a lot of people counting on you." Randy walked out of the office, determined to do that.

Chapter 27

Randy savored bacon and eggs at his mother's kitchen table. "Mom, there's no need to pay somebody to put up the Christmas lights. I've done it plenty of times."

She refilled his coffee cup. "No, I'm used to paying the boys, and they know how I want them. Besides, we can't have our big star falling off a ladder." She giggled, then took another bite of toast.

He gave in. "Okay, I have a full day, anyway. Bob Rogers is coming at eleven, and this afternoon I want to visit with Mr. Hoover for a while."

She jerked around to face him. "And why is Bob coming here? I told you I'm not moving."

"No problem, Mom. Bob will be here to give me some pointers on a project I'm thinking about."

Her eyes sparkled. "You're buying a house here? Wonderful."

"No, but I do have an idea to explore. He can help me think it through and put me in touch with the right people."

"Well, I'll leave it all to you, I guess. Have you shared any of it with your sister?"

"No, and don't go saying anything. This is me thinking out loud right now."

Randy met him in the driveway. "Thanks for coming out, Bob." Randy and the real estate man walked to the barn.

"No problem, Randy, although you were a little mysterious on the phone. I thought Mrs. Walters wasn't ready to sell."

"No, she's not. An idea keeps going around in my head. I thought you might help me clear it up. Here we are. Sorry for all the dust in here. Let me get a light on."

"Randy, if you're thinking of converting this to living space or something, you know I'm not in construction or anything. How can I help?"

"Sit down at the workbench there, Bob. I have to ask you to keep quiet about what I'm about to share with you."

"You can count on me. So, it has to do with this barn? You know, this is a small town, Randy. Even secrets travel fast."

"I know, but before anything gets out, I want to be sure. You know, any change in my life will be front page news these days."

"I get it. So, what do you have in mind?"

Randy paced the dirt floor as he described a little of his plan. "I'm thinking this could be a great music venue if done up right. A studio in the back and maybe an apartment upstairs. I can see people driving from LA and surrounding towns to hear good music. There's plenty of unused pasture to make into parking." He looked at Bob for his response. "Your thoughts?"

"This sure came out of left field. Are you talking about being here to run it? What about Nashville?"

"Now you understand the secrecy, Bob. I would be here often while keeping my career going. I can't alienate the Nashville crowd by them hearing rumors before I have a chance to explain it all."

Bob looked around the extensive structure. "Well, this will be a gigantic job, and expensive. Do you have a contractor?"

"No, I hoped you could give me some names. The money, well, I can't say money's no object, but I met with my sister yesterday who's been keeping my books, and I should be able to pull it off. I'll need an architect, too." He began writing in a notebook.

Bob stood to walk around the space. "This could really be something, Randy. I'll see what names I can find for you. First, have you spoken to the zoning commission? Can you even do it in this area?"

Randy wrote it down. "I'll take care of it right away." He broke the lead on the first pencil and grabbed another. "I think it should work way out here, but I'll make sure. This is good. What else?"

"I can get my office to put out a survey in the area to test the waters. You need to know the likelihood of the public responding to something like this. You know, the old 'build it and they will come' myth is just that, a myth."

"This is why I wanted you to come by. You know more about this than you let on. You invoice me for your time and anything else involving your office."

Randy laid out his plan as they walked around inside. He saw the gleam in Bob's eyes as he offered suggestions on the layout. This was a good start.

In the afternoon, he pushed open the door to his favorite place downtown. "Hi, Mr. Hoover. How are you?"

The man stood from his stool behind the counter. "I heard you were in town. Glad you stopped in, Randy."

"Yeah, I thought we could shoot the breeze a little if

you've got time."

"Always for you. Jimmy is learning fast. You can be proud of him."

"Oh, I am. While I'm here, I'll get him a couple of sets of strings for his stocking, and how about a new strap? Something wild, like him."

"I have a few here, but let me show you this." He brought out a catalog and turned to a page of handmade straps.

"You sure know him well. How about this one and with his name on it? Will it be here for Christmas? I want to see his face when he opens this."

"I think so. Christmas orders might have them backed up, though. When I call it in, can I use your name? Maybe it'll help."

Randy flushed. "You bet, if it works. Listen, I wanted to discuss the store if we can."

"Sure. What exactly? Let's sit down over here." They took chairs in the guitar department. It reminded Randy of discovering his first instrument there, and now Jimmy had, too.

He paused to find the right words. "I know you plan on selling out soon. Have you done anything about it?"

"I had a couple of appraisers in to see what it might bring. One was a no-go. It turned out to be a liquidation company. They want to come in and hold a store-closing sale and keep most of the money. No way. Not only is this our nest egg, but I'd like to dream there's a buyer out there who will keep things going."

"I know what you mean. And the other one? They gave you a value?"

Mr. Hoover sat back to stare at his young friend a moment, then asked, "What's on your mind, Randy?

These aren't friendly chat questions, are they?"

Randy shifted his hat back. "No, sir. I've been thinking. Lakeview wouldn't be the same without this store. I'm doing all right now and need some investments, anyway. Maybe it's time I give back to my hometown. I may want to be your buyer, Mr. Hoover."

The store owner sat back and removed his cap to run his hand through his hair. "You know what you're doing? This place doesn't make much. Although I can imagine some improvement with your name on the sign."

Randy leaned forward and nudged his friend's leg. "We don't have to decide today. You said you were ready to retire. I'll bet Mrs. Hoover has a honey-do list all made out."

"Shoot, you know it. Actually, Randy, she has followed my music dreams all these years. We'll travel some together. Enjoy the time we have left."

"When can we sit to talk more about it?"

"My part-timer will be in here Saturday. Why don't we meet for lunch at Miss Millie's? I'll tell her we need a table in the back. I'll bring the books, too."

"Good. I'm going to be setting up with an accountant this week. He'll need to see the books, too."

"Fine with me. Young man, if we're going to talk business, I think you've known me long enough to call me Eldon."

"May take some getting used to, but I'll try. One thing. I know you'll talk with your wife, but otherwise, we have to keep this private. If I decide to go ahead, there's a bunch of people I need to talk to back in Nashville."

The man put his cap back on and reached to shake

Randy's hand. "I get ya, boy. See you Saturday."

When Randy got in his vehicle to leave, he took a deep breath and wiped his brow with his sleeve. *Whew, hope I know what I'm doing. It feels right.*

****

The next day, he went to the city hall where a clerk in the zoning office gave him good news. "Yes, Mr. Walters, it looks like zoning will allow what you're wanting to do in your area." They shook hands as Randy rose to leave. "I hope it comes through for you. This sounds like a good idea."

"And this is private, right?"

"Of course, young man. No problem at all."

Back in the pickup, he checked the task off his list. He looked forward to meeting contractors and architects before he returned to Nashville.

****

Jimmy sat beside him for movie night at home. "You must be the tallest kid in your class now, Jimmy."

The boy thought for a minute. "No, Susanne Miller is the tallest. Everybody says she'll be a basketball star someday."

"Good for her. Hey, do you mind Mom and I decided against the charter school?"

"No, Dad. I didn't want to leave my friends anyway, and I know the place is probably expensive."

Randy hated to see one so young pick up on such issues. "The cost doesn't matter, son. You know I can help Mom more now. We thought maybe you'd stay where you are a couple more years. The teachers get you, and that's important to us."

"She said maybe for middle school. That's okay with me. Can we go Christmas shopping for Mom? I've been saving my allowance."

"Sure, on the weekend. Can I chip in a little, too?"
He's such a good kid.

****

"David, thanks for seeing me." Randy was in the Ventura office of Sarah's husband. "I have some accounting business to go over with you."

"I'm so glad you came. Sarah is looking forward to you staying a few days since we finally have you here."

"Tonight will have to do this trip. I have a lot going on at home. I want to talk to you about what may happen there soon."

David sat up at his desk. "Let's hear it."

"First, my sister has been taking care of my money. You know, paying bills and balancing the checkbook. It has become overwhelming for her."

David laughed. "Too much money. Now there's a good problem to have."

"Yeah, but now, I need somebody who deals with numbers who knows what they're doing. I thought we could work together."

"Well, I'm sure we can, Randy. What else do you have?"

Randy paced as he talked. "Here's the deal. I'm thinking this will take some real financial oversight. I need someone to tell me it even makes sense. If it works, I'll be in California more."

"Oh, Randy, that sounds awesome. But what about Nashville?"

"I know. People will think I'm crazy. I think I've got it worked out in my mind. First, I want to buy the old music store in town. I'll need you to look over the books and such. I'll listen if you say it doesn't make sense.

Then, I'm going to convert the barn on our home place to a music venue. I can start the concerts in the back of the store like at McCabe's music store in LA. Have you and Sarah been there? You should go. They bring in name acts and pack the place. After we complete the barn, we move the shows out there."

"You don't dream small, do you? Okay, have your sister send me what she has. I'll at least look through everything. Then how do I get in touch with this store owner? You want a soda? Sarah will be here soon."

Chapter 28

"Mom, you know I won't be here for lunch, right? I'm meeting with Mr. Hoover. Any more toast over there?"

"Sure. Will there be more people traipsing through my barn today?"

Randy sensed the uneasiness in her voice. "Not on a Saturday. I guess we better talk about all this."

"I wish you would. What's the big secret?" She set the coffeepot on the table and sat down with him.

"Well, I think I've found a way to keep my career going, but be here a lot more." She beamed and clapped her hands. "Now wait, Mom. There's a lot to work out yet. This may not happen at all."

"Well, tell me. Are you planning on living out there?"

"No, I have other plans for the barn. First, I'm talking with Mr. Hoover about buying the music store. He plans to retire in the spring, and I hate to see the store close. We'll see how it goes today."

She still held questions. "And my barn?"

"Yes, Mom, I know it's your barn. If we can make some kind of leasing agreement, or something, I want it to be a music venue. Where we do shows on the weekends."

Her brow furrowed as she asked, "It'll be yours one day, anyway. You shouldn't have to pay me."

"That's nice, Mom, but no. It will be a business deal, and you need to profit from it, too. My accountant will help us figure it out. I know this is a lot to take in right now. I didn't want to bother you without more information. Also, I worry about your privacy. We won't go forward if you don't like it for any reason. This is your home."

She smiled and asked, "You'd be living here? I'll make it work. Don't you worry." She got out of her chair and threw her arms around his neck. "Can we rent it out for events? You know the church does a barbecue every year. And weddings. Oh, won't that be fun?"

"Hold on, Mom. Those are great ideas, but let's not get ahead of ourselves."

She waved him off. "Oh, you'll make it happen. You always get what you want when you decide to work at it. Like with your singing. Uh-oh. What about your career?"

Randy squirmed in his chair. "I'm still thinking it through. That's why you can't say anything to anyone outside the family. Please, Mom. You hear me? I can't afford to make the wrong people mad in Nashville."

Randy wanted his agent's agreement on the idea, but needed a more detailed plan before he presented it to him. Neil continuing to manage his singing career was a must. For Randy to keep his contract with the recording label while building the life he wanted required Neil's expertise.

He paced in his mother's living room, waiting for his agent to answer. "Neil, how are things back in Nashville?"

"Great. I'm meeting with Josh next week to set up the recording schedule for January. Do you want me to push for mid-month? Then you and the band will have some time to reacquaint yourselves with everything when you get back."

"Good idea. How much of next year's schedule do you have worked out?"

"Quite a bit. We got Buckboard again. I left a week after that open, like you said, for a visit with family. I think I've spread things out like you wanted. We can go back in and add if you decide. I hope you know what you're doing."

"Me too." Randy stifled a laugh. "I was thinking. The songwriting is paying off. What would it take to set up my own publishing company?"

"What? You're killin' me. If I could get you to concentrate on one th…"

"Calm down. Not right now. I asked a simple question. See what you can find out, and we'll talk when I get back. Have a good Christmas, and I'll see you after the New Year."

Christmas at home proved to be everything he remembered. More family came around than he'd seen since his father's funeral. As always, food took center stage at each gathering. At night, he and his mother sat on the front porch swing to enjoy the property aglow with colorful lights and decorations.

A visit to Bakersfield was a treat. "Jennie, it is so good to see you. Where's Tom this afternoon?"

"He has lessons at the shop today. He said he'd be in about three thirty. Take your jacket off and sit down. Tell me all the good news."

"Mom sent you some of her oatmeal cookies, and Santa brought you a little something, too."

"Oh my, you shouldn't have done anything for us." She snickered. "Put it there next to your gift under the tree."

He found his usual spot on the couch. "Things are going great. I have some ideas to run past you two. I may make some changes."

"Jennie, your roasted chicken was exceptional. You used some different spices, didn't you? Excuse me while I loosen my belt. Good food is going to be the demise of me on this trip."

Tom teased Jennie. "She keeps getting better, right? Lady, when are you gonna put out a cookbook? You could pay for my retirement."

After Randy snickered, he asked, "So, Tom, how is it being off the time clock?"

"Great, like I thought it would be. I stay so busy, though, I don't know how I ever had time to work. How about things with you? Everything still moving fast?"

"Yes, sir. The albums are selling like crazy. Sold-out shows everywhere we go. I love the friends I've made songwriting."

Tom set his coffee down and looked at his young protégé. "So, what is it? You have something on your mind."

"I never could fool you." Randy leaned toward Tom, elbows on knees. "I have a pretty wild idea. If I can make it work, though, I think I'll be a lot happier. Did I tell you I've done some writing with Verlon Thompson? What a talented songwriter and such a great guy. You know he has a studio and performance place in a barn on his place?"

"Yes, he named it Barnegie Hall. Very clever."

"It got me to thinking. You know I've been looking for some way to find a balance in my life. I want the music, I need it, but I need family, too."

Jennie joined the discussion. "So, are you buying a barn or moving your family to Nashville?"

Tom offered, "I don't think that's it, is it, Randy? What have you got up your sleeve?"

Randy took his time laying out the entire plan. He wanted Tom's blessing on the project. "You're looking at me like I'm crazy. What do you think?"

Tom left his seat and walked around the room, shaking his head. "This is risky, son. It sounds like you've thought it through, but I don't know if it'll go the way you think. It may be too soon, is all I'm afraid of." He sat again.

"You mean I'm not as established as I think? Maybe Nashville won't continue to support me."

"And your fan base might not. Randy, you're new to being on top. Fans are fickle, the whole bunch of them. They expect you to be out there in their cities performing and making more CDs. They find it hard to imagine you needing anything else but them. I don't know."

Randy stood, his body stiff. "So, I can keep going like I am, get filthy rich, have a gold record or two, win some awards, and then when my son is all grown up, I finally get to come home. Is that it?"

Jennie reached for his arm. "Don't get upset, now. He's playing devil's advocate, aren't you, Tom? Listen to our experience. We were part of Nashville for, what, twelve years?"

"I'm saying I want the life you came to California for without giving up my music. You made it work, and others have, too."

Tom downed his coffee before turning to the young man to say, "If by others you mean the likes of Verlon, Dean Dillon, and Garth, even George Strait, they did it after they established themselves firmly. It was different for us. What Buck offered me was a regular paycheck completely away from Nashville. No risk. I knew exactly how it would go. You can make something work, but think of the risk. Can you absorb it?"

"Well, I guess we'll see. I'm going to talk to Neil as soon as I get back."

"I have to admit, it could be a good idea. We'll always worry about you is all."

"I know. Not much will change this coming year at least. I'll get a manager for the store, and I'll keep planning the rest. It won't all happen right away." He acknowledged the look of fear for him on their faces. "I have to try."

****

Back at his mother's, the adults gathered at the dinner table while the kids played on their grandmother's new Xbox in the other room. Randy laid out notes and drawings. "I'm sure you're wondering about all this. I have a proposition to tell you about. Mom knows some of it."

His sister spoke first. "Nothing surprises me about you, Brother. Mom was a little coy with the dinner invite, though." Dan nodded in agreement.

Randy took a deep breath and began. "I have a plan to convert the barn into an event space. Concerts mostly and a recording studio. Eventually I'll be here to run it, but I need help to get through the construction phase. I only have rough sketches from architects right now. I haven't chosen one. I've interviewed a few contractors, too, but nothing has been right yet." He looked at Dan, whose face appeared to have lost all its blood.

Sherry, never afraid to speak, "Are you crazy?

Mom, you approve of this? People will be all over your place. It will cost a fortune." The light bulb went off in her head. "Wait. You'd be living here? Really? Randy, when?"

"Slow down, sis. I have a timeline all laid out." He shoved a large spreadsheet toward them. "Of course, things can change. Dan, you're awfully quiet."

"I'm thinking of everything it'll take to convert that old barn."

"That's why I need you. You're already seeing it. You've been in construction all your adult life. I know you've been foreman on extensive jobs for your boss for the last few years. You see how it ought to go and the way to get guys to do it. I need somebody I trust to take my place in overseeing the entire operation. I'll still be out touring."

Dan and Sherry shared a look, which Randy thought was somewhere between fear and excitement. Dan said, "My job, Randy. My family depends on my income. When this gets rolling, it won't be a part-time thing."

His mom added, "You're asking a lot, son."

Randy moved the papers aside and leaned forward. "I know the risks, Dan, Sherry. I also know I have no right at all to ask you for anything else. You've been there for me at every turn. I believe in this so much. I think it will give you something better. An opportunity to have your own business like you've wanted, Dan. I'll pay all your fees to get your business and contractors' licenses before we start. So, after you finish this project, you'll have something to show other potential customers. They'll be breaking your door down to build their next home, office building, whatever."

Dan's head made a slow movement from side to side

as he pushed back from the table. Elbows on his knees and hands clasped, he said, "This is so much to think about, Randy."

Sherry laid her hand on her husband's shoulder and turned to Randy. "We can't give you an answer on such short notice."

"No, I don't want you to. This is still in the planning stages. I'll have to clear everything in Nashville. Do you think you can at least let me know how you're thinking before I leave on Sunday? Run the numbers on salary and health benefits. Consider time, stress, and everything you think might change for you. I love you guys, and I want you comfortable with the decision. Take all these plans with you. You can bring them back with your answer. If it's a go, I want to get started as soon as possible."

His mother refilled the coffee. "He didn't tell you the rest of his news."

Sherry thumbed through the pages. "I don't know if I can take anything else." She looked up with anticipation. "What, are you getting married to the singer you've been dating?"

The punch to his gut emptied his lungs. He searched their faces for strength. "She died unexpectedly a few months back. Sorry I said nothing. Hard to deal with is an understatement. One thing about it though, something her dad said to me made it plain I have to do whatever it takes to give me the life I want." The only sound was the beep, beep of the video game in the next room.

He recovered with a smile. "So, no, what Mom means is I'm buying Hoover's music store. We sign the papers tomorrow so I can take possession at the end of April. You'll see on the timeline that I want to have the renovations there completed before we start the barn project. My new accountant has looked over all this. The only negative is he thinks the store is heavy on inventory." He shrugged. "I guess that will make for some good grand-opening sales. Anyway, yes, this will all be expensive. But he said if the albums keep selling and the shows sell out like they have been, I'll be able to handle it just fine."

They reviewed the plans in greater detail and discussed a hundred what-ifs until Sherry went to check out the silence in the den. "Look. The kids have sacked out in there. We'd better get them home."

The men shook hands. "I'll get with you before you leave, Randy. Thanks for the vote of confidence in me. It means a lot. I do hope we can work this out."

****

Randy left for Nashville with a full commitment from Dan to take the job. Dan could handle a lot of the planning and still keep the other job for a while. He had plenty of time to study for the contractor's license test and set up his business. Randy wanted him to immediately take over decisions on bids and hiring. When the first hammer fell on the project, Dan would be there to manage it all.

As the plane left the ground, relief, fear, and exhilaration rushed through his body. He could see his new dream coming true.

Chapter 29

The first morning back in Nashville, he arranged the hard discussion with his agent.

"Hello, Barbara. Is Neil in?"

"He sure is, sweetie. Was Santa good to you?"

"He was, and you?"

"Spoiled me rotten. Here he is now."

Neil's voice flew through the phone. "Hey, are you back?"

"Yes, and we have some things to talk about. Are you available tomorrow?"

"Sure, come in about eleven. A good year is what we'll have, Randy."

"That's my plan."

Neil met him at his office door. "Come sit down, my friend. How the heck are you?"

Randy laid his hat on the empty chair beside him in front of the desk. "I couldn't be better. I spoke to all the band last week. We'll start rehearsals tonight. Did you get everything worked out with Josh and the studio?"

"I did. You'll start recording on the 16th. They're expecting a lot from this one."

Randy's voice rose, and he squirmed like a kid at the circus. "I have some killer songs planned, and the third time may be the charm. I don't think it will even stop at gold."

Neil slapped his hand on the desk. "There's what I

want to hear. Let the label do their thing for the album. We'll promote the hell out of you after your success last year."

"So, let me see what you've got on the schedule so far."

The calendar glared on the computer screen. Randy leaned in to see. "I can print this out if you want to take it home."

"No, not until you finish the thing. Thanks for the gaps in there. I can schedule some good writing time."

Neil shifted his head to one side and asked, "What else is on your mind?"

Randy stood to speak. "I have some new ideas for change in the next few years. Before you fly off the handle, listen to me." He sat again to look the man in the eye as he laid out his new plan.

When he stopped for a breath, he asked, "Well, I know you're thinking something. Start talking, please."

Neil turned his chair to the window and didn't make a sound for a moment. "This is a kick in the teeth." He jerked his chair around to face his client. "Honestly, Randy, I don't know when I've seen anyone so unhappy with success. After all our hard work, you finally make it, and you want to give up and throw it all away. What am I supposed to say to that?"

"I'm not giving up, and never said I was. I see it as a curve in the road, a slightly different direction. I'll always have music performance in my life. As much as I love music, I need my home and family. No matter what might happen here, I can catch a flight when I'm needed. And don't think I don't appreciate everything you've done for me. It will be a new way for us to work together. I still need your support."

Neil's head swung from side to side. "I will have to give this some thought. I don't think you know what you're doing. What about Carnival? You don't think you owe the label something?"

"I'll give everything to this new album like always. I don't plan on letting them down." Randy shifted forward in his chair. "This is between us for now. If I can see things aren't working out, I'll drop it before anyone becomes the wiser. If everything is going as planned, we'll approach it with all players well before it hits. Come on, Neil, lunch is on me."

Randy watched as he still shook his head before saying, "My appetite flew out the window. Give me a little time with this. I'll call you."

Later, Randy took flowers to dinner with Julia and Marsha. "Thanks for having me over. I've missed our cookouts."

Julia shivered. "If you don't mind, January is a little chilly for eating outside. You'll have to make do in here."

"Sounds good to me. Hey, who is this?" He bent down to pick up an orange-striped kitten.

Marsha answered, "We decided it was finally time to replace Loretta."

"And what's this one's name? Tammy?"

"No, this is Reba. Not terribly creative, but they're both redheads, after all."

The kitten squirmed out of his hands. "You two are so fun. I hope you won't send me off too early tonight. I have some ideas to run by you."

Marsha nodded. "I knew you had something under your hat when I picked you up at the airport the other day."

"Yeah, I wanted to tell you together and also thought it best to present it to Neil first."

Julia took his arm. "This sounds like something I don't want on an empty stomach. Let's eat first."

After dinner, he laid out his plans as he had with his family and his agent. Like them, the ladies at first expressed concern for his future. Their skepticism didn't deter him.

"I've thought about this a lot. I know I'm not a businessman or a builder. I surrounded myself with the right people here in Nashville, and I'll do the same on this project. I won't go forward if those smarter people convince me it won't work, but I have to try."

Julia's voice took on a serious tone he had never heard from her. "I thought you had learned more about how Nashville works. You're really not allowed much of a personal life at first. The music overtakes everything."

"Yes, I've seen that, but I believe I can make it all work together."

"It will affect your touring and recording, and fans forget so quickly, Randy."

Marsha said, "We're surprised, that's all. We'll always be here for you. Let us know what you need."

"I'm not giving up on the career. I want to build on a unique part of it, and I'll need you."

****

Randy walked into the studio this time like it was a familiar old house. The hard work fed his soul. He and his producer, Dave Easton, grew even more comfortable with each other's techniques and skills. The response from his amazing musicians to the songs he'd chosen to record made him happy.

Neil stopped by on the third day to listen. "Randy,

you're right. This might be the one for you. I have you set up with a couple of interviews as soon as you wrap it up. We need to get the public excited."

"Sounds good. When is it we hit the road?"

"Why? You have plans?"

Randy pulled his agent outside. "We never finished our talk. Let's do it right now. I can't deal with this tension between us and you avoiding my calls. I asked a simple question, and you get smart. Don't be a butt through this. I told you, no letting down. I am in this all the way."

Neil shook his head. "I'm sorry. You leave April 22nd. Listen, I've given it a lot of thought. I can see you're serious, and I'll work with you. But you've got to understand what happens to you affects me and my reputation in this town."

"I'm well aware of that. I don't want to have the fans thinking I was just another flash in the pan. Recording and touring will continue, but not as much. If we promote things right, it will work."

The two shook hands as Neil said, "Don't forget, your photo shoot is on Saturday. I know you wanted the day off, but that's when they could fit you in."

"Yeah, fine. Aaron's playing the Opry Saturday night and gave me tickets. You and your wife want to go with me?"

"I'll ask her. She'll go for it, I'm sure. Thanks. I'll let you know tomorrow."

Randy realized it still might take some work to get Neil fully on board. He couldn't worry about it, though. For now, there was an album to record and promote.

Randy loved hearing Aaron's music on the Opry. He went backstage to say hello and thank him for the tickets.

"You sounded great tonight. Are those songs on your new CD?"

"Yes, how's yours going?"

"Good. We'll finish on Monday. The tour begins in late April. Here we go again, right?"

"Exactly. Another summer of fun. We start in April, too." Aaron reached to shake his hand. "Sandy's been wanting to have you over."

"Great. Let's make it happen soon."

Randy returned to his seat. He enjoyed spending time with friends. Friends who would always have his back.

After leaving the auditorium, Neil said, "Thanks for tonight. This is a rare night out for us. Hey, tomorrow is the super bowl. We're having a few friends over. A little food, some beer and wine. Why don't you come over?"

"That would be fun, but I told Jeff we'd watch at home. If I know us, we'll probably turn the volume down and work on some songs. He's a much-overlooked singer/songwriter. You should check him out. Thanks for the invite, though."

As he walked across the parking lot, Randy heard his name called out several times as other artists recognized him. A quick greeting and they moved on. In the truck, he reflected on his good fortune. *I rub shoulders with heroes from my youth and the new chart busters. I live a good life here.* On Monday, he contacted Dan to see how things were developing. The ball was rolling in California.

****

Randy phoned Frank in Bakersfield. "Hi, Frank. How are Sue and my namesake?"

"Sue is great. Randy is growing like a weed. How

are things with you?"

"Rolling along fine. I have something to talk to you about. Pretty important. Have you got some time?"

"Sure. What's up?"

Randy told him about his plan little by little. He'd learned not to overload his friends with too much information at once. "I know you have a good job there, but I'd like you to come here to manage the store for me. We'll have to talk salary."

"How cool. Thing is, I got another promotion. Sue's folks are here, too. Man, what a move this would be. It sure sounds fun, though. Let me think about it."

"I thought maybe I could get some of the oil field from under your fingernails. April would be your start date, but talk it over with Sue. I need to know your answer pretty fast."

Frank's call the next day was not all bad news. "I'd love to do it, Randy, but I can't see it right now. We need more money than you can afford out of the place. Sue's folks help a lot with watching the baby while we both work. I have an idea, though, if you want to hear it."

Randy took a moment for the nausea of disappointment to leave him before he responded. "I get it. I knew it was a long shot. What else you got?"

"This may sound crazy, but how about our old roommate, Johnny Haywood? You know, he's been working at Boot Barn for the last couple of years. They keep wanting to make him a manager, but he says it would interfere with his music. He seems a little frustrated with the gigging grind. He helped in his dad's grocery while growing up. I think he might have more of a business head than you think."

Something like relief washed over Randy. "At least

I know him. I think it might work, Frank. I'll call him right now. Listen, when we get the concerts going, you'll drive down to perform on Saturday nights, right?"

Frank laughed. "Now that we might work out."

Chapter 30

Randy's band members loaded their gear onto the bus as Julia dropped him off. He hugged her and promised to stay in touch. The driver, Tony, took Randy's bags as he stepped up into what would be his home for the next few months.

"Hey, everybody. Looks like you're all here." He smiled and kidded, "There's always that moment when an artist thinks, what if the band doesn't show?" They greeted him with laughs, handshakes, and hello slaps to his back.

Roger said, "We notice you got them to put windows in the back. You'll enjoy those. Up for a card game or some jamming this afternoon?"

Randy jumped into the groove again. "You bet. We'll have plenty of time on the way to St. Louis."

The new windows in his room were a wonderful source of light for writing. The dark blue drapes ensured his late morning sleep. He put away his personal things. *The CD is number one already, the band is top-notch, this feels good. What a great tour this will be.*

St. Louis, Kansas City, Tulsa, Dallas. The days were clicking off the schedule. Most shows sold out as soon as the tickets went on sale. An up-and-coming female singer opened for him at about half of the stops. They used local talent to open the others.

Fans told him the new CD was their favorite so far.

He agreed. He purposely chose songs to appeal to a variety of listeners to add new fans. This album gave him another chance at a top award. More, it meant money to put toward his projects back home.

In mid-June, he spoke to his crew as they sat around a lunch table in Meridian, Mississippi. "Okay, guys, Birmingham tonight. You know what that means. After the show, we'll get out of there quick and drive most of the night to get home. This has been a fantastic start to the tour. I believe we're making some right fine music, don't you? A trip home is next for me, then I'll fly into Fort Smith to meet you in a week and a half. I owe you more thanks than I probably say. Let's keep it fun."

"A new motto for you, keeping it fun? You've sure had a good outlook this time," Jack said, looking at the others who added their agreement.

Randy nodded. "Yeah, an excellent motto. I think I've found the balance I've been looking for. Or at least a direction to get me there." He couldn't reveal too much yet.

****

In Nashville, he spent two days writing with Jeff and other friends. With everything happening back in California, things would happen fast over the summer. He welcomed a relaxing dinner with Julia and Marsha before heading home.

He took a minute to call his mother from the waiting room at Neil's office. "I can only be there a few days, Mom. You know I'm coming mainly for the grand opening of the store. I'll be there around noon on Thursday, so have lunch ready."

Randy attempted to keep the grand-opening event under the radar. The local newspaper gave it a splash in the entertainment column, but he had to believe Nashville wasn't reading his hometown news. Word in the national press about him buying a music store in his hometown might draw attention to what else he had going on there.

A new storefront and a revived business excited the city council.

At the grand opening, Eldon and Mrs. Hoover shook hands with friends and customers who were part of the history of the old business. Randy offered giveaways and musical games for the kids. He performed a few songs on the new stage. The hours of shining the instruments paid off. They looked great sparkling on the walls. His mother beamed with pride, and Dan took in all the compliments on his remodel of the store and handed out business cards.

Randy approached the former owner sitting alone on his favorite stool talking to the new manager, Johnny. "Eldon, I hope you approve of what we did with your old place. I thought we had to give it a fresh new look."

Eldon moved his cap back. "You did fine. Refinishing the old wood floors makes everything look new. The additional soundproofing in the classrooms is great. Cutting back on the music books was probably a good thing, too. Some of the sheet music had been here for years. I can't believe you want to have concerts in the back area. Gosh, I could have been doing the same all along."

"Yeah, I hope it goes. I wish we'd done this before the ladies took the space next door to put in the salon. That would have been a perfect place for the stage area."

Johnny surveyed his new business home. "This will do just fine."

To close out his weekend at home, father and son sat on the bank of the pond where Randy used to fish with his dad. "Son, how is your mom doing? Looks like I won't get to see her again before I leave unless I stop by her store."

The boy reeled in his line and tossed it out again. The float settled into the ripples moving across the water. "She's fine. Works a lot."

"Well, she's working hard to make things good for you."

Jimmy's clear blue eyes met Randy's. "That's what she says about you, Dad. I understand why you can't be here much." He turned back to the water.

Randy had made Jimmy aware of his plans but wondered what he really understood about it all. He couldn't wait to be there for ball games, skinned knees, and school programs. "Son, I'm trying to make it so I can be here more. Maybe a lot. How do you think that would be?"

At once, Jimmy's float went under the water. "Whoa, Dad, help me. He's a monster fish." He spread his feet and turned the handle of the reel with all his strength.

"Keep the rod up. Don't let him get away. Reel him in. I'll get the net." They laughed and cheered as the trophy jumped up out of the water, glistening in the sun.

After getting the fish to shore, Jimmy propped up his arm, holding the weight of the fish.

He said as Randy took his picture, "This is how it will be, Dad. Perfect."

****

Back on the road, Randy directed his business partners to call in the afternoon so he could sleep late.

Things were busy with the barn project, now in full swing.

"David, I got your message last night, but I figured you guys were in bed already. What have you got? Am I out of money already?"

"No, nothing so dire. I need you to sign off on some papers. I got an account set up with Charles Schwab for your investments. You can't start too early saving for retirement."

"Good idea. Email them, and I'll get it done at the next stop. Anything new with you and Sarah?"

"She graduates after this semester. We're excited about that."

"Oh, yeah, that is good news. Will I see everyone at the Buckboard Festival again?"

"You know it. We're looking forward to a great time."

"Listen, I have another call coming in. Send those forms."

Staying in touch with the project while touring was hard but fulfilling when he thought of the future result.

Jack stood in the doorway to Randy's room. "Hey, boss, you gonna come out of your office for some cards? We've got popcorn."

"Give me a few minutes. I need to take care of this on my phone."

"Sure thing. Man, you need a secretary. I thought your agent took care of things for you."

"This is some business I have to handle myself. Go ahead, I'll be out there in a sec." It was getting harder to keep his secret.

****

With the tour more than half finished, the cities flew

by in a whirlwind blur. One afternoon, the phone interrupted his fun with his crew.

"Let me get this, guys."

Roger led in the teasing. "Yeah, we know. Another of your fans. Could you send at least one of those girls my way?"

Randy joined their laughter. "Hey, I wish. Hello, this is Randy."

Neil was on the line. "Are you going to be in Nashville for a few days on your August break?"

"Two or three days, maybe. Why?"

"The Opry again. Can you make that happen?"

"Of course, you know I won't turn them down. I need to get home to California for a few, but I'll make it work."

"How's it going back there? When will the place be ready?"

"Early next summer is the goal. My brother-in-law has done a great job with only a few hiccups along the way. They'll have the floor in by the time I visit in August. Then we can lay out the studio."

"Randy, I have to tell you I had my doubts. Now, I'd bet if anyone could make a go of this, you'll get it done. By the way, your album is fifteen weeks in the top ten."

He shook his head at the phone. "I was happy with it being number one for four weeks. This is amazing."

"You better be building a trophy cabinet in that music hall of yours."

"A short time ago, I wouldn't have thought it possible."

"Nashville is the city of dreams, Randy. Thing is, a lot of performers sleep right through it all. The CMA nominations this year are going to have your name all over them. You've worked hard."

Randy thought of Angie, Jeff, and so many other friends. *Sometimes, no matter how hard you work, it comes down to luck. I've sure had my share.*

****

"Welcome back to Cheyenne, Mr. Walters. We are so glad to have you here tonight. Anything you need, you let me or my assistant Gary know. Your dressing room is right this way."

"I'm sure everything will be fine, Mark. We loved this beautiful arena last time. Do you know how many we'll have tonight?"

"Oh, it sold out on the first day. The young lady opening for you is already here. Things should go like clockwork."

Randy's phone vibrated in his pocket. "Excuse me, Mark. Hello, Dan, is everything okay? I was bragging about you to my agent the other day."

"Is this a good time? I wanted to let you know there was a glitch with the electrical inspection, but we worked it out."

"How much did that cost me?"

"A couple thousand. What I wanted to discuss is the flooring. I've got the reclaimed barn wood you wanted coming from Virginia. I hope you realize the cost is through the roof."

"Yeah, I figured. The thing is, I think it will add to the look and the sound. Anything else?"

"No, I wanted to keep you in the loop. Oh yeah, one thing, I thought we might start out with everything from church pews to split-log benches for seating. Whatever we can find. Kind of down to earth and it fits the rustic feel we're going with, don't you think?"

"Dan, I love keeping it homey. How's the family?"

"The usual, kids growing like weeds and the women keeping me in line." He gave a jolly laugh.

I'll be there in time to enjoy some of the kids growing up.

****

As the bus made its way through Arizona on a September morning, he heard his phone on the table beside his bed. He managed a sleepy, "Hullo?"

"Randy, get up, get up." Neil sounded like a kid with a new toy.

"What time is it? This better be good."

"It is so good. Sit up. I want to make sure you get this. You up?"

"Yes, for cryin' out loud. What is it?"

"They announced the nominations a couple hours ago. I told you, didn't I tell you? 2013 is your year."

Randy shot up out of the bed. "I got something? What? Who am I up against?"

"I emailed you the list. Pull it up, quick." He couldn't wait. "Song of the Year, Album of the Year, and Male Vocalist of the Year. Wahoo!"

He scrolled the screen over the categories and names. "Look at my name alongside these guys. No way. No way."

"My phone has been ringing off the wall all morning. I have you totally booked the week you get back. Interviews, benefits, photo shoots. I fully expect the Opry to call again."

"You set everything up, and I'll be there. I promised you this entire year and an awesome CD. We've done it. You're the man, Neil."

"And then we talk, huh? What's next?"

"I don't know. We may have to talk to Josh and everyone else before long. Mom said a reporter showed up at the place last week. She wanted a personal interest story about my family, but she noticed the activity around the barn. Mom said she handled it." He chuckled. "She told her she's putting in a bed-and-breakfast. Mom thinks fast on her feet, but if this gal goes to snooping, we're in for it."

Neil took a deep breath and released it slowly. "It was bound to happen. We've been lucky. I hoped we could wait until after the awards show in November. We'll decide when you get here. You pull in on October third, right? I'll see you then."

Chapter 31

Activity filled the month of October throughout Nashville. Everything centered on the upcoming CMA awards on November fifth. Agents wore out their phones promoting their clients. The award nominees saw little rest, but Randy carved out time to write with new friends like Lester Ashford.

Lester met him at the door of his home in one of his signature sweaters, appropriate for the cool fall weather. "Come on in here, Randy. Sit anywhere you like. I've got coffee or cider, which soothes my raspy old throat. Unless you want water."

"Cider sounds great. Thanks for having me out. I've been looking forward to this."

"Me, too. Let's sit and catch up a bit before we get to work. How did your tour go this year?"

The talk soon turned to what each of them was writing. The ideas and music flowed until Randy's phone rang.

"I'll have to get this. It's my mom. Hi, Mom. Is everything okay?"

"Yes, of course. I wanted to know what time you'll be in next week."

He shook his head, rolled his eyes, and mouthed words to his host. *I'm sorry.* "Noon on Wednesday. Mom, Sherry has my itinerary. I'm sort of busy here."

Lester waved for Randy to hand him the phone. "Hi,

Mrs. Walters, Lester Ashford here. We met last year."

She screamed. "Oh, my Lord. I can't believe you remember me."

Randy heard her response and grinned as he imagined his mother straightening her hair as if Lester could see her through the phone.

He sat back and laughed. "I never forget a pretty face. Will we see you at the awards show again next month? I hope so. I'll give you back to Randy now."

"See you next week, Mom. Yes, ma'am, he's real nice. Bye."

"You plan to bring her again? Maybe I shouldn't have said anything."

"No problem. I'll talk with her about it on my trip home. I'm thinking I might bring my young son back with me."

"Bring them both. You can always arrange another ticket for the show. These are the good days, Randy. Don't miss anything."

****

Randy made a quick trip home to check on the progress. After a walk-through of the barn, "Dan, it looks great. I knew you could do it."

"Glad you like it. There's still a lot to finish inside, and then we'll paint and refinish the exterior. You want it red, right?"

"An authentic barn red with white trim so people can see it when they drive by."

"Got it. The parking area will be last. Sherry and your mom have been scouring all the antique stores and flea markets for fixtures and finishes. I'll let them set up the loft sleeping quarters, too. I need you to look at the plans for the studio. We may end up with one less cubicle than you wanted."

"I'm sure we can work it out."

After dinner, Randy took his ex-wife aside to talk. "Carrie, I want Jimmy to attend the CMA night with me. I know it means taking him out of school for a few days. It might be good for him, though. He could write a report for extra credit or something. What do you say?"

She grinned from ear to ear. "That's amazing. He'll have so much fun. Are you not taking your mom this year? You'd better let her know. She's looking forward to it."

"I'll take them both when I go back. Then she can fly home with him. He's only nine."

"Yeah, nine going on sixteen sometimes. But, yes, that's a good plan."

"Good, then I'll tell them both right now."

****

Nashville buzzed with activity, and Randy enjoyed taking his son and mother sightseeing and shopping across the city. He took them to the studio where he recorded, and they spent an afternoon at the Country Music Hall of Fame Museum. After breakfast on the morning of the awards show, his mother told her boys to go enjoy some time alone. She'd get her hair done, then rest for the night's activities. By noon they were back at the hotel where she scurried around to put out clothes for each to look their best.

"What have you got there, young man?"

"Dad got me a new guitar."

She swiveled her head to her son. "You do remember you own a music store."

Impish pride covered Randy's face. "But, Mom, this one came from Nashville."

She shook her head. "Grandson, you get to tote this stuff through the airport."

Randy put his arm around her. "Let's get something to eat, then we can start getting ready. Jimmy wants spicy chicken again."

The television reporter on the red carpet remembered Mrs. Walters and wanted to interview her. Randy thanked everyone for welcoming her again.

"Come on, Jimmy, we'll get our picture taken over here. Look at the cameras and change up your position some as they snap."

"Who's this, Randy? Turn this way, kid."

"This is my son. He's nine, and this afternoon I learned now he wants us to call him Jim Randall Walters. I think he's already got his stage persona all set, too."

"So, he's named after you, Randy? Over here, Randy. One more with the kid, Randy."

"Yes, me and my dad, James. Hey, Mom, get over here. Get in the pictures."

She obliged the cameras before the trio took their seats.

Jimmy couldn't sit still. "Gosh, Dad, did you see Miranda Lambert over there? Geez. She's even prettier in person."

"Hang on, son. We'll see how many we can meet later."

His mother asked, "Are you too nervous? I mean, this is three awards."

"Three nominations, but yes, I feel like my stomach is going to turn over any minute. I'm glad you guys are here with me. It got my mind off it some of the last couple of days. I'll be performing my song and giving out one award, so I'll be kind of up and down through the show."

People continued to stop by to speak to Randy and wish him well. Some recognized his mother and spoke to her. When the music came up and the lights dimmed, he worried people around him could hear the pounding of his heart. He tried to calm Jimmy down when Carrie Underwood stepped onto the stage to emcee the proceedings.

It thrilled Randy to be presenting the Duo of the Year award with Martina McBride. When it was time to sing his nominated song, the thrill of live performance was there, but being before this audience of peers almost took his breath away. Jimmy stood and applauded like his hands were on fire.

The night rolled on, and Randy's leg bounced until time for the Song of the Year award. He brushed his hands down his thighs again and again until his mother reached over to calm them. When the announcer said, "And the winner is…hey not only did he perform it…"

Randy's throat tightened.

"…he also wrote it. Randy Walters' 'Hometown Hero.' Come on up, Randy."

Randy's fist shot into the air, then he turned to embrace his mother and son. He took the walk toward the stage and leapt up the stairs. The award was cold but precious in his hands as he tried to gather himself to speak.

"Thank you to the CMA, my manager, Neil Farrell, and Carnival Recording Company. Thanks to my family for supporting me. My mom and my son are here tonight." He shook the award toward them. "This is all for you. Thank you, everyone." The presenter led him backstage, where more cameras awaited him. When he got back to his seat, Jimmy squeezed his arm, a smile covering his face.

"Wait till the guys hear this."

Randy found it hard to focus through the next few awards, then Brooks and Dunn came out to present the Album of the Year award. Again, Randy's heart quaked. He heard them say in tandem, "Randy Walters and his album, *Hometown Hero*."

This time, he moved slower to get up from his seat. He paused at the microphone while he calmed his voice. "I can't tell you what this means. We worked so hard to make something for the fans. Dave Easton is like the best producer ever. The team at Carnival was there every day, making it more than special. Thank you all for this." He looked up and held the award high as he walked offstage.

Later in the show, Randy seemed to give a sigh of relief when the Male Vocalist of the Year award went to Blake Shelton. After the show, photographers and reporters surrounded Randy. Friends embraced him and shook his hand. His mother talked with Aaron and Sandy, who again asked her to dinner the following night.

The clock struck midnight when at last Randy got free. "I'm sorry. You two must be tired. I'll get you to the hotel."

His mother said, "This boy is still flying high. Maybe some hot chocolate would help him sleep. I could use some decaf coffee myself."

"Okay, it'll have to be Waffle House at this hour. Here's our car. Let's go."

****

The next night, Aaron met them at the door. "Welcome, everybody. Mrs. Walters, let me take your jacket. Sandy's in the kitchen."

Randy's mother took Aaron's hand. "Now, you know I'm Helen. Jimmy, say hello again to Mr. Franklin."

The boy stood awestruck by the star. "Uh, hullo, Mr. Franklin."

Aaron bent over to shake Jimmy's hand. "Finally, I get to meet you, Jim Randall. The kids are out back. Why don't you go introduce yourself?" He stood to face Randy. "Great kid you've got there."

Sonny's voice filled the room as he put an arm around Helen's shoulder and joked, "Our two girls are out there, too. Is he like his daddy? Do we need to watch him?"

Randy shook his head and looked after his son. "He's a mighty nine-year-old. Maybe we should. Great to see you, Sonny."

Julia sat with the men in discussion of the music business. Helen joined the other ladies in the kitchen.

"Sandy, I brought you a little something. I was hoping we'd get to visit again. It's not much, just some pot holders I made."

Sandy's eyes lit up at the sight of the handmade items. "This is so nice, and they'll come in handy. Aaron is always charring my others at the grill. These will be for company."

Marsha gave Helen a hug and pointed to the woman mashing potatoes. "You remember Sonny's wife, Jean. Listen, I tried the brownie recipe you gave me. Those things are dangerously good."

After dinner, Randy shared his plans with Aaron and Sonny. "What do you guys think? Julia already read me the riot act a while back."

An eerie silence filled the room. Aaron got up to stand by the fire. Sonny sat back and stared at Randy, his hand drumming a rhythm on his thigh. At last, Aaron asked, "And the concert hall or whatever, you're almost finished with it?"

"More than halfway complete. I'll be making some final decisions when I go home for Christmas. The store has been open a while and holding its own. So, I know you're thinking about something. What is it?"

Aaron sat again. "Man, oh man, Randy, what a risk." He watched Randy while Sonny and Julia remained silent. "Honestly, friend, I wish I'd had the guts to do it myself. Sandy and I both miss home, too. We love our place here, and now we've built her folks a house on the back acreage. I've got the studio now, and it's far enough from the city to be comfortable, but, man, you're going to be home. I'm jealous, Randy. Who have you told?"

"You guys and Neil. We're planning how to tell the Carnival folks when we meet with them. I know it'll be tough, but I can't turn back now. Family is everything, and the songwriting is becoming more and more important to me. I'm thinking of starting my own publishing business."

Sonny added, "You might as well. Lots of artists are doing it. Now you have those two awards on your shelf. You have more power than you know."

Aaron looked at Sonny and Julia. "Have our people get with his people to schedule me for his grand opening."

Chapter 32

The next day, Randy joined Neil in the office. Neil stood looking out the window, then flopped into his office chair to argue another point. He rose to walk around the circle around his desk. Randy squirmed as they discussed the future.

"Randy, I've never been through anything like this. I'll have to work hard to convince the record company you're still in for 100%. You know, though, I've never seen someone so determined to have life on their own terms. When do I get to see your place?"

Randy set his hat on the chair beside him. "You're invited to the grand opening. So far, I've traded nightmares of a failed career for sleepless nights about carpenters and plumbers, but I've enjoyed every minute. I do think I'll start a publishing company sometime soon. And if I have to record and tour on my own, so be it."

"You've got more guts than a Georgia Tech football team." Neil picked up his phone and looked up Josh's number. "Josh, ole boy, how the hell are ya'? Did you see our guy snatch those two awards the other night? Yeah, I get it, you're busy. So we were thinking we'd come over soon to talk. Got time Monday?"

Josh sat as stiff as a city hall statue and listened to everything Randy said. His only response was, "I'd better get my boss in here."

Neil stood to respond, "Oh, now, surely we can

figure this out."

Josh's hand flew up as if to say, *Stop, sit down.*

Neil looked at Randy as hard as he hit the chair. "I knew this was going to happen. I'm finished in this town."

"Take it easy. You'll see. It'll all work out."

Neil turned in his chair with a look of disbelief on his face. "Were you born with all this blind optimism, or do you have something special you drink every morning?"

"Ha ha. Hold your horses. How bad can it be?"

The tension in the room over the next two hours revealed the answer. Executives and legal minds filled the office. Randy stayed positive and firm. He explained his plan, which included another album with the label while his career was still climbing. Neil added he already had Randy booked in large venues and festivals all over the country to continue to support his albums.

Josh was pacing now. "Man, I talked you up with my boss and got you a recording deal. This is how you repay me?"

Neil tried to explain. "It is fewer tour dates, but believe me, he's gonna work as hard as always. The sales will be there."

"All the fans will hear is he left Nashville. They'll think he retired and give up on him."

"That's where good promotion comes in. We'll have to set them straight. Look, he only wants to live and work out of California. He's a family man."

The company president who took over Josh's chair interjected himself into the conversation. "Yes, and run two other businesses out there." He turned to face Randy. "Where do you think your focus will be?"

Randy slapped his hand around the arm of his chair and leaned forward. He'd heard enough. "On the music, sir. I'll do right by it and you. I know fans may think I'm quitting, but we can fix that. Listen, this can work for all of us. We've been successful together and made a bushel of money. A few days ago, I won two prestigious awards. If we strike with another album while the iron is hot, we'll make a bunch more. Then..." He stretched back in the chair. "Then you can kick me to the curb if it's not working for you, and my life will be my own. That's nothing but fair, guys. This is what I want."

The corporate head looked to the legal minds. Each gave him a quick nod. "It certainly sounds like you've thought it through. Give us a copy of your tour schedule and a few days to take this all in. The contract changes no matter what. When will you be moving to California?"

"Depends on whether we're doing the album. I'll stay until that's finished." Randy stood.

The boss moved around the desk to shake Randy's hand. "The album is on."

****

During the rest of November and the first two weeks of December, Neil scheduled Randy for shows around the country, radio and TV interviews, and a benefit for the Boys and Girls Club in Nashville. In the last half of the month, Randy went home to celebrate the holidays with his family.

"Mom, this has been a whirlwind year. Next year will be crazy, too. Dan has the barn right on schedule."

"He has worked hard, and I think he's afraid he'll disappoint you. You should say something to him."

"I do, all the time." He endured her raised eyebrows

and stare until he said, "Okay, Mom, I'll go see him."

He walked into the barn and smelled the newness of it all. He heard his latest CD blaring. "Hey, Dan. Dan, where are you?"

Dan stuck his head out of the upstairs area. "Randy. Give me a minute. I'll be right down."

Randy turned the music down, looked up, then watched Dan climb down the ladder from the loft.

"I was putting in another electrical outlet up there. I have to follow up on these subs all the time. Good to see you. How long can you stay?"

"I have to get back for another recording in mid-January. This is looking better than I ever dreamed." His eyes caught something. "You didn't take down Dad's workbench?"

"Nah, I didn't have the heart to destroy it. I can still see him there, hunched over some leather project. I thought by moving it over next to the door, we could use it for selling tickets, CDs and stuff."

Dan's sentiment touched Randy. "That's awesome. You've done such a good job, not missing a thing. I don't know how to thank you."

Dan smiled. "The paycheck takes care of it, but I know you mean it. Thanks."

Randy went back to business. "We aimed for a June concert. Still a good target?"

Dan reached for his clipboard. "Should be good. I scheduled all the sound equipment and signage for mid-May. Gives us time for at least a couple dry runs in June before grand opening."

"Yeah, a few concerts for locals will give us an excellent test. Then we'll have the opening wing ding on July 4th weekend. What do you think?"

"We'll have it ready, boss."

****

Recording the new CD went like clockwork. It was a compilation of songs he'd created with other Nashville writers. He titled it '*And Then We Wrote...*'

Dave Easton was a forever fan now. "This is another good one, Randy. Glad I got to work on it with you."

Jeff agreed to hold off on finding a replacement roommate until Randy finished the CD and made preparations for his tour. "You know, you'll always have a couch here. I owe you for all the times you covered me when I was short on the rent."

"You're a good friend. I hope including the song we wrote on this CD will get you some traction. Did I tell you? We're releasing it as the first single. You deserve that and more. Your offer might come in handy when I come back to record or play the Opry or something."

Randy talked with Neil about the upcoming tour. "I had to replace Steve on bass. I couldn't blame him. He got a good deal with Brad Paisley and will have more play dates. I'm glad the other guys are hanging with me."

"You're lucky it was only him. This lighter schedule has its drawbacks."

"Yeah, but I have three dates set to write with Lester Ashford over the summer. You know how many guys would kill for that?"

"Yeah, you've got me there. Come on, let's finish this list. How many CDs do you think you'll need for the Charlotte show? You went through two cases there last year."

****

In March, Randy moved his belongings back into his old room at his mother's. "Now, Mom, you know I'll be in and out. I'll be touring some this summer, and when I'm here, I'll be helping a bit at the store."

"I'll take what I can get. The ladies at church think I'm the luckiest gal around. A couple of them have daughters they want to bring around. I didn't do that, you understand."

"Mom. You'd better not. I'll see you later. I'm going down to the store."

"Johnny, how's it going?"

"Over all pretty good. I have four guitar students for later this afternoon. We're advertising, so more folks come out for the concerts from all around, even LA. I'm scrambling right now. My act for Saturday's show fell through. Hey, what about you?"

"I guess I could. Do I get to keep the tips?" They shared a good laugh.

Leaving on tour was tough this time because of the good things happening in his life. He flew to meet the band at their first show in Richmond. Living between the bus, Nashville, and his home in California became the norm. The day he could spend most of his time at home was close.

One afternoon, Jack knocked on the door to Randy's room on the bus. "Boss, are you busy?"

"No, come on in. What's up?"

"I wanted to be up front with you. We've been out a couple of months now. I'm not sure this limited tour is working for me with pay being on a per-show basis. You know, I got married last year, and Mary is pregnant. Now I need to think of the money to support my family."

"I can't say I didn't see this coming."

"You'll let me stick it out as long as I can? I love working with you."

Randy didn't have to think about that. "Yeah, we've really built something together. How about I make you the road manager, too? More responsibility, but you'll be a great help to me. A bump in pay might make staying worthwhile. Am I right? To get us through this tour?"

"Sure, thanks, Randy. I didn't want to let you down."

Randy handled these minor challenges one by one. He was determined to make it work.

****

June came around fast, and the barn was near completion. He had a week of finishing touches before inviting local friends and family in for a concert. Keeping it low key and a small crowd at first allowed him and Dan to evaluate or improve things. He contracted his old friend Bobby Wilson to drive over from LA to lead the band of musicians they both played with over the years. This gave him a chance to ensure the mix was good.

"Bobby, you're gonna be our guinea pig on the bed in the loft. Let me know how you like it."

"Heck, man, I'm sure it's the nicest and cheapest motel I've stayed at in a long time." He threw his head back and let go the laugh Randy had missed.

Over a late cup of decaf coffee, Randy asked, "Mom, did you have a good time tonight? It wasn't too much for you?"

"It was a lot of fun. Did you see my ladies' class in the first row? They're asking when to show up for the next one."

"You understand, this was a small crowd. The place will hold a hundred fifty. The parking lot will be full. You still on board with the whole thing?"

"Bring 'em on. Sherry and I were talking. Maybe we should have cookies, brownies, or something for the break. She says we could charge for them, like a bake sale."

"Woah, there, lady. I don't want you overdoing it. But I'd say that sounds like a good idea if you're up for it."

Chapter 33

Julia met Randy with open arms. "Come in here, stranger. How long are you in town for this time?"

"A couple of days. Then I meet the tour in Phoenix for a show on Friday."

Marsha called from the kitchen. "Just passing through, huh? Glad you could come by for dinner."

"We're making a video for the new release. So strange, but kind of fun. You guys are coming to the grand opening of my place, aren't you? Aaron and I are both going to play."

"Of course. You said we can stay in the loft, right? It sounds so fun."

"Yep. My friends Tom and Jennie are staying in Mom's extra bedroom. You'll love them."

Marsha asked, "So, is it really working out for you?"

Randy nodded. "It is. Of course, I've had to handle a few calls from Dan about construction issues, and I catch a lot of sleep on airplanes, but yes, it is going to work."

****

Randy made it home for the opening concert with a few days to spare. Preparations continued right up to the event. Setting the grand opening of his barn during the Fourth of July festivities made it even more exciting.

"Tom, Jennie, come on in. Come out of the kitchen. Mom, they're here."

He took Tom out to the barn while the ladies continued preparations for dinner. Before they entered, he pointed out the brass plate next to the door.

"Nice touch, don't you think? It still has the name covered until we reveal everything. The rest says Established Saturday July 5, 2014. I wanted to always remember the date."

"Good idea. I love the old pickup by the gate. Does she still run, or does it only hold that 'Live Music Here' sign?"

"I had it fixed up, so it purrs like a kitten, like when my dad drove it. I thought it was a neat touch out front."

"Well, let's see the inside of this barn of yours. I can't wait."

Randy pulled open the door and stepped back. Tom walked in and let out a whistle at what he saw.

"This is much more than I expected. And I love the rustic touches. How's the acoustics?"

"Better than I ever dreamed. Dan did such a good job. He spent time with experts who build studios and performance venues around Los Angeles. He learned a lot."

They continued to tour the place, and Tom marveled at the studio.

"Randy, this is top-notch. You won't even need Nashville for your albums."

"I'll go back for the studio musicians, but I think I can record anything here and make money."

Tom stood with his student and said, "Son, I am proud of everything you've done. I knew there was something special about you the first day you walked into the Crystal Palace. I'm not sure I could have imagined all this for you, though. You made this happen on your own."

Randy blushed. "Thanks, Tom. We'd better get back to the house. You can help me set up the tables in the front yard. Lots of friends and all my family will join us for dinner tonight. I'd better get back there to play host when they arrive."

After the feast that night, the women made quick work of cleaning up. The group sat outside to enjoy the evening breeze until darkness overtook them. His mother, Jennie, and Marsha seated themselves in the dining room with their heads together, as if plotting something. Jimmy played games with his cousins until he heard the jamming start in the living room. He grabbed his guitar. Randy beamed with pride as Jimmy joined right in and grasped his turn at a song. Everyone else gathered to enjoy the music and chatter. The hit of the night was Frank and Sue's little Randall.

Tom sat beside Jimmy. "So, you want to be called Jim now, eh?"

"Yep, Jim Randall Walters. I think it'll look good on CD covers, don't you?"

Tom laughed. "That's a fine guitar you're playing."

"Yeah, I got it when I was in Nashville last year for the CMA awards."

"You don't say." Tom looked over at Randy and winked.

The musicians worked on some of Randy's songs to prepare for the concert. Bobby Wilson was bringing the drummer in time to rehearse the next day.

When the music stopped, the crowd thinned. Randy asked, "You all got checked into your rooms? I hope they're okay. Be here around eight a.m. for breakfast."

Sarah spoke for everyone. "You didn't have to get

us hotel rooms, Randy. But yes, they're nice."

Randy walked Carrie and Jimmy to her car. "Thanks for coming, Carrie. I hope you like my friends."

"I do and had a great time. Some of them seem to think our relationship is a little odd."

"I don't care. No matter what, we'll always be family."

Randy woke early the next day, his bed bathed in the California sun. His eyes roamed the familiar souvenirs, pictures and childhood mementoes which adorned the walls of the room where he grew up. He jumped up and took down posters of past heroes like Clint Black, Rosanne Cash, and Cal Ripken, Jr. He carefully removed an 8x10 glossy of Linda Ronstadt and laid it in the top drawer of the dresser. His high school diploma and the dried carnation from senior prom joined Linda next to stacks of *Country Music Roundup* and *Hot Rod* magazines.

He removed the blue plaid spread from his bed and turned to see his mother in the doorway. "Oh, hi, Mom. You're up early."

"I have a horde of people coming for breakfast, remember? How about you?"

"I thought it was time to put some things behind me. I'm starting a new chapter in life today." He reached in the closet for a large package from Bed Bath & Beyond. His mother helped him position the new beige comforter on the bed.

"When did you get this?" She smoothed it under the pillows.

"Last time I visited. I hesitated to make changes. I didn't want to hurt your feelings. You've always kept things so nice for me."

"Son, this is your home. You need to be comfortable. I was thinking of asking Dan about building a small house for me out back. Then you could have this larger place for entertaining and maybe a family one day?"

He sat on the bed with her. "Mom, I'm not taking your home. If the place is too much for you, I'll bring in a weekly housekeeper. Otherwise, let's put off this talk until I have that family. How does that sound?"

She hugged him. "You're as stubborn as your father."

Bobby Wilson and the drummer, Dean, arrived mid-morning. After introductions and a late breakfast for the two musicians, Randy took them to the barn where the others were setting up. Soon, sounds of rehearsal filled the space and wafted back to the house.

Aaron's bus and motor home pulled into the parking lot around noon. Randy met him as he stepped off the bus.

"Hi, Aaron. How was Santa Barbara last night?"

He shook Randy's hand. "Fun, a great crowd. Do those tables under the trees out front mean what I think they mean?" The two friends started the walk to the house. "We snacked for breakfast. You said you'd have a spread of food here. Oh, man. I can smell the fried chicken from here."

"You won't believe the food coming out of that old farm kitchen. Let me introduce you to everybody."

After lunch, Aaron's band set up their instruments for sound check. He looked around the barn with wide eyes. "We sent the equipment truck on to the next gig. You said you'd have a full setup, and you weren't kidding. Randy, this place is amazing."

Rehearsals and sound check completed, the troupe visited the music store in town. Johnny and his helper showed them around. Randy pointed out the newly remodeled room where he took lessons as a kid.

Frank asked Johnny, "How do you like it here? I hope I didn't steer you wrong in taking the job."

"No, I love it. The town is for sure my style, and the business is great. Randy gives me free rein to manage the place."

"What do you have planned for the stage area now the barn is opening?"

"I've got some open mic and showcase nights started. I'm working with the music teacher at the high school, too. One night will be for the kids to come in for their own open mic."

Julia said to Randy, "You know I've got some ideas for promoting this place a little more."

Randy grinned and nodded toward his manager. "You talk to Johnny. He runs the operation."

Back at the barn, Randy gathered everyone outside for the unveiling of his dream come true.

"This is it, folks. All the hard work comes down to tonight. Dan, get up here. I want you to share in this. You know he's not only my brother-in-law, but my friend, and now my contractor. He totally rebuilt this place for me." The crowd clapped, whistled, and cheered. "And don't forget, his company is ready for another project. See him after the show." Laughter rippled through the crowd.

"Mom." The crowd split to let him step toward her. "I hope you're pleased with how it turned out." He wrapped his arm around her as they turned to face the building that held so many memories for them.

She wiped a tear. "Your father would be so proud."

"I hope so, Mom. Dan, you want to pull the cord and show us the sign up there? One, two, three, go."

There was a collective gasp as the vinyl cover fell away, revealing the art work. His mother folded into his arms at the sight. The wooden sign with bright red letters spelled out *Dad's Barn and Music Hall*, and below, in blue letters edged in white, *The Home of Right Fine Music*.

****

The time had come. Cars and pickups snaked into the parking area where David, Jimmy, and a local Boy Scout troop kept them in order. Sherry and Marsha sold tickets as fast as their hands would move. Carrie and Sarah ushered people to their seats. Julia took care of the merchandise table. Family and friends who were such a vital part of this night sat in the front row. Everyone knew their jobs, and the event started without a hitch.

Backstage, Randy paced around and fussed over every detail. Aaron came to his side. "You ready, pardner? Don't worry, you'll be fine. After all, you've played the Grand Old Opry. This should be a breeze."

"Somehow, this feels more important. Aaron, are you sure about going on first? You're a bigger draw than me."

"Not here, I'm not. These are your people. This is your night. So, I'm only going to do about forty minutes. Then the stage is all yours." Aaron slapped Randy's back and moved toward the stage to wait.

The sold-out crowd watched as Aaron christened the stage with his well-known hits. The full house responded with cheers and applause.

Tom stood beside Randy backstage, watching it all

unfold. "You okay, son? Thank you for including me in this. I think this may be the proudest performance of my career."

Randy threw his arms around his friend and mentor. His words caught in his throat each time he tried to speak.

After Aaron's last song, they took a scheduled break. The ladies sold cookies and bottled water. Randy's band for the night got into place. Bobby on bass, Frank on rhythm guitar, Dean on drums, Johnny on steel and fiddle, and Tom on lead guitar. They were ready. The crowd returned to their seats and chanted, "Randy, Randy, Randy."

Tom struck up a lively rendition of Buck Owens' instrumental "'Buckaroo'." As the band joined in, Tom stepped to the mic to announce, "Here he is, CMA award winner, your own Randy Walters."

To Randy, it seemed like the sides of the old barn bellowed in and out with the pulse of excitement flowing through the crowd. No packed arena of his career sounded so loud or heartfelt to his ears. He walked to the mic, overcome by the response. The camera flashes from reporters made it hard, but he looked across the room to see old friends, musicians, neighbors, his fifth-grade teacher, the mayor, and Neil and his wife. It took a full minute to gather himself and quiet the crowd back in their seats.

"Thank you for being here tonight. I hope you're having a good time so far. Isn't Aaron amazing?" The people went wild again until he could wave them down. "You're going to hear a wide range of music from me tonight. I think it fitting Tom and the guys started us off with a Buck Owens tune here in California. You'll hear more Bakersfield with a Merle Haggard tune here and there. I want to share my influences and the journey to my current music. But first, I think it's only right I start our time together tonight with the song that won me two awards last year. After all, I was thinking of a lot of you when I wrote it. Guys, let's do 'Hometown Hero' for them." The audience left their chairs to yell and sing along. He was home.

Epilogue

The five years since grand opening night were good for Randy and his family. He recorded two more albums in Nashville. More awards came his way for his songwriting and one as Male Vocalist, before he decided he'd endured enough airline time back and forth, prompting him to cut ties with his label. With the success of Dad's Barn, he could establish his publishing company and record in his own studio. The fees from renting the studio to other artists added to the royalties from the recording and songwriting, which sustained a good lifestyle for him. He continued a limited performance schedule around the country for income, fun, and to keep his name before the public.

Randy lost Tom three years after moving home. It was like the death of his father all over again. Their closeness he missed most and still reached for the phone to call his friend for advice or to share good news. As a teacher, Tom could be tough on Randy, but that's what made him an excellent mentor. He was sure Tom's lessons had been crucial to him on the road to success.

Randy took his mother to visit Jennie as often as possible. Like his own mother, Jennie now lived with one of her sons. The two women worked together on a cookbook. Marsha designed it for them and got it published as *Cookin' for The Band*. Julia managed a brief book signing tour around California.

Julia and Randy stayed close, and she gave him advice on promotions for his new endeavors.

With Dan's business taking off, he and Sherry built their family a large home on the lake. The stylish new place made her happy, and he gained the fishing boat he always wanted.

Jimmy grew into being Jim Randall full time. Randy regularly put his son on stage with him at Dad's Barn after he turned thirteen. When he reached sixteen, he began playing open mics at the store and other places around the area. Randy passed on some of the same pointers Tom gave him, including being positive he really wanted a career in music.

Carrie remained a constant in Randy's life. She left the Dollar General when Randy made her the manager of Dad's Barn. The gossip around town about them remarrying fell short. The relationship they built seemed to work for them.

Sarah and David added a boy and a girl to their beach house. They visited Dad's Barn often. Frank and Sue gave little Randall a sister, and Frank agreed to play at the barn most weekends.

Now Randy could sit on the porch swing, look over his life, and be happy. Music, friends, and family were around him every day. He showed a strength of conviction in standing up for what he needed. He felt his dad's spirit around him, beaming with pride for all Randy accomplished. Of the many things his dad taught him, the most important turned out to be the love of family and right fine music.

A word about the author...

An Oklahoma native, Gency takes a down-to-earth look at life and exists comfortably on the page with the fictional characters she creates. A career that took her across America gave her a life enriched by a variety of personalities and cultures. Since retirement near Albuquerque, NM, those characters and stories have jumped from memory to the written page. She is a member of Southwest Writers, Oklahoma Writers Federation, Inc., and The Author's Guild. A lifelong musician, her performances and leadership roles with the International Western Music Association, Oklahoma City Traditional Music Association, and Southern California Bluegrass Association give her a front-row understanding of a young man striving for success in music.